THE LOCKDOWN ARTIST

JAY WAMSTED

THE LOCKDOWN ARTIST
by JAY WAMSTED

ISBN: 979-8-9931973-0-2

A publication of Jay Wamsted.
Art Direction & Design by Station16 (Station16 LLC)
Illustrations by Erin Rahill
© Copyright 2026 Jay Wamsted

The poem, "XV, Men of careful turns, hater of forks in the road," reprinted by consent of Brooks Permissions.

For more about the author visit
www.JayWamsted.com

---

instagram · @jaywamsted
tiktok · @jay.wamsted
x · @jaywamsted

SCAN TO FOLLOW JAY

To My Students

CONTENTS

PART THREE   193
THE PROGRESS OF LIGHTS

THROUGH THE LOOKING GLASS

"I could tell you my adventures -
beginning from this morning,"
said Alice a little timidly:
"But it's no use going back to yesterday,
because I was a different person then."

- LEWIS CARROLL

CHAPTER I

FIRST DAY

I wasn't surprised to see that the new kid looked afraid.

Today was going to be a rough one for him, but that feeling of fear would definitely serve him well. This place was pretty scary, after all, and the rest of the room already knew it. Things might go okay for him if he could learn just one fact quick: in this place, fear is one of the few things you can count on to keep you safe.

Williams had pulled him up in front of the class, and was droning through an introduction, encouraging us to show the new kid the ropes on his first day of school. His name was Liam, and we were supposed to be kind and help him out, all that stuff teachers say because it seems like the right thing to do. Nobody was looking straight at them, of course, but you could tell that everybody was paying close attention. We didn't get new kids in this class often, and when it happened they were almost never Guests.

He was big, like grown-man big. I would have believed he was 18 or even 19 seeing him from a distance, but up close his face had a distinct pudge to it that made him seem more like an overgrown middle schooler. It would be odd for him to be as young as all that, of course. Nation was a junior level class and most of us were at least 16 years old. He was shifting his weight back and forth, clutching his clear backpack, like someone might all of a sudden snatch it out of his hand and just run wild with it. His eyes jumped at random around the room, as if afraid to rest on any one thing for too long. He probably didn't want to miss out on some important clue he would need later.

Like I said, he seemed to be carrying a healthy dose of fear. And there was no lack of things for him to be afraid of here at 231.

Williams gestured toward an empty desk near the front of the room and went back to business. "Okay, okay, everyone, where were we before the Z.A. brought Liam in?"

A long beat went by, space filled primarily with the sound of the new kid getting settled into his seat. A couple of folks coughed before someone finally called out from the back, "Democracy."

Anyone willing to speak into the void of this place was a relief, and Williams pounced on it. He was a small man of uncertain age; someone told me he had a family on the outside, but it always felt hard to believe. Maybe another teacher, but not Williams. "Of course, yes, democracy," he said, swiping at his screen, scanning for the next part of his lesson plan. "The thing that Winston Churchill once described as the worst form of government."

Dead quiet reigned. I wasn't sure if he was making some kind of joke or just leading us awkwardly through some canned introduction; either way it wasn't worth the risk of getting involved. Then, as usual, a girl's voice carried across the room, little more than a whisper but impossible to miss in the silence. "Except for all the others," she said.

Williams looked up, his eyes flashing. We all knew he would be staring straight at Jazz.

Liam glanced over, trying to identify the voice. To a new kid, though, the speaker wouldn't have stood out in any meaningful way.

She was kind of tall for a girl, and thin, like she could outrun you easy. But it was hard to tell all that in the crowded room—pretty much everyone looks the same when stuck sitting in a desk. Like a lot of Peeks, she kept her hair in short, tight braids, and her government-issue uniform was a size too big. Though Guests were granted more leeway in our dress code, Peeks weren't allowed to wear makeup or jewelry—even if they needed glasses, those had to be standard issue. To a new kid, the Peek side of the room must have run together into one big blur.

"What?" Williams said, clearly annoyed at Jazz. I saw Liam flinch.

Pretty much any other student would have shrugged and let it go. Like most of us, I had long since learned the futility of arguing with a teacher here. Jazz was not just anyone, though. I took a risk and turned to face her, figured the Globe wouldn't be watching me at this point anyway. They say a Peek had never been at the top of a class here at 231. Jazz was the first, and it was obvious that most of the teachers didn't like it. Williams was for sure one of those teachers.

"The rest of the quote," she said, "goes like this: *except for all the others that have been tried.* Churchill's point is that democracy might be a terrible kind of government, but all the others are even worse." Jazz was speaking in a quiet, even voice; her hands lay flat and still on the desk. *"Democracy is the worst form of government—except for all the others that have been tried.* It's a joke about World War II."

"I'm pretty sure that can't be right," Williams said, jabbing at his screen, frustrated. Another long silence. "There!" he crowed, finally pulling an article up on the display for us to see. A grainy black-and-white photo of a bulbous man smoking a huge cigar bore the headline, "Churchill Says Democracy Is the Worst Form of Government." Williams pointed at the display triumphantly, spun around to face us almost as if he expected everyone to clap. No one did.

Instead, Jazz laughed, a barking little noise that sped through the silence of the room. "Mr. Williams," she said, "just because someone put it on the Stream doesn't make it true. Any dumbass can post an article and butcher a quote." Still looking straight at him, she laughed again. "You need to ask yourself who benefits from changing that old man's words. Everybody serves somebody, you know?"

At first Williams didn't answer, just settled into his desk and leaned back, hands laced behind his head. I could tell he was agitated by his tapping foot, but the rest of his body stayed still as he kept his eyes trained on Jazz's prone hands. Suddenly, he shot back. "Why would it be the first thing to pop up on the Stream when I search, though? Unless it were true?" Turning my eyes away from Jazz and Williams for just a moment, I stole a glance at Liam. He looked miserable, like he might cry.

What an introduction for him. There's no way he saw this kind of stuff back where he came from.

We all waited while Jazz took a couple of slow, deep breaths. She cut her eyes to the ceiling, waited, then brought them back to the front. Finally, she said, "Whatever, Mr. Williams. That quote can be whatever you say it is. I'm all good." Her orange jumpsuit rippled as she settled her body back in her chair. All the while, those hands stayed glued to the desk.

A long moment went by where nobody spoke—most of us half holding our breath—but then Williams smiled. "Okay, Jazz, thanks for an important lesson. We have to be able to verify the history of our Nation in order to know that it's true!" With a flick of his finger he swiped the article off the display and replaced it with a list of names and "potential topics." He went on, "I've split you up into groups. You have the remainder of class to prepare a short presentation on one of the many failings of democracy. Rough drafts are due to me tomorrow before the Meeting, and you'll present during our time in here."

The whole class seemed to move together at once; it was like a switch had flipped from off to on. I glanced at the display only to see that my group was pretty much the same as it always was—my roommates Madison, Randall, and Kiki, plus Orion from the Peek side of the room. Notably, I checked and saw that the new kid had been placed with Jazz.

Liam stood up and looked around, lost; nobody from his group made a move to bring him in. He turned helplessly to Williams, who only motioned in the general direction of the Peeks. I watched him walk cautiously toward them, looking like he was doing his level best not to panic. When he got close, however, Jazz placed a hand square in the center of his chest, pushing him back at us.

"Y'all taking the new kid," she called to me. It was a statement, not a question. I looked to Williams, who shrugged; there were certain things he usually just let slide. Orion had been headed our way and Jazz beckoned him back to their corner, laughing.

There were well over forty students crammed into our class, even though the room had probably been built for only twenty-five. We were split roughly half and half, but the Peeks huddled together on the side near their door, pushing desks together to create a kind of solid mass. Williams allowed it because it gave the rest of us enough space to breathe. I think it also gave him an excuse not to walk over there and check up on them. He spent most of his time at his desk, swiping and tapping, standing only occasionally to peer over shoulders on our side.

We circled up, Liam taking the seat between Randall and Maddy. I checked my notes to see whose turn it was and nodded at Kiki.

"I'm on it," she said. She pulled her earbuds out of her pocket and popped them in one-handed, sliding frames around her screen with the other. I turned to Liam.

"Tell us your story," I said. Again, it was a statement and not a question, but we needed to know who we were suddenly being asked to live with. Fear was one way to stay safe here; information was another.

Liam glanced away from me. "Shouldn't we get started on the assignment?" He looked nervously over at Williams, who was sipping coffee from his thermos and trying to pretend he wasn't just sitting there scrolling on his screen.

"No, Kiki's got it. We take turns with stuff like this," I said, and she cocked a finger at us without even looking up. "It's busywork and everybody knows it. If she needs our help, she'll ask."

"Oh," Liam said, shifting around in his seat, trying to get comfortable. They probably had better chairs where he came from, too.

"So?" I said to him, sliding a note to Randall. *What do you think? He seems like he might be okay, right?*

Liam swallowed hard and stared at the Guests' door. Instead of answering, he asked us a question. "Where are we?"

Randall took my note and turned to Liam. "You're learning about our Nation, friend," he said. "We're in Nation class with the illustrious Mr. Williams." He motioned toward the front, where Williams had given up all pretense of paying attention to us. He was holding his screen way out in front of him the way adults do, laughing at whatever he was watching. Randall scrawled something on the paper and handed it back to me.

"No, I mean, where is this place? The actual building I mean?" Liam looked around the room as if a window would suddenly appear, allow him to somehow get his bearings by looking at the sun.

The note read: *Your guess = Good as mine.* I shrugged, looked up at Liam. "You've been assigned to join us here at Federal Education Site 231. At least, that's how it will read on your paperwork. Everyone here just calls it 231." Out of habit I took the scrap of paper, rolled it into a ball, and popped it into my mouth. It probably wasn't necessary with such a small little note, but every new kid learns soon enough—you can never be too careful.

Liam looked aggravated. "No, I know that. I'm sorry. I mean, like, *where* are we? As in what part of town? They just picked me up at my old school and put me in a van. Felt like we were driving forever to get here, and nothing I could see out the window looked familiar after the first ten minutes."

Madison cut in. "We're on the southwest side, by the old quarry. You probably came straight down the channel from the Northern Arc?" Maddy had gone to elementary school in the Arc; I briefly wondered if somehow their families knew each other.

"Yeah," Liam replied. He looked at Williams again. "It's crazy—I mean, I woke up this morning and everything was just so normal. My parents dropped me off at school like always, and later I was sitting in math class and then they called for me on the announcements, told me to bring my bag and my jacket. I didn't even say goodbye to anyone, I thought it was just a doctor's appointment or something and that they had forgot to tell me about it." His words were tripping over each other on their way out of his mouth now. He was starting to warm up to us a little bit.

"Kiandria!" Williams called out from behind his desk. "Take that hood off your head." Kiki had slunk down in her chair, trying to cut us out while she did our work. Guests may not have to wear jumpsuits, but we weren't allowed to do just any old thing, either. Hoodies were acceptable so long as we didn't put them up over our heads. Kiki shrugged her shoulders and the hood fell away; she didn't even break stride with her tapping and swiping.

"Your parents missed a tuition payment," I said to Liam. Again, not a question. That's pretty much the only way a Guest would end up with us mid-year: one overdue check to their old school and they got grabbed in the middle of the day and shipped here. It might have felt novel to Liam. Not to us.

He winced, looked down at his newly issued screen. It was still dark; he hadn't even turned it on. "I guess?" he said.

"Hey," I said, leaning in to force eye contact. My voice softened. None of this was his fault. "Your parents probably didn't even know anyone was coming to get you until it was too late. Usually there's no word until it's over, when someone shows up at your house to grab your clothes and stuff. They're probably as stressed as you are right now."

Liam nodded and blinked back tears he didn't want us to see, looked away from me. We politely ignored him; we'd all been there at one time or another. He changed the subject. "Hey, so, are they really…

11

like, for real?" He pointed over into the corner where Jazz and Orion were sitting with their group. Just like us, one of them was working away at a screen while the others were talking. Unlike us, the typist kept looking up to ask questions. Usually, Jazz answered.

I smiled and nodded. Every time we got a new Guest, they eventually asked the same question. "Yeah, they're really for real."

"And they just sit here in class with us? Every day?"

"Technically," Randall said, "we're the ones sitting in their class. They were here first." He was looking over Kiki's shoulder at her work, apparently believing he had something to contribute. She kept throwing her body into his way, however, angling her screen away from him. Maddy watched, idly, nodding along to the scratchy beat coming from Kiki's headphones. Liam seemed like he was about to say something when we were interrupted by a dull noise coming from the Globe, like a bass guitar stuck at its lowest pitch. He looked up, around, and over at the door, clearly startled. No one else in the room reacted at all.

"Sounds like one of the Drones is having another feedback accident," Randall said, grinning. Williams looked over at us and cackled.

"Admin is so proud of those Drones!" he said. It was the only energy he'd shown us at all today. "The Head talks about them every week in our Site meeting. He's convinced that once the program goes wide, all the Associates—"

Suddenly the Globe overhead lit up like fire, the emergency light blinking on and off, bathing the room in a violent red color. A siren wailed from the invisible speaker, cutting off all conversation, and over top of that an automized voice intoned, "CODE RED. CODE RED. PLEASE FOLLOW PROTOCOLS AND ASSUME THE POSITION FOR YOUR OWN SAFETY. CODE RED."

The bass thrum had meant nothing to us, but a Globe screaming Code Red meant everything.

My group hit the ground immediately, Randall delaying just a beat in order to pull Liam down with us. We crawled under our desks and wove our legs together to sit cross-legged, wrapped our arms around our bodies. Anyone over about five feet tall had to curl into a ball in order to get into this insane position; if you were wearing a full-body Peek jumpsuit it was even more unwieldy. I tried to relax—it was always a miserable wait with that siren going, and we never knew how long something like this would last. The noise was overwhelming, repeating and blaring in time with the light flipping from normal to blood and back again.

By this point Liam was legit crying. I felt terrible for him, but there was nothing any of us could do to help him right now. He seemed like a good kid; I could only imagine what was going through his mind.

Williams's voice carried out from under his desk, over the wail of the siren. "Jazz!" he yelled, "get on the ground!" I looked over to her corner only to see that she hadn't moved so much as an inch—she was still sitting in her desk, hands again placed carefully in front of her. "You know they'll give you an Infraction if you don't get under that desk!" His voice was crossed up with something like panic.

Jazz didn't even look up from her hands. "You think I care about an Infraction?" she said quietly. I didn't think that Williams could hear her from beneath his far more capacious desk, but I was pretty sure she wasn't talking to him. No one made it through a semester at 231 without becoming something like an excellent lip reader. Every student with a sight line understood her perfectly.

The alarm dominated the room, insisting over and over that we maintain our positions for our own safety. Liam was shaking so hard under the desk next to me that its legs clattered back and forth, like a table in one of those old-timey haunted houses. Randall caught my attention, smiled and shrugged. Maddy whispered something to Liam that I couldn't quite catch.

I heard the clanging buzz on the door and turned just in time to see it fly open and smack against the wall. Two Associates burst through in full tactical gear. The overhead light changed from blood red to a dark purple, and one of them raced for Williams, checking to see if he was okay. The other pushed across the room, weaving through the aisles to get into Jazz's face and shout, "Down on the ground! Now!" His voice filtered through his gas mask, taking on a faint metallic quality. He sounded a little like a stormtrooper.

Jazz turned her head and looked at him, suddenly all smiles. For a moment it seemed like she wasn't going to react with anything more, but then she slowly raised her arms in the air, palms out to show her empty hands. From a sitting position at her desk, her fingers were just about level with the Associate's face.

"Down on the ground! This is your last warning!" the metallic voice commanded. For what felt like forever Jazz kept her hands in the air, motionless. Then she turned slowly, angling her head so that her eyes could cut over to Williams's desk. I don't know what she was looking for; he was hidden from view.

The overhead audio continued to blare as two radios squawked simultaneously, "Area J-3: Clear!" The effect was one of scratchy surround sound, like going to the movie theater with my dad, ages ago.

The Associate in front of Jazz grabbed at the radio attached to his shoulder harness. "Sir, we have a small problem over here in Area K-7," he said, never taking his eyes off her as she carefully turned back to face him square again.

She opened her mouth to speak, but the only word any of us heard was, "If—"

"Infraction," the other Associate said, rounding behind her, and he shot his taser into her back. She flew out of her desk and hit the ground, twitching wildly.

———

CHAPTER 2

THE CAFETERIA

At lunch I asked Kiki to go and get the new kid from the cafeteria line, then tossed a couple of backpacks to the ground to make space for him at our table. This was one of the few places we could talk without too much fear of being overheard, and after the scene in Nation I was betting that Liam had more than a few questions. We didn't owe it to Williams to show him the ropes; I didn't know anybody who would have gone even a little out of their way for that man. Be that as it may, my friends and I were going to help Liam all the same. Somebody had done it for each of us back when we were new to 231, and we knew we had to pay that forward.

Randall plopped down next to me and sighed. "You know, it's not that I expect good food here or anything. I know better than that at this point." He picked up his nachos, thirty tortilla chips congealed into one giant mass, rotated them to prove their adhesive quality, and ceremoniously dropped them back onto his tray. I heard an audible squishing sound. "I just wish that it could be edible every day. Is that too much for a man to ask?" He started poking at the cheese with his fork.

A couple of kids around us looked over and grinned, started prodding at their own cheese product lunch. I gave Randall a little shake of the head and cut my eyes over to the nearest Associate. We weren't in his microphone range at the moment, but I didn't want him having any reason to suspect we might be disturbing the peace. We needed whatever semblance of privacy we could get. Randall nodded, left his nachos to their own devices and began to peel an orange.

Across the cafeteria I saw Orion moving. I jumped up, made for the middle of the room, said over my shoulder, "Get Liam settled, okay? I'll be right back."

The only spot where the Peek cafeteria intersected with ours was at the coffee station. We ate from different meal lines, sat at different tables, but for whatever reason they let us prepare our caffeine together. Orion was headed straight for it. We could see into each other's side of the room, of course, look right through the chain link fence that ran floor-to-ceiling down the center. We could hear each other's conversations if they got loud enough, although usually that much volume got tamped down pretty quick. But the only place a Guest and a Peek could speak without an Associate moving you along was while getting a coffee. I had been keeping an eye on Orion from the moment I got inside, hoping he would grab a drink before we headed to Mason's class. Finally, I had my chance to talk.

Walking slow like I didn't have a care in the world, I dodged two Associates and a Drone, but still managed to reach the station within seconds of Orion. He was pressed up against the counter, pouring something into a paper cup. Our side had the option for mugs, if we wanted them—we could even take them to class if we scanned them out and returned them promptly—but I moved up next to him and grabbed a paper cup to match his.

"What are you drinking?" I asked, a little too loud. I winced and stole a glance at the Associate on the far side of the station; he was staring across the cafeteria toward the Peek exit. Orion looked over at me, holding my gaze but not saying a word.

"Hey, is Jazz okay?" I tried again, this time a little quieter. The Associate seemed to be paying us no attention.

Orion stopped stirring his drink, tapped the little straw out, threw it away. He looked pointedly past me and paused a beat. "What the hell do you care?" he finally asked. He flicked his eyes at my shoes and smacked his teeth. "You can go on with all that mess, Ben. Run on back to your side and play with your friends."

I poured coffee—it might have been decaf, I didn't know how to tell the difference—and added a random amount of cream. I didn't usually drink the stuff and had no idea what I was doing. "Orion, hey—" I stopped, unsure what to say. "Just tell Jazz that I'm sorry, okay? Would you do that for me? Please?"

Orion finally squared to face me. "You're sorry? Sorry about what, exactly?" He was loud enough that the Associate looked up, started our way. Not ideal, but it saved me from having to answer Orion's question.

When the Associates were on standard duty they disengaged their gas masks and goggles, allowing us to see faces framed inside their helmets. The goggles slid up and clicked into place over their foreheads, but the gas masks swung freely away on a set of hinges. They were able to lock into place on the side, but most Associates left them loose—the easier to snap into place in an emergency. Trying to keep the masks from rocking wildly turned their walk into a kind of strut, like a kid trying not to crease his new shoes. The guy heading toward us looked young, not much older than me at all. His smile seemed genuine, even if he had a taser and a truncheon holstered to his belt. In between the weapons he sported a whole row of tear gas and smoke grenades, a couple of flash-bangs. Standard duty still came with some scary equipment.

"Hey guys," he said as he got closer, "that's probably enough to get you through your next class right there."

Orion smiled back at the Associate. "Yes sir, Derek, sir. Ben and I were just on our way to class. Headed to Literature. Getting ready to hit those books with Mr. Mason."

Derek? I looked for a nametag on the Associate's uniform and didn't see one. Who knew this guy's name was Derek? Weird to think that on the Peek side of the chain link they would get to know the Associates.

"Ah," the Associate—Derek—responded, pointing to a couple of sleeves that had come loose from the stack. Orion straightened them up. Derek went on, "Everybody loves class with Mr. Mason, that's one thing I know for sure about this school."

I stood there awkwardly for a moment before Orion walked away without so much as a glance. Derek, though, turned and glared at me. I quickly nodded at him and raised my coffee in a sort of weak salute. "Yes, sir. We're just getting ready to go talk about *Frankenstein*. It's exciting stuff."

He kept his eyes leveled at me for a moment and then, without a word, lazily turned away.

In my absence, Kiki had found Liam and brought him back to sit with us. She put him between her and Randall—who, predictably, had begun talking about the nachos for his new audience. Kiki was laughing at the routine for some reason, but at least they were doing it quietly. The seat across from them was left open for me, the rest of our Block scattered up and down the table. Madison's bag was leaning on my seat. So, obviously, I pushed it over with my foot.

"Hey, watch it, Ben!" she said. "You don't see me messing with your coffee!" She looked into my cup and busted out laughing. "Ben Walker! How much cream did you add to this coffee? It looks like you're drinking hot milk!"

I hung my head in mock shame and shot back, "You'd better keep your stuff out of my zone, Maddy. You don't want the Z.A. coming over here to check through that bag."

Maddy looked around, like the mere mention of the name could summon the beast. "No, I do not." She pulled the bag tight under her seat, shook her head, and went back to laughing about my coffee.

Liam skittered his eyes back and forth between us. He hadn't so much as touched his lunch, maybe hadn't said a word to anyone at all since the Infraction. Nothing strange about that; this day would have been a lot to take in even without Jazz and the Code Red.

Not every student came into 231 as dramatically as did Liam. Many of us, me included, had moved here naturally after we levelled up from our neighborhood schools. Most parts of the City still had functioning elementary schools; it wasn't until kids hit middle and high that parents had to start thinking about whether they would be able to afford to pay for private. The government offered aid, of course, but tuition at the better schools was so high that most families couldn't afford it. If you lived in certain parts of the City, you might end up at a Federal Site right after elementary—many middle schools had closed years ago. Some people were luckier than others, though, and my parents lived in a place where I was able to go to school for free through 8th grade. After that, though, they decided to send me here.

Maddy and Randall had started with me on that first day; Kiki was already here, had been since 6th grade. About half of our Block joined later, much the same way Liam did. Apparently that was pretty normal for the 9th and 10th grade years: parents would bust their budgets and stretch to make those first couple of payments, but at some point the money ran out and they had to give up. Liam was the first new student we had seen in a while, though—both Guests and Peeks had been stable so far our junior year.

Liam looked up from his now completely solidified nachos. "So, can I ask you a question?" He said it to nobody in particular, but everyone in earshot turned his way.

"You want to know about the Infraction?" I said, checking to make sure there wasn't a Drone hovering nearby. He nodded.

"First off," Kiki said, touching his arm, "keep your voice down." She tilted her head over at the Associate—was that Derek? did he follow me over here?—and turned back to Liam. "He can't record us from there, not with his mobile listening equipment, but we don't want him coming any closer or we'll have to cut the conversation off completely."

"Record us?" Liam said. "Like, he can record what we're saying?" He looked aghast.

"Yeah, like, he can definitely record what we're saying," Madison said, gently. She blew her bangs away from her face as she watched him. "Don't worry, though. It's not the same as in the classroom. If you just talk quiet, the Globes won't bother trying to listen. They could filter out all the noise and hear any one of us, of course. But there's hundreds of kids in here. They won't run diagnostics unless you look suspicious. Just act normal. We're safe just so long as the Drones or Associates don't get too close."

Liam's eyes somehow opened wider. "They record us in the classroom, too?"

I pointed up at the ceiling. "See those?" Liam looked up. Spaced every fifty feet or so around the cafeteria, making a grid of the entire space, were the Observation Globes. If you didn't know any better you'd think they were simply architectural—glossy hemispheres decorating the upper reaches of the room. You might think so, that is, until you noticed that they were everywhere at 231.

Liam stared. "I thought those were the emergency lights. Isn't that the thing that changed colors back in the room? When that girl was, you know..." He trailed off.

Randall elbowed him. "Don't ever look at one of them for too long. Just because they don't really listen to us in here doesn't mean they aren't watching." He poked at his food and forced a big smile. "If the Algorithm thinks we're doing something unusual, any weird aberration to our behavior? It'll notify the Z.A., and they'll send someone over to check us out."

"The Globes hold the cameras and the spread mics, and they also double as the signal lights," I interrupted. "They're in every classroom, every hallway, every dorm. They're even going to watch you brush your teeth." Liam's eyes lit up again. "There is no privacy here. That goes for all of us, Peeks or Guests."

"The good news, though," Kiki said, smiling back at Randall, then pointing at me as if I'd just said something really funny, "is that usually we can talk in here, and in the common room." She stopped performing and looked around, laid eyes on all the nearby Associates. "Just so long as those guys keep their distance."

Liam seemed as if he were about to ask another question, but stopped. Kiki grinned for real and offered him the orange from her tray. He took it and started ripping anxious chunks off the peel with his thumbnail. I wondered what his last meal at home had been like, whether his parents had been there, if he had any siblings in the house. I would find out soon enough. It wouldn't be long before we all became Liam's new family, like it or not.

"So the Code Red and the Infraction were two different things," I said. "I mean, they came into the room because of the Code —that's how they always case the building—but I don't think they were specifically after Jazz or anything. That is, until she decided to make them come after her." I looked around at the others and added, "I have no idea why they called the Code Red in the first place. We'll hear something later, probably?" Everybody shrugged in turn.

"But not always," Madison muttered.

"Truth," Kiki said, pointing at her and shaking her head.

"You're telling me that wasn't a drill?" Liam asked, his voice rising again. "We did those once a month at my old school. I just assumed that they were clearing the building for an exercise or something, and then that girl…Jazz…did what she did."

Randall laughed. "No, rookie, that was not a drill. There are Code Reds here often enough that we get plenty of practice the old-fashioned way. I am here to announce that there is no need for drills at

231." He finished in a kind of mock salute to the table.

Liam looked like he might cry again. "And Jazz?"

I glanced at Kiki one more time, thinking she might know more, but she was watching the Peeks. I followed her gaze to see them clearing tables and lining up at their exit. It was a quiet process, punctuated only by the occasional call from an Associate, hollering for someone to come back and clean something up that had been missed in the initial departure.

Turning back to Liam, I said, "I don't know about Jazz either. Obviously, she was supposed to be under her desk just like the rest of us."

"So that was a taser they used on her, right?" he asked, and I nodded. "Is every Infraction like that? I mean, do you always get tased?"

Randall cut in. "An Infraction ends however they want it to end. It's best not to press your luck and find out."

There was a lull, and, as if on cue, a Drone whooshed by. We all took advantage to sit there in silence for a moment.

"Yeah, but why?" Liam said, once Maddy touched his arm and nodded an all-clear. "Why would she do that? Did she know they would tase her?"

"Oh, she knew," Kiki smiled, turning back toward the rest of the group. "She knew exactly what she was doing."

The alarm went off on our side of the cafeteria. It was something more than the bell I remembered from my middle school back home, but a lot less than the wailing siren we heard during lockdown. In stark contrast to the Peeks, we were allowed to make a reasonable amount of noise taking our trash up to the front and crowding our way to the exit. In the push and shove I grabbed Liam to help guide him through the motions.

"We'll talk more tonight in the dorm, okay?" I patted him on the shoulder in what I hoped was a comforting manner. I was the youngest of four siblings; this elder statesman role wasn't exactly in my wheelhouse. Thinking of my actual family, though, reminded me of something. "By the way," I asked, "believe me when I say that I'm not trying to be rude. But, seriously, how old are you?"

He fell in step beside me as we moved toward the doors. "Fourteen," he said, hanging his head just a little. "You?"

"Sixteen," I replied. "You skip a grade at some point?"

He nodded. "And I have a late birthday. I don't turn fifteen until next summer." He looked around. "Is it that obvious I don't fit in?"

I laughed as we fell in line for the exit. "Liam, it would be weird if you fit into this place right away. Just wait. A couple of weeks? You'll blend in just fine. And things will never be the same." And, for the first time since I met him, Liam smiled.

There was only one way out of the cafeteria, Guests and Peeks alike through adjacent doors, and everyone was queueing up along the chain link fence to get through our side. The pair of double doors gave way to a double set of hallways, still separated by the chain link fence. We rarely moved around the building at the same time as the Peeks, but when it was necessary Admin made sure we weren't able to mingle. The Guest side of the hall was spotted with windows looking out over the security buildings and the Recks Area. The Peek side was straight cinder block.

About three-quarters of the way down our hall, their side hit a dead end and turned to the left. Ours kept going straight for a couple hundred more feet. The chain link stopped where their side turned, and our hallway became regular again. Before this transition, however, there was a brief moment where you could catch a glimpse down into their part of the building. I glanced over to see that though they had left the cafeteria some time back, it seemed like a lot of them were still in their hall, standing in line waiting—for what? They should have been in class already. I stopped for a second and tried to make out what was going on.

"What gives?" Kiki asked, bumping into me and throwing her

hands in the air. She had been staring out the windows, probably thinking about how Recks was going to be super boring without Jazz.

"What's going on down there?" I asked, pointing down the Peek hall. She glanced over and shrugged.

"No telling. I'm sure Mason will know." She grabbed my arm and pulled me along. "Come on, I actually care about this class. It's the only good part of our day and I don't want to miss a second of it!"

Liam was waiting for us at the end of the hallway. He could have just followed the traffic flow, but it was obvious that he didn't want to walk alone. The classrooms were all off to the left,   but as we turned I pointed to the right. "That's the way to our dorms. We're not allowed in there during the day without being authorized, just so you know."

"We're not allowed anywhere in this building without an authorization, Ben," Kiki said. She turned to Liam and added, overly serious, "The only safe place to be is wherever you already are."

I laughed. "For real, though. Don't try to get over anyone or you'll end up with all kinds of problems."

"Who can write me a pass?" Liam asked. I cut a look at Kiki, saw her grin at his use of such a quaint expression. There was nothing here like teachers scrawling passes on spare scraps of paper. We waited for the rest of the Guests to move past us and then pulled up at the back of the line.

"Depends on the time of day. But most of the adults can authorize you with their scanner. Teachers, Associates, Z.A.s, G.A.s" I paused. "They gave you your Credentials?"

He held up his wrist, wriggled it back and forth to show the thin plastic bracelet that was a permanent part of everyone's wardrobe here at 231. "This?" He tugged at it to demonstrate the tight fit. I showed him mine as a mirror image.

"That's the one. That's your ticket around the building. Anywhere you go separate from the rest of the Block, you'll have to get your Credentials cleared."

"But Liam?" Kiki asked, pausing outside the door to Mason's class.

Liam stopped and looked at her. "He's going to say otherwise, but if some kid named Kenny tells you he can get your Credentials authorized? That he can trick the Algorithm and get you a pass for snacks or something?" Liam nodded earnestly and Kiki went on. "Don't listen to him. He's been trying for years to hack the system, and all he'll do is get your canteen allowance wiped."

He looked at me and I shrugged. "Like I said, give it a week or so. Soon you'll fit right in." I gestured grandly to the open door and Kiki waltzed in ahead of me, smiling and waving to someone I couldn't see. I looked at Liam, nodded toward the opening.

"You'll like it in here," I said. He took a breath and stepped inside.

CHAPTER 3

MASON

In general, the Peeks arrived first to Mason's class, through a separate door that led from their hall. Guests always got a few extra minutes at lunch, delaying us just enough so we could arrive after the Peeks got settled into their desks. At the end of class we would run the play in reverse; Guests left a few minutes early and they would wait us out. Given this system, it was unusual to enter the classroom and see even a couple of empty Peek seats, though I had expected it today given all the bodies in the hallway. Walking into class, however, I was shocked to note that at the moment the room held only Guests.

I froze in the doorway, stared over toward the Peek entrance. It was still shut and locked. Mason was at his desk, feet kicked up, writing on a clipboard. He motioned to me to close our door and stood up, walked toward the front of the room as he scrawled. I clicked the handle into place and heard the soft whir of the automatic lock. Then I sat down and waited.

For the most part we travelled from class to class in the same group of students—Guests from K Block and Peeks from Zone 7, around twenty of them and twenty of us. There was a kid from E Block who attended Mason's class with us, someone who had credit from another school that made his schedule run a little off from the rest of his Block. I didn't know his name; we only saw him in here and he was pretty quiet. All the other Guests had been present in Williams's class just an hour ago during the Code Red, had witnessed what happened to Jazz. Seeing the E Block kid made me wonder what the Lockdown had been like in the rest of the building.

For what felt like forever, Mason just stood at the front of the room, bouncing back and forth on the balls of his feet and writing on his clipboard. I tried to keep my eyes on him, for the Globe, but couldn't help myself from glancing over at the Peek door; still no sign of life. The entire Zone might be right on the other side, though—it was all but impossible to hear anything through the reinforced steel. We could have been chatting while we waited—though there were teachers who always enforced strict silence in the classroom, Mason wasn't one of them. The vibe in the room was strange, however. Timewise, we were already late getting started, but with half the class missing it didn't seem like Mason was in any hurry to begin. I was just about to write a note to Randall when Mason hugged the clipboard to his chest and looked around.

"I know that all of you were anticipating us advancing our discussion of *Frankenstein* today," he said. The sound of bags being unzipped and books flapping open followed his mention of our text. "It seems, however, that the events of this morning have destined us to be little more than mice." He paused and cocked an eyebrow at us. We all knew that look—we were supposed to be reading something into what he was saying.

On a normal day Jazz would beat us all to the punch, but with her absence Kiki had space to think. "Best laid plans!" she called out, and Mason smiled. Everyone knew he lived for this stuff.

"The best laid plans of mice and men, often go awry," he quoted. "You probably remember the line from our study of Steinbeck last year, but these incisive words were written by Robert Burns in 1785. Like Mary Shelley, he was also from the British Isles." He paused for a moment and added, "This was long before Russia annexed them into Greater Europe, of course."

Mason waited another beat, clearly trying to decide how long he could get away with this diversion. A shake of his head and he went on. "At any rate, our discussion of *Frankenstein*—this gothic master-piece, a work of early science fiction written when the author was scarcely older than you are today—sadly, it will have to wait. It seems that the Code Red has unexpectedly delayed us."

David immediately raised his hand. Besides the one kid from E Block, everyone else in the room was in my dorm. Meaning that, much like family, we lived and ate together every day, stuck with each other even when we might not like it. David was definitely in that camp; everything about him rubbed me the wrong way. Mason nodded in his direction, and he spoke a little too loudly for the half empty room. "Can you tell us what's going on out there, Mr. Mason, sir? I happened to notice that many of the Peeks were still in the hallway for some reason. Do you know why?" He seemed pleased with himself that he had acquired this completely obvious information. I tried not to roll my eyes.

Mason sighed, though I couldn't tell whether his frustration lie with David or the situation with the Peeks. "It seems that the…In-fraction…incurred by your classmate,"—he glanced over to where Jazz typically sat, and then back to the room at large—"has raised the threat of inspection for some on the other side. They will be joining us shortly, I am told."

The class immediately broke out into an uproar. I couldn't remem-ber the last time we heard about an unscheduled inspection. Usually they did them at night, and we would only hear about it later across the chain link fence. Mason held up a hand, but Kiki spoke over it. "All because of Jazz?" she asked.

Mason waited in that obvious way teachers do and the class quickly went silent. "No. And yes." He paused for a moment and looked at the Globe in the ceiling, seemed to consider something for a moment. He turned back to us and went on. "The Code Red didn't have anything to do with Jazz. But the G.A.s seem to be...curious...about why Jazz chose the moment of the lockdown for her...actions. Shall we call them a protest of sorts?"

"That's bullshit," Kiki said. I saw Liam tense at her words. No way kids were that real with adults at his old school. "They were just looking for a reason to bring her in and she gave them one. They would have done it any which way."

"That is entirely possible," Mason said, looking back toward the Globe. "Quite often there exists more than one interpretation of any given event."

Mason was one of the few Black teachers at 231. He was tall and thin, always wore a shirt and tie with his Chuck Taylors. He had glasses that stayed perched on his nose, and he was constantly changing the angle of his head to look either over or through them. A routine move involved surveying the whole class over the frames; when a student said something particularly insightful he would move closer and lean back, look them straight in the eye through the lenses. Everyone liked him. It wasn't just that this was most everybody's favorite class. It was that, for the bulk of us, this was one of the only places in the building we felt seen by something other than the Globes.

He started walking up and down the aisles, another favorite move. When he got next to Liam, he stopped and looked down at him through his lenses. "Hello, young man. Welcome to our class." He turned to gesture toward the empty seats in an exaggerated fashion. "Such as it is today, at least. I can assure you that usually we are accomplishing more from a literary point of view than we are right now."

I could see Liam visibly relax. Mason was everything that Williams wasn't; he must have reminded Liam of home. He stuck out his hand and said, "Hi. I mean, hello. I mean, good afternoon. Sir. Good afternoon, sir."

Mason smiled and shook his head, stuck his hands forcibly into his pockets. "I don't do that in here, sorry." He smiled and looked up at the Globe over his head. "Too many eyes, in communication with too many lawyers." A couple of kids laughed. Even Liam smiled.

Mason strolled back over to his desk and sat down. "You all can look over your notes while we wait. I don't know how long they'll be. Remember our guiding question for today: *in a world where so many things fade away, why does this old novel continue to capture our imaginations?*

The class split off into conversations, none of which had anything to do with *Frankenstein*. The possibility of an inspection had us all a little rattled. Whatever the Code Red had been about, it must have been serious for them to be pulling a whole class out at once. Word was that years ago even a single inspection could take hours—they would make someone take off all their clothes and get searched by hand, sit them down under lights and ask a barrage of questions. The body searching stopped when the government banned it—fears about lawsuits over due process trumped the expediency of the results—but what happened these days was somehow supposed to be worse. I'd never been through an inspection—few Guests had—but I'd heard plenty of horror stories about the device.

The rumble around the room was split into pockets, mostly indiscernible. There was plenty to talk about—a class wide discussion about our day would have been nice—but we had all become expert at keeping off the Globes whenever possible. I was surprised, then, to hear Randall's voice rise up above the rest. He was arguing with Madison and suddenly shouted out, "You know it as well as I do, Maddy! It's total bullshit that they might get inspected when we're just sitting here in class like normal."

Every conversation in the room immediately ground to a halt. I looked at Mason, worried, wondering how he would react. I was pretty sure I knew what he thought about inspections. What he would say about it in a classroom full of students was another matter altogether.

He dropped his magazine to the desk—he was always either writing or reading; I never saw him scrolling on his screen. He looked casually toward our door, pointedly keeping his eyes away from the Peek entrance. "Appearances may be deceiving, Randall," he said slowly, trailing his gaze across the room, looking over his lenses at each of us in turn. "And yet, they are sometimes demonstrative," he finished. Then he switched perspectives on his glasses, picked up his magazine, and went back to his reading.

Liam turned to me. "Does he always talk like that?"

I was watching Randall, half worried someone was about to bust through the door and grab him for his outburst, but I turned to Liam and replied. "Yeah, it's kind of his thing. Keeping up with his code isn't part of your official grade or anything. But everybody hustles extra to understand in here. You'll see—it's just the way it works with Mason."

"What does he mean? About appearances being demonstrative?"

Randall turned around, away from Madison, and cut in. "Just watch. You'll know what he's talking about when they get back."

Liam looked across the room. "The Peeks you mean?"

"Yeah," Randall replied. He was flipping idly through *Frankenstein*; I couldn't help but notice that he'd marked up far more of the book than I had. "The only way you could miss it is if you weren't willing to pay attention."

Liam looked as if he were going to ask another question, but he was interrupted by a insistent ring coming from the Peek door. Mason stood and walked over, put his eye up to the retinal scanner that would allow entry from the other side; only a G.A. could access a classroom from the hallway without a teacher's permission. The door buzzed and swung into the room. Two Associates stepped through, squared up and angled their bodies. Momentarily, the Peeks shuffled silently in, moving slowly past the Associates toward their section. I turned my head sharply over to catch Randall's eye. Atypically, every Peek was wearing handcuffs.

The room had been quiet before but somehow got even more dead, the silence cut only by the sound of jangling chains. Liam turned to me and looked like he was about to say something, but I shook my head, pointed to his notebook. It took him a second to catch on, but then he scribbled something on a scrap of paper and handed it to me.

What did Mr. Mason mean? What am I supposed to be looking for? Do they always wear handcuffs when they come to class?

I shook my head to answer his last question and, in a fit of inspiration that I thought would have impressed Mason, I wrote back. *But that's not the thing. It's that appearance, like beauty, is often only skin deep.*

I passed the paper back to Liam and mimed squishing it up, tossing it into my mouth. He nodded and read the note. For a moment it felt like I could see his mind working as he sat there thinking, then looking up and around the room. I watched him stare over at the Peeks as he crumpled the note, saw the disgust as he tried to chew it up. It almost made me laugh to wonder if he had ever tasted paper before. Everyone was just about seated when his jaws stopped. He swallowed hard, his eyes went a little bit wider, and he cut his glance toward Mason. I knew then that he finally saw it.

Our side of the room—the Guest's area—was pretty diverse. About half of us were white—Liam, Madison, and me among them. Half of the rest were Black, like Kiki and Randall. Carlos and Diana were Hispanic; Ellie and Jon were Asian; Kai was Indigenous. It was like a meeting of the model U.N. over where Liam and I were sitting. You could take any random picture, put in on a brochure, and it would be like a commercial trying to sell Federal Education Sites to worried parents.

On the other side, however, there were twenty Peeks, sitting stock still in their desks. One of the Associates kept a hand on his taser while the other went around to remove their handcuffs. The Peeks were all wearing matching orange jumpsuits. Everyone's face showed a similar look of exhaustion. As their handcuffs were removed, each of them quickly placed their palms flat on the desk. No one spoke. Nobody so much as even breathed a little too heavy.

All but one of the Peeks were Black or Hispanic.

———————————

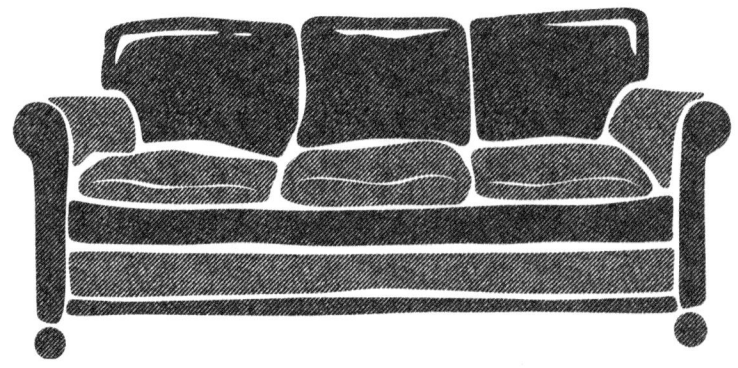

CHAPTER 4

FIRST NIGHT

"I'm sorry, guys," Liam said, "but I still just don't understand."

The entire Block was sitting in our common room. We had finally made it to the end of the day, through dinner and Recks. By the time the Peeks had settled into Mason's class—the removal of handcuffs was a theater that always took some time—he decided to push *Frankenstein* to the next day. He officially assigned study hall for the rest of the period, but I think he knew that the Peeks just needed some space to talk after what turned out to be a threatening bluff. In the end there was no inspection, but Admin was definitely looking for something and it had everyone spooked. Cancelling class was the only way that Mason could give the Peeks anything like a break.

Dinner and Recks had been super quiet. The entire school seemed on edge, and even though folks took to the court and shot around during Recks, a game never materialized. We sat there for a while watching Randall play a series of one-on-ones with Orion, but without

Jazz it seemed like nobody else was feeling it. Half of K Block came back to the dorm even before curfew. We gave Liam a quick tour—there wasn't much to see so it didn't take long—then found his stuff from home and got him settled into his new space, such as it was. After that we made for the common area. We still had over an hour until lights dim.

"What don't you understand?" Kiki asked. All twenty of us were back by now, scattered around the room, broken off into four or five conversations. Between three sofas and a handful of chairs, there were almost enough seats for everyone—just so long as you didn't mind being up in your roommate's business. Like I told Liam, there was no privacy here at 231.

Liam looked up at the Globe overhead, cut his eyes back to me. I laughed. "Excellent instincts, but you're actually safe here. The Algorithm is still watching us, for sure, but the dorm is the only place in the whole site where they're not allowed to listen." He looked at me incredulously.

Carlos called out from the corner, bent over his screen, working on something or another. He was always working on something. Like Mason, he didn't waste time. "Ben's right, rookie," he said. "Somebody won a lawsuit at some point and the court ruled that 'freedom of speech' extended all the way into 231." He looked up. "It was a wild victory for us. The Algorithm even has to blur our mouths in here so nobody can read lips from the footage."

"Everywhere else is government business," Kiki said, waving her hand around to indicate the small room. "But this? This is our own little kingdom."

"But still, you have to be careful," I warned, leaning toward the Globe in an offhand way. "The Algorithm still watches your eyes and your body. If it picks up too much variation it'll think something is going on and send someone to check up on us. Just make sure you look super laid back at all times."

"Like this," Randall said, kicking his feet up on the coffee table and sliding down into his chair. He was in a good mood after winning two out of three against Orion. Picking up his screen, he swiped cartoonishly and smiled in an exaggerated rictus.

Liam laughed. "Okay," he said slowly, leaning back into the sofa. "Laid back. I can do that." Randall looked up.

"You could not look less laid back, rookie," he said. "But for your first day? I'll give you proper points for trying." Liam held his hand up in the air and imitated Randall's swiping, cracking everyone up.

He turned back to Kiki. "I guess I'm surprised. I didn't expect to come here and see something so...prejudiced...as that classroom." Half the room broke out in laughter, but Liam went on. "I'm serious! When they passed the Prison Expansion Act they said we needed it to maintain equality or whatever. They told us that—"

Randall cut in. "Son, you can go the fuck on with all that." His tone changed on a dime as he waved his hand dismissively. The room went still, all eyes on him. "And you can cut that shit out with *prejudice* or whatever. What they do here is *racist* and that's all there is to it. They've always put more Black people into prisons, time out of mind. It's just what they do to us." He gestured at Kiki, who nodded. "How you going to expect prison schools to be any different?"

Tossing his screen on the coffee table and pulling a pencil out of his pocket, he twirled it through his fingers, all along keeping eye contact with Liam. I knew Randall well, and even still his vibe was unnerving. I couldn't imagine how Liam felt right now.

Randall was probably my best friend here at 231. My first day here was terrifying for all the same reasons that were swirling Liam's head right now, and Randall and I had met during intake. He was scared, too, though I couldn't tell it at the time; his confidence was contagious, and it got me through those first terrible weeks. It was only later that he admitted to me his own fears. I could tell he liked Liam. But I also knew that he wasn't going to give him anything like a free pass on his ignorance of Federal Sites. Being new came with a steep learning curve.

Liam looked away from Randall awkwardly. He glanced up at the Globe again and cleared his throat, quite obviously changing the subject. "Hey, I have a question about rooms and cameras and...showers... and..." He trailed off, and I cut in laughing. It was time to give the new kid a break on his first day; it wasn't his fault he that was so overwhelmed.

"You mean how it all works?" I spread my hands out to cover all the conversations bubbling back to life. "You want to know why they've got twenty of us sleeping in the same room, right?" Liam blushed and nodded.

Kiki spoke up. "It's simple really. See, they just don't care about who likes who here. It doesn't matter to them that Ben likes girls, or that I like girls, or that Maddy for whatever reason likes these boys." Here she rolled her eyes over at Randall, sitting as close to Maddy as they could manage with the Globe watching. Maddy blushed and Randall grinned.

Kiki waved her hands and finished. "Hell, they don't even care that Carlos doesn't like none of y'all."

"Not true!" Carlos interrupted. "I'm just keeping my options open until one of you finally impresses me with something special." He looked up. "And it's 'who likes whom,' if you want to be proper about it all."

"Go on with your proper," Kiki said, snatching the pencil out of Randall's hand and chucking it at Carlos. "Anyways, the thing is that they can put us all into a room to live together because there is not a single moment where you will ever be alone with anyone else." She pointed at the Globe. "The only privacy you will get is in the shower, the toilet, or that tiny-ass changing room that connects them. And if they catch you going in there with someone else..." She grimaced and drew a finger across her throat.

"Don't stay in there too long alone either," Randall said, grinning, holding out a hand for Carlos to give back his pencil. "They monitor hot water and toilet paper here, too. If the Algorithm thinks you've been spending too much time in there they'll dock your canteen allowance."

Liam looked at me, panicked, and I shrugged. We had always heard this was true, though no one quite knew what the threshold for "too much" might be with regards to toilet paper.

"Five minutes, y'all," said Randall, suddenly. He jumped to his feet and picked up his screen. Kiki sighed and stood up, pushed Maddy's legs off the coffee table. Normally she would have objected, loudly, but instead she rolled off the couch and got to her feet as well. All around the room everyone except Liam was following suit—David was organizing screens and books, Kai was throwing away trash. We all started arranging the furniture, which had slowly scattered around the room throughout the evening, facing all the seats toward the blank wall opposite the hallway.

"Get up, rookie," Randall said, tapping Liam on the arm. "Four minutes."

Liam stood up and looked around. "Four minutes until what?" he asked. He picked a cushion up off the ground and seemed perplexed. I pointed toward a sofa whose upholstery pattern in no way matched the object in Liam's hand.

"That goes there. Don't ask why," I said. "Four minutes until the News. Don't ask about that either. You'll just have to wait and see."

Liam nodded. It had been a long day, and he was probably relieved to stop talking about it all, even for just a little while. He wasn't going to feel quite so sanguine in three more minutes; it felt like a small kindness to let him have this moment of peace.

The room more or less arranged, everyone went to their usual seats. I was on the couch between Kiki and Randall. Carlos was squeezed in on the other side of Kiki, almost sideways against the arm, Ellie leaning right up next to his legs. I motioned for Liam to sit on the floor in front of us next to Madison. Like I said, there weren't enough seats when we were all present. Nobody was stupid enough to give the News anything less than full attention, though—not just because of an uncomfortable seat assignment.

"Hey Liam?" Randall asked. Liam looked over at him and Randall went on. "Whatever you do, just keep your face pointed toward the display."

Liam looked around the room. "What display?" he said, but suddenly the blank wall lit to life. Everyone turned immediately to stare at it, shoulders straight and hands in our laps. Out of the corner of my eye I saw Liam looking around at several of us, clearly bewildered. It only took him a few moments, however, to adjust his posture to match ours.

The display was filled by the same two faces that spoke to us every night. In fact, no one in my dorm could remember a time that it wasn't Donna and Dan on the wall delivering the News. They leaned intensely toward the camera as the theme music swelled, the shot slowly zooming out to show off a giant map of the United States. She was a bottle blonde, wore too much makeup, smiled incessantly. I'd heard some kids describe her as pretty, but her look just wasn't really my thing. He had slicked back hair and a clean-shaven face. He didn't smile as much as she did, but when he did they both had identical rows of blazing white teeth. Their vibe was one of a perpetually disagreeing married couple; they could have been brother and sister, though, for the way they gave the same energy.

Donna went first, speaking through her teeth at us.

Good evening, City! So wonderful to be with you again after another beautiful day. Both the weather and the news were excellent today—let's get into it! Employment is up, productivity is up, the stock market is up. Temperatures are up too, probably rising with all of that good news! The economy has never been in better shape, according to this recent report from the President's Council of Civic Adjustment. Let's go to my interview from earlier today with that Department's Director, who spoke to us from inside the White House, of all places!

The display cut to a clip of an old white man talking loudly at the camera. He had the same strange teeth as Donna and Dan, his hair swooped sideways over a conspicuous bald spot. He repeated what Donna had already said but in a slightly different order—productivity, stocks, then employment—before the camera cut back to the studio and a shot of Dan.

He was straightening a stack of papers in an aggressive, repetitive manner. His gaze into the camera lagged just a second or two behind the cut to his face; for a moment the News was just a picture of Dan staring intently at a stack of papers, shuffled over and over by his angry hands. Suddenly I was overcome with the idea that these papers must be blank. I felt the corner of my mouth twitch, like I might laugh in spite of myself.

It lasted only a second, though. One glance at the Globe overhead was more than enough to chill that urge right out of me.

Finally Dan turned to the camera and scowled, his disappointed mouth framing bared teeth. He spoke in a low voice, laced with obvious disgust at the information he was for some terrible reason forced to bring to our attention.

The economy is good news, Donna, but unfortunately there is far more going on in the City than just our booming business sector. As all of you know, our City is also a festering mess of criminal activity. These are citizens who have shown themselves unwilling to work—they have no desire to secure an honest job for the the good of their families. This despite a record low level of unemployment! These malefactors could find a job if they wanted to. It seems, sadly, that they would rather commit crime. Tonight's stats are grim, but the City General has a plan. Let's cut to my interview with him from this morning.

It went on like that for fifteen minutes. Donna would smile and tell us about how great things were going—tell a story about a family saving an abandoned litter of puppies from the City Pound, let us know that they all found nice new homes. Dan would give us the myriad of dangers faced by those homes, interview a principal at a failing school in an adjoining neighborhood. All the while, various talking heads came and went to reinforce what Donna and Dan were saying. I was numb to it at this point, able to keep my body focused even as my mind flitted about aimlessly. I knew everyone else was doing the same; most nights after the News we could barely hold a conversation about what we'd seen for all the attention we were collectively giving it. Liam, however? I could only imagine how he was taking all this.

I was shocked out of my reverie by Dan's final segment of the night, though—last in a string of supposed threats to the City, he had begun to talk about our school.

And we're bringing you breaking news here, City. Today, over at Federal Education Site 231, a startling incident has led to more questions than answers. It seems that a routine Code Red was interrupted by an intentional act of terrorism, committed by a Student-Prisoner whose name is still being withheld due to the nature of an ongoing investigation. The Head Admin for 231 has assured us that all Guests are safe and secure, and that steps have been taken to ensure that this S.P. will be disciplined to the fullest extent allowed by the Expansion Act. Fortunately for all of us, this premeditated crime was caught on camera by one of 231's Observation Globes. We have been assured here at City News that this footage will lead to swift and certain punishment.

Dan stopped suddenly and looked down at his papers, started re-stacking them yet again. Then the News ended the same way it did every night. Dan turned to Donna and smiled, his face completely out of sync with his tone from just moments before, and they held each other's gaze for an instant before turning together to look back into the camera.

Well, that's our City News for tonight, Donna said.

Keep in mind, City, that it is our solemn duty to eliminate the darkness, Dan added.

—but never forget to praise the progress of lights, Donna finished, with a smile.

After a beat the display clicked softly and became again just a blank wall. Instantly Randall stood up. "I don't know about those puppies, y'all!" he said. "How come we never get puppies here?"

"Puppies?" Diana asked, perplexed. She was typically the best at tuning Dan and Donna out.

"Weren't you listening, Randy?" Carlos threw a pillow and hit him in the back. "Our school is a known terror camp. We're really going to have to shape up or they're never going to give us a puppy!"

"No puppies?" Randall said, his mouth open wide in mock surprise.

"Guys?" Liam asked, looking around. I didn't need to see his face to know he must be freaking out. Most kids straight from the outside had never seen the News before in their lives.

Maddy interrupted him. "Don't let the Algorithm catch you being upset, Liam" she said, angling her head back toward the Globe. "Just stand up and stretch. Maybe throw a pillow at Randall first—that makes everyone feel better." She turned and chucked one at him. He caught it deftly and immediately handed it back to her with a flourishing bow.

Liam stood up and started doing deep knee bends. "Guys, what was that?"

Kiki burst out laughing. "Rookie, I don't think Maddy meant to literally stretch!" She started doing toe touches. "But I don't want the Algorithm to pick you up just for being some kind of weirdo, so I'll help out." A couple of kids laughed and started doing jumping jacks.

"That was the News," I said. "We watch it every night from 9:30 to 9:45, and then we head back toward bed. It is…" I balked at how to describe it. Too many words went through my mind.

"Dispiriting?" Carlos offered. The rest of the dorm was slowly filtering their way out the back hallway. I touched Liam on the arm, pointed to follow them. He stopped doing knee bends and fell in line.

"I was going to say 'a dumpster fire,' Carlos. But I'll defer to your superior diction." I turned to Liam. "The News is just one of those things you'll get used to," I said.

"And we have to watch it like that?" Liam asked, looking back over his shoulder at the empty room, as if he were already forming negative connotations with that wall.

"It is not worth the trouble to disagree with the News," Randall said. "If they think we're not paying attention, they'll send Associates in to watch with us. Nobody wants that." He shrugged and pushed ahead to catch up to Maddy.

The short hallway gave way to our bunkroom—a large, rectangular space with three skylights spaced evenly across the ceiling. There were twelve bunk beds, six pushing out into the room widthwise from each of the opposite walls. They were so close together that with a medium-sized lean you could slap the person next to you awake. Against all available wall space were scattered 24 small wardrobes atop 24 small chests; if you had more stuff than space you had no choice but to get rid of stuff. Straight across the corridor of beds were the privacy rooms, such as they were. We got six of these, also. Crammed in between each pair of doors was a small sink and mirror.

Liam looked up at the Globes. He pointed in what he probably thought was a surreptitious manner. It came off more like an oversized marionette lurching at the sky.

I laughed and shook my head. "This room is for sleeping only," I said, choosing my words carefully. "We get ready for bed, maybe read a book if you're up to it, then we go to sleep. Lights dim is at 10:30 and wakeup at 7:00." I smiled in my best impression of Donna.

Liam got the picture and nodded. The microphones were on in here.

The drill at the end of the night was pretty basic. It's not that we literally couldn't talk, rather it's that it felt like a waste of time to speak in here after the relative freedom of the common room. We took turns in the privacy rooms, bundled up on our bunks—Liam got a whole bed to himself and chose the top—and everyone read or wrote in the shuffling silence. Screens were forbidden since they were proven to be bad for sleeping, so most of us would doze off even before mandated bedtime.

At 10:30 the fluorescent lights clicked off and the Globes turned up, casting a low golden glow into every corner of the room. I could all but hear Liam's unspoken question: *they watch us even while we sleep?* He was catching on quick, though; he kept quiet.

For a long time I lay there and listened to my roommates breathe.

I knew Randall was asleep when the first big snores hit the dorm; I could hear Maddy adjusting her blankets over and over as she tried to get comfortable. David was counting to himself under his breath, just barely out loud, muttering his mind to a state of relaxation; Kiki was slowly stretching her arms and legs, a relaxation routine she had taught herself at the start of sophomore year. Liam lay there longer than the rest, of course. Learning how to sleep in the light of the Globes took me a month, and I couldn't even imagine how fast his thoughts must be racing. It was a wild understatement to say that he had been through a lot today.

Eventually his breathing slowed, too. I didn't need to look over to know that he had finally dozed off. After two and a half years at 231, I could identify a sleeping roommate with unerring accuracy. I was the last one awake pretty much every night, had probably listened to the sound of someone falling from wake to sleep thousands of times.

Then, just like clockwork, when I was finally alone, I felt it hit.

I closed my eyes tight, took a deep ragged breath. The day flashed through my mind in fast-forward, from breakfast to Liam to the Code Red, the Infraction, then to Jazz being called a terrorist on the News. I managed to keep control for a minute, tried to focus on everyone else in the room, listened in turn to all of my roommates breathe.

Eventually, however, just like every night, I gave up. Turning over onto my stomach, I buried my face into my pillow and cried myself to sleep.

———————————

CHAPTER 5
THE MEETING

The line to get through security for the Meeting was much longer than usual.

The common room had been a riot that morning. We all took turns trying to explain the News to Liam, tripping over ourselves to do our impressions of Dan or Donna; we brainstormed together to wonder what it meant that Jazz had made the program. Everyone assumed the situation would run forward into the Meeting. Liam had no idea how unusual yesterday had been—something big was brewing, something more than just a Code Red or Jazz putting her hands up in Williams's class. We all hoped that today we would learn something more.

The walk to the auditorium involved going back toward the cafeteria but staying straight at the turn, heading past all the classrooms. Eventually our hallway joined back up with the Peek side, and the chain-link fence led us right to the long line of people waiting to get inside the giant room. This was one of two places where all the students at 231 could be seated at once. The cafeteria was small enough that they had to feed us in shifts; the only other place we could all gather was the gym.

"What the hell?" Randall said, craning his neck to see. He was half a head taller than anyone except Liam, able to see into the auditorium even from here.

"Are they in there already?" I asked. The entire walk I had been worried that the Peeks were being inspected, that Admin had decided yesterday's threat level needed escalation.

"Yeah, it looks they're all in there—that's not the delay. They're checking everyone's Credentials at the door, I think."

"Is that not normal?" Liam asked. He had been pretty quiet all morning, managed to keep his questions to a minimum. If his first night was anything like I remember mine being, he'd slept only in patches. They said that the golden glow was supposed to be restorative for the neurons in our brains, but for most of us lights dim wreaked havoc on R.E.M. cycles. It might be weeks before he got a solid night's sleep.

"No," I said. "Usually everyone just walks on through. They'll grab a couple of random people for Credentials and retinal scans, but mostly for show. This can't be good." I reflexively twisted the bracelet against my wrist. I was in the right place—right along with my entire Block. Still, the fear of getting flagged for walking around without proper documentation was strong. Even on a normal day that could cause a lot of trouble.

Today was definitely shaping up to be abnormal.

The line inched forward slowly but surely. They had eight pairs of Associates running Credentials, and it seemed like every other kid they ran got grabbed for a retinal scan. In the time we stood in line three or four of those students were pulled straight off the scanners and escorted elsewhere, presumably for some sort of further examination. I wondered if they were getting inspected; I'd heard that they couldn't do that from a failed retinal scan alone, but things were definitely way out of order at this point. Maybe the rules had changed. I tried to take some deep breaths, slow my heart rate down. Even if it was only a routine interrogation and not an inspection, I did not want to miss this Meeting. Whatever was going on, I wanted to hear about it firsthand.

Liam and Randall made it through with just their Credentials, so I wasn't surprised when they asked me to step aside for a retinal scan. It only took a moment, the Associate pushing the goggles into place over my eyes without so much as a word of warning. There was no strap, so he just held them tight to my face, his other hand pressing the back of my head for stability. They fit like an ancient VR headset, except I couldn't see anything but the blinding light as it read my eyes. He pulled it away after a moment and we stood there waiting as the data processed. The flash was still burning in my brain when the Associate started reading my results to his partner.

"Pulse, 85. Blood pressure, 130 over 80. Blood-alcohol, zero. Cholesterol, normal. Sugar, high-mid but acceptable. Testosterone, high-mid, borderline unacceptable. Dopamine, normal. Serotonin, normal. Cortisol, high, unacceptable." He paused and looked at me, the clacking of his partner's keyboard breaking off into an obvious void.

"You okay, son?" he asked, stepping just a little closer. His gas mask wobbled a little bit to the side; he was near enough that I could see the stubble on his chin from where he had missed a spot shaving. "You seem a little nervous. Anything you want to tell us? Something you think we need to know?"

"No sir," I said, doing my best to appear calm. My stomach was doing flips, though. Nothing like this had ever happened to me before. The afterimage from the flash of the scanner was slowly fading away, but it was making me slightly dizzy as I stood there, knees locked in fear.

He glanced down at his screen, seemed to be reading through the results again, and then looked back up at me, waiting. It was clear I was going to have to say something to defend myself. I tried not to glance at the kid next to me as he got pulled away.

"Well, yes sir, I guess I am a little nervous," I said, forcing my frozen muscles to fidget just a little, hoping to demonstrate some anxiety for him. "We got a new student yesterday—a new Guest—and during the Code Red, I was just a little stressed out for him, I suppose. He seems like a good guy and I just wonder how he's doing with all this. It was a crazy first day, you know?"

The Associate watched me through my little speech, blank-faced. When I finished he nodded and turned away, back to his partner. "EKG, normal. Hemispheric brain waves, normal." He glanced at me. "You're good to go, son. I hope your new friend catches on quick. There's no reason to be nervous about anything here at 231. Not if you're acting right." He kept his eyes on me for just a moment as he cleared the scanner, and then he went back to the line.

I hustled to find my seat with the rest of the Block. I could feel my heart pounding; my throat felt dry but I was shaking too much to even reach for my water bottle.

"What'd they get you on?" Kiki asked as I was getting into my seat. Apparently they had been able to see me through the open door.

"Cortisol," I said. "He asked me if I was nervous about anything."

"Cortisol!" Randall barked. Several kids turned around to look and Madison shushed him, anxiously looking over at the nearest Associate. Randall waved her away. "Maddy, come on! How could you not have elevated cortisol here? How they going to flag you for stress in this place?" He started laughing.

It was like a balloon bursting—all my worry just disappeared, chased away by the sound of that little bit of joy. Kiki and Madison started laughing, too; even Liam cracked a smile.

"Truth is they should flag you for having low cortisol here," Kiki said, slapping Randall's hand. "That would mean you're too stupid to be stressed. Or you must be on drugs or something." She leaned against me she was laughing so hard. For a moment everything felt totally normal—we were just a bunch of friends having a good time at school. Randall was about to say something else, but then the Globes shifted to a bright blue color. In that flash of light the entire auditorium went dead silent.

The Meeting had started.

Four Associates marched out on stage and posted up in the corners—gas masks and goggles engaged, tactical gear at the ready. The H.A. strode out to the bulky lectern positioned at the center, paused for the drama of it and looked around at us. The Head was a large man with gray hair cropped short; as one of only a handful of civilians in the building, he tended toward boxy suits. He snapped his fingers and the blue light winked out. After carefully adjusting the microphone, drawing out the silence, he spoke.

"We would like to begin today's meeting by acknowledging the eight thousand, four hundred and twenty-eighth day of the Braswell Administration. We also gratefully acknowledge the peace and prosperity that our President has wisely brought to this great Nation." He looked around, all but daring one of us to say something. No one was foolish enough to try him. He smiled and went on, "For our opening moment I would like to welcome a member of our most illustrious senior class to the stage."

He gestured to the front row, where the oldest students sat, and today's randomly selected speaker came to the stage. She fidgeted with the microphone, looking nervous; I couldn't help but wonder what her cortisol levels were right now.

She read from the piece of paper that stayed permanently taped to the top of the lectern. "For our non-denominational moment of silence today we remember those who have gone before us." We all could have said the words by heart—she was only reading in order to make double sure she didn't make a mistake. "We know that it is only our actions that determine our character, and it is only our character that determines our place in the world. We pause, also, to consider those who will one day come after us. May their burdens be lighter by virtue of the times we spend in refinement."

She stopped reading and bowed her head; everyone followed suit. I felt a tickle in my throat but fought it off. One time a kid started coughing during the moment and they removed him pretty much immediately—the last thing I needed right now was to draw any more attention to myself.

After thirty seconds or so the student said, "Always."

The entire room, save for Liam, responded, "We remember."

She said, "We remember."

"Always," we replied.

She stepped away from the microphone and the Head returned, smiling, to do the announcements.

He went on first about our preparations for the Testing, scheduled in a couple of weeks. Then came Visitation, up next month—unfortunately subject to change due to the recent circumstances. Admin would keep us posted about any alterations to the schedule on a need-to-know basis. Next, he read out a lengthy list of college acceptances, pausing here or there to nod at a particular student. As usual, the list included more than a few high-profile schools—Dartmouth, Princeton, Cal Tech. Liam turned around to look at us several times, clearly surprised, but that was just naiveté on his part. The big-time scouts knew it just as well as we did: if you could succeed here, you could succeed anywhere. Score high enough on the Testing and you could basically write your own ticket out of this place.

The Head went on. "Some years back, before any of you were born, our great Nation used to acknowledge something they called 'Black History Month.' In recognition of this quaint history—a time before President Braswell did away with the need to recognize race under the law—the Admin asked one of your teachers, Mr. Mason, to come to the stage and read a poem. He has assured us that this is a reading with special significance to the…African-adjacent…community." He tripped over the phrase and, seemingly to cover his mistake, backed up suddenly and looked anxiously around for Mason. After ceding the lectern he went to the wings and awkwardly stood between two

Associates, partially hidden in the shadows.

Mason, on the other hand, could not have looked more relaxed. He had on a black shirt and gray pants, the red of his tie perfectly matching his crisp Chuck Taylors. After walking slowly up to the lectern he pulled a couple of folded papers out of his pocket, smoothed them out and placed them on top. Only then did he look up at us and smile. In stark contrast to the Head, it looked like he actually meant it—you could see it in his eyes.

"In 1950," he began, "a poet named Gwendolyn Brooks became the first Black American to win the Pulitzer Prize. She won it for her poetry, specifically for a collection entitled *Annie Allen*." Mason paused for just a moment and I couldn't help but think of Dan, just how different he felt when he read from his papers. Mason went on. "Today I would like to recite for you the last poem from *Annie Allen,* a piece known only by its first line—'Men of careful turns, haters of forks in the road.'"

He paused again and then put down his papers. He stepped away from the lectern, almost swaggered across to the front of the stage. He glanced over at the Head and gave a formal nod—the Head coughed and waved awkwardly back—and then he began to recite:

Men of careful turns, haters of forks in the road,
The strain at the eye, that puzzlement, that awe —
Grant me that I am human, that I hurt,
That I can cry.

Every word was like music, rising and falling to a rhythm hidden in Mason's mind, some sound that seemed to echo in my own imagination. He turned and paced to another portion of the stage, and I swear you could somehow hear an auditorium full of heads turning to follow him. I had always thought we were dead quiet for the Head, but I was wrong. That was a silence born out of compliance; it was filled with the noise of wandering thoughts. This was a stillness that could come only from respect.

He went on for more than a minute, taking long pauses after lines he must have considered important— *fearing sudden fire out of the uncaring mouth.* He circled the stage several times—*so our fathers said, and they were wise, we think*—before making his way back to the lectern—*the toys are all grotesque and not for lovely hands, are dangerous.* At times he was something like shouting; at others he seemed to be speaking to us in a conversational tone. Then he lowered his voice to the barest of whispers, leaning into the microphone for the first time so we could hear him. The effect was electric as he spoke the final phrases of this strange poem:

Rise.
Let us combine. There are no magics or elves
Or timely godmothers to guide us. We are lost, must
Wizard a track through our own screaming weed.

He bowed his head and went still, his heaving chest the only motion visible in his body. It was clear that no one knew what to do, but then the Head began a slow, moderate beat of applause. Everybody else in the Meeting joined in immediately, but at the same stately pace. It was a strange, muted expression of how I felt about what had just happened; it seemed like I was taking my first breath in the time since Mason had come to the stage. He looked up, nodded at us in a short bow, and walked off the stage. The Head ceased clapping immediately and within seconds we had all followed suit.

"That was...interesting...Mr. Mason," he said, slowly adjusting the microphone back so it angled up toward his prodigious height. "I'm not quite sure I followed every turn of Ms. Brooks's imagery, but, then again, I never was much for poetry. I always found myself more attracted to the mathematical mind and the certainty it yields." He paused awkwardly, as if waiting for a laugh, but when none materialized he went on, pulling a single sheet of paper out of a folder. Unusually, he began to read from the script in front of him.

"Yesterday we here at 231 experienced a routine Code Red event, one triggered by an unfortunate accident. It seems that a Drone broke down in Zone 7, which triggered the nearby Globe to enter into a state of partial malfunction. This breakdown led to a cascade of Globe failures throughout Zones 5, 6, and 7. When the Algorithm became aware of the fact that it had lost touch with more than three Globes, it followed protocol and called for a full, schoolwide lockdown."

The Head paused almost as if for effect, and the room was just as electric as when Mason had been speaking moments before. It was in an entirely different direction, though—then we had been facing forward, rapt, but now we were all doing our best to resist the urge to turn to our neighbors. I had been at 231 for over two years now and I'd never even heard of a Globe failure. I finally snuck glances at Kiki and Randall; they each shrugged in turn.

"After the Code Red was cleared," the H.A. said, silencing the sideways murmurs, still reading straight off the paper, "and upon a survey of the equipment hall, Admin noticed that some mundane electrical items had gone missing during the confusion. Because a revolving series of Globes had been offline during the event, we were unable to acquire sufficient video footage of the areas in question, and thus were unable to identify the new location of the items. Regardless—" Here he paused and looked up and around the room before going on. "Any student able to provide information on said materials—considered to be punishable contraband from this moment forward—can expect to receive a reward from Admin commensurate with the subjective value of the items."

This was as bizarre as the Globes failing. Though of course we often heard rumors about students who got extra canteen allowance or even unmonitored free time in exchange for information, these stories were always difficult to verify. Understandably, the recipients of such favor—if, indeed, they even existed—were reluctant to let themselves be known to those of us they might be informing upon. But everyone was convinced that it happened; too many people got busted by the Associates for it to be just coincidence. There were traitors among us. We just didn't know who.

The fact that the Head was up on stage, however, asking for help? This was entirely unprecedented.

The Head gazed out into the silent crowd for a long minute, moving his eyes around the room. He seemed to be looking into every face, almost as if he would ferret out the thief by sheer force of will. I knew it was only an optical illusion created by distance, but when he turned his focus toward our section it was all I could do not to shudder. Even despite my best efforts not to turn aside, I couldn't keep my eyes on him. Instead, I tapped lightly on my leg, twice, and began to signal to Randall.

For months the two of us had been working on a system to communicate during times like this—places where passing notes would be conspicuous and reading lips impossible. We hadn't started it up out of any specific need—we spent all day together and had plenty of time to talk even after these forced silences. I guess there was something about being told you couldn't talk to your friend, though; necessity is the mother of invention, as Mason would say. So one day during the Meeting, I elbowed Randall and tried to tap out his name in Morse Code. He immediately reciprocated, and it entertained us so much that we decided to keep it going. We added some American Sign Language, mixed it up with some homemade signals of our own. Whenever possible we would sit side-by-side and signal—me left-handed and him right-handed. If you happened to be passing by you would think we were just burning off energy. If you looked closer, though, you'd know we were up to something. That's why every so often we would pound a game of rock-paper-scissors—to throw the Algorithm off the trail. Also, it just made us laugh.

By this point, what had started as simple Morse Code had developed into a secret language that was completely indecipherable to everyone but us. Kiki tried hard to break it, watching us whenever she had the chance. Every once in a while she would get something correct, coming up to us later and busting us for some small part of the conversation. But for the most part she, too, was in the dark. Actual words, Morse Code spellings, homemade slang—it was confusing, and sometimes we tripped even ourselves up. We figured that the jumbled vibe was probably for the best. Anything that made too much sense was a prime target for the Algorithm to decipher.

What is going on? I asked. Through long practice, I was able to keep one eye on the stage and the other on Randall's hand.

He shrugged and signaled back, *No idea. These stolen things must be a pretty big deal. I wonder what they are?*

I rolled my eyes and tried to laugh with my hands. *Maybe someone got into their secret stash of snacks and drinks? Maybe Admin has nothing special to eat today?*

Randall's shoulders shook as he tried to suppress an actual laugh. *Maybe someone will start selling on the side and we can buy some of them. Keep your eyes open—can't wait to get all the good Admin snacks.*

Suddenly the Head cleared his throat and placed the paper down on the lectern. He had finished his visual tour of the auditorium. "We will now begin our scheduled day of classes by being led in the Pledge," he said, turning peremptorily and stalking off the stage. The junior who had been selected to lead was slow on the uptake; he clearly didn't expect this transition to have occurred quite so rapidly. Stumbling from the stairs toward the lectern, adjusting the microphone—it seemed to take forever. I felt terrible for him.

We had stopped signaling even before he cleared his throat and spoke, his voice cracking through the first syllables. "Please stand for the Pledge of Allegiance."

The room roared to life as hundreds of bodies stood up at once, seats clapping into their upright position, rocking back and forth into place. The auditorium was built for bodies, not acoustics; the echoing clatter was tremendous. The boy waited for the noise to die down somewhat before he risked speaking. The display dissolved to a giant video of a flag rippling in the wind as we all joined in.

"I pledge allegiance, to the flag, of the United States of America. And to the Republic, for which it stands. One Nation, under God—"

Half the voices dropped out for the word "God." I don't know if this was an actual right we had been awarded after some lawsuit, or whether it was the one civil disobedience Admin allowed us. In any case, there were Jewish kids here who wouldn't speak the name of God at all. There were Muslim kids here who wouldn't speak the name of God connected to something like a flag. There were atheists, too, who thought that the God whose name the others feared to say didn't exist at all.

I didn't speak the name either. Not that I was an atheist; I believed in God. It just felt wrong to say his name attached to a place like this.

"—indivisible, with liberty, and justice, for all."

I knew plenty of kids who said "injustice" rather than say "and justice." It wasn't much of a protest, but it was the best we could do here at 231.

Liam made to sit down but Madison stopped him, shaking her head and pointing at the door. The Peeks, however, took their seats again, ready to wait out the lengthy process of us being dismissed. Now that I was standing up, I could turn to see Orion and the empty place next to him, the spot where Jazz should have been sitting. I wondered at the conversation the Peeks must have been having during the last 24 hours, tried to imagine living under the constant threat of inspection.

One of the G.A.s—I couldn't remember his name; they all looked kind of the same—came to the microphone and spoke.

"We are going to dismiss in reverse order today, students." He glanced at the Guests and indicated with his hands that we were to sit back down. We did so, confused looks shooting back and forth. Then he turned to the Peeks and said, "Yesterday's interrogation of Zones 5, 6, and 7 yielded several inconclusive results, and the entire lot of you are to report to the gym for further questions. Your Z.A.

will explain further on a need-to-know basis." He turned back to the Guests. "I trust that you will make good use of your time. Feel free to talk amongst yourselves as you wait. Obviously, the Peeks will be late to first period."

With these words the doors to the auditorium opened and Associates began to file in, more than I had ever seen in this room at one time. Every row of Peeks got two guards, one on each end, tactical gear engaged. After marching in and assuming their positions they waited for all the Guests to get back in their seats and settle in; despite the G.A.'s advice, our conversation had ceased immediately upon their entering. I counted eight Drones whooshing around, but there could easily have been more—I didn't feel free to look around too closely. The G.A. swept his eyes across the rows before pointing to the Peeks in the far back.

The furthest Associate used his truncheon to tap the Peek closest to him and, without waiting for a response, spun on his heels and walked to the door. The row of Peeks rose to their feet as one and turned to follow, the other Associate bringing up the rear. The room was so quiet we could hear the stomp of sneakers on the worn carpet. After the last of them had cleared the edge of the seats, the process repeated with the next row down. It was orderly, rapid, and bizarre. On our side, no one spoke for watching.

About halfway through the room, however, one of the Peeks tripped on his way into the aisle. His foot must have caught something in the narrow space, and he stumbled to his knees, arms splayed out in front of him to keep his face from hitting the ground. The Associate on the next row whirled around, and for just a moment I foolishly thought he was going to help the kid up off the ground. Instead, he put a boot in his belly, several times, knocking him fully prone. Then he extended his truncheon and rolled him over, spread the weapon across the kid's chest, and dropped the full weight of his body on top of it. The Peek was screaming from the shock—even from this far across the room it was a horrific sound.

Except for the lines of Peeks and Associates who were still walking out of the room, no one else moved.

The G.A. gave a curt nod and two Associates jumped off the stage, ran toward the Peek on the ground. They picked him up, one on each arm, and quickly dragged him out the door. By this point he had stopped screaming, but it was unclear if that was because he had recovered his common sense or if he had lost consciousness.

When he was clear of the room the Associate turned back around to his row, pointed his truncheon at the Peeks, and spat, "You lot. Move." The Peeks walked out as if nothing had happened.

Liam looked over at me and caught my eye. He seemed close to tears again as he mouthed a single word: *Why?*

I shrugged, spread out my hands. I don't know if he understood me or not when I soundlessly replied, *Because they can.*

Because they can.

CHAPTER 6
DEMOCRACY

Admin pulled a slick move on us after the Meeting.

First they told us that complete silence was required on our walk to the cafeteria. They said that leaving the auditorium a little later put us out of sync with teachers planning and that we weren't to disturb them. I didn't think much of it until we got into line for breakfast—nobody would have been foolish enough to talk about the Meeting in the halls anyway. By the time we got to our table, though, we realized that we were trapped. There was no official mandate to enforce our silence in here, but all the same it was eerily quiet in the cafeteria as we poked through our bagels and eggs. We needed cover for what we really wanted to talk about—the Peeks getting marched out of the auditorium, the stolen contraband, the bribe Admin was offering to snitch on whoever it was that had managed to put one over on them. Occasionally someone tried to strike up a conversation about something else—Carlos talking about yesterday's math homework or David trying to plan for the upcoming Testing—but there just wasn't enough noise in the room to feel comfortable.

I kept thinking that if only everyone would begin to speak at the same time we would be safe, but there was no opportunity to coordinate anything like that. Not without some kind of point person, and I wasn't willing to take that risk. Corporately, if we'd all started talking at once it would have been okay for everyone to join in. Individually, though, each of us was unwilling to be the first to broach the subject of the Meeting, afraid of being caught on a spread mic. I watched the door, expecting the Peeks to march in and provide some noise that could mask our efforts to build a conversation, but they never came.

So, for lack of a leader, together we ate in something like silence.

Math class went by the same way math class always went by—totally boring but also completely unremarkable. I was surprised to see the Peeks already in place when we got there, confused at how unconcerned they seemed to be about the "further questions" they had been asked. How could something so important have also taken so little time? I tried to make eye contact with the ones I knew best—Orion, Anthony, Brie—but nobody seemed interested in giving me anything like a clue as to what had happened. They were just chatting quietly when we walked in, laughing amongst themselves and eating their brown bag breakfasts. Whatever went down in the further questions must not have been that big a deal to them.

Jazz never said much in math—she would just sit there and finish her work lightning fast, setting us all up to feel slow—so her absence wasn't really all that noticeable there. On the other hand, Williams's class felt like it was running underwater without her presence. Every question he asked was followed by a long, painful silence, and he had no shame in letting that empty space just drag on and on. Some teachers would adjust if folks didn't get on board with their lesson plans; they would listen to what their class was saying between the lines of the silence. Not Williams—something about our discomfort seemed almost energizing to him. From his perch sitting at the front of the room he got more animated the more we didn't know, swiping at his screen and flashing dense slides up on the display.

We were just about to start our presentations when the buzzer for the Peek side clanged. The class went quiet instantly. We watched Williams kick his feet to the ground, slide his screen back into his pocket, move slowly over to the door. He pressed the button on the console, and with a flat, beeping sound the intercom flared to life.

"Requesting access for one of your students, Mr. Williams," the voice on the other side crackled through.

Williams looked pointedly at Jazz's empty desk and smirked, pressed the button again. "Oh, really? Which student?" he said, an exaggerated look of surprise plastered on his face.

"Jazzlyn Lewis, processed for an Infraction on yesterday," the voice said. "Cleared for return today by order of the G.A." Williams rolled his eyes theatrically and muttered something under his breath. He placed his eye on the scanner and the door buzzed, began to swing away from the wall.

Two Associates pushed through, each holding one of Jazz's arms. They were engaged in full tactical gear. She was wearing handcuffs and ankle fetters.

The crush of the classroom slowed her walk to a shuffle. It was all the Associates could do to inch her along to her desk, squeezing in between rows in order to place her in her seat. When they finally got her situated one of them leaned down and unlocked her ankles, but only so they could immediately be attached to the desk. The other freed one handcuff, ran the chain through a U-bolt soldered to the top of the desk, and re-attached the cuff to her wrist. After testing the four points for security, the Associates turned, nodded to Williams, and vacated the room. The door swung shut behind them, locking into place with that ominous whirring click.

Jazz had stayed perfectly still throughout the entire process, an inscrutable look on her face. It seemed impossible to think that she wasn't furious at this treatment, but judging by her vibe she just as easy could have been entertained. The only obvious sign of distress I could see—aside from the handcuffs, of course, and the rumpled, day-old orange jumpsuit—was her hair. I had never seen it even a tiny bit out of order before, but today several of her braids had started to come undone, sending curls out from her head at wild angles. As the Associates were leaving I caught her flick a smile and wink at Orion, but the by the time Williams returned to the front of the class her face was impassive again.

"Well, Jazz," Williams crowed, "words fail to describe what a pleasure it is to see you. You look...well." He cut his eyes to her handcuffs before glancing away. "Your classmates have been working diligently in your absence. They were just about to begin their presentations when you...arrived. I'm sorry to say that it will be two full letter grades deducted for you and your team in light of your failure to present today." He looked around at all of us, a triumphant sort of grin on his face. "But I'll be more than happy to hear your thoughts tomorrow, after you've had the chance to get better prepared. As always, I'm sure your insights will be most illuminating."

"We're prepared today, though," Jazz said quietly.

Williams stopped cold. "What did you say?" he asked.

"We're prepared today," Jazz replied. "Right now, in fact. We'd be honored to present first." She glanced over at her group and the looks on their faces were pretty uniform: this information was news to them.

Jazz went on. "Sorry we couldn't send you the rough draft before the Meeting this morning like you asked. I tried, of course, but I guess I was a little...tied up?" She grinned and raised her hands into the air; they caught at the end of the chain and the room broke out into laughter. It took Williams more than a few seconds of glaring around at us in order to quell the noise.

"Well, I guess that's just one letter grade lower, then," he grumbled. "I still get to dock you for the lack of a draft. You'll be going third." He sat back at his desk and looked around at the rest of us. "All right then, you lot. Failures of democracy. Get on with it!"

A group of Peeks went first and gave a routine presentation about voter access. We had always heard that too many voters had too many options in our Nation's early elections, and that one of the brilliant moves of President Braswell was to implement an effective way to keep elections under control. His reforms were simple: reduce the number of people who could cast a ballot, eliminate most polling places, and then require the remaining voters to pass a series of retinal scans. I had heard all of this before; it had been covered in Nation every year for as long as I could remember. I never thought it made much sense to try to limit voters, but Williams nodded emphatically along and took notes. He gave them an A- and waved them brusquely away.

We were second. As per our usual arrangement, Kiki flicked over brief roles to each of our screens—the only way to get full credit was to prove that you were participating in some way. She took the lead and ran the class through a brief history of what used to be known as the "separation of powers." In the past, the Nation was split into three equal governments, all watching over each other in a system of what they called "checks and balances." The Braswell Administration had eliminated most of this during their third term; I was explaining their new laws when Williams interrupted.

"And these old separations were proven by history to be mistakes, correct?" he asked. "That's why, over time, President Braswell had to assume control of the judicial branch. So that he could maintain order, right?"

Williams angled his eyes at the Peeks and I froze, stared at my screen, wondered how to answer. It was no secret what he wanted me to say—I knew the whitewashed, history-primer answer by heart—but I wasn't sure quite how to say it without selling out. It's not like everyone agreed with Braswell. My father worked for the opposition party, and I had grown up hearing about various plans to defeat the President. But what I could hear in my own home and what I could say in this building were totally different things. After a long pause, Williams audibly tapping his foot while he waited, Kiki cut in to save me.

"Yeah, well, of course we all know that mistakes were made in the original founding of our Nation," she said, cautiously. "Ben was just saying to me earlier that democracy has always been a fragile experiment. Weren't you, Ben?" I nodded eagerly as she continued. "And when the Founders tried too hard to protect that experiment, they made some mistakes. Mistakes that later needed correcting by President Braswell."

It was a beautiful answer, meaningless enough to be worthy of any politician, and Williams just ate it up. "You are absolutely right, Kiandria," he said. "Almost from the day of its signing, mistakes were made in the implementation of our great Constitution. It is why we expend so much energy trying to recover the intent of our brilliant Founders." He looked around at us, beaming, cut a glance over to Jazz. It was almost a dare to say something. She didn't.

"Well done, students. You receive an A+ for your delightful insights." He pivoted smoothly back to Jazz. "Next up? Ms. Lewis?" She held her hands up in mock resignation and he laughed. "Ah! You will not be able to present from the front of the room as is traditional in these situations. Never fear, however. I will allow you to present from your corner, and, in my magnanimity, I will dock no further points from your group for this obvious delinquency." He made a show of turning his chair toward the Peeks and kicking his feet up on the nearest desk. With a grand flourish of his hands he gestured at her to get on with it.

Jazz handed her screen to Orion, and they followed our lead with the charade that their entire group had somehow contributed to Jazz's presentation. Each of the five Peeks said a few words about democracy and its relative inferiority to other forms of government common throughout history. Notably, they came in hard on the side of monarchical rule and the stability it could bring to a country. Orion got stuck having to explain both why the Founders were so wise to break away from Britain and, at the same time, why King George was leading such an obviously superior system of government, one that President Braswell was actively imitating. It was a tricky business, but I saw Williams smiling throughout. Soon enough, though, the screen was passed back to Jazz, who glanced at it cursorily before placing it on the desk and looking up at Williams. She held his eyes for a moment and then began speaking, sweeping her gaze around the room at the rest of us.

Like Mason reciting his poem that morning, she didn't read a word of what she was saying off the screen. She spoke entirely from memory.

"With all due respect to my illustrious classmates, both those who have gone before as well as those still to come," she said, indicating us in turn with slight nods of her head, "there is only one true failing of democracy. It is neither the issue of voter access nor the separation of powers. These are items worthy of attention and concern, of course, but they are nothing so much like *failings.*"

Williams coughed and Jazz paused, looked over to him. He tried to stare her down for a moment, but then he seemed to lose his nerve. Instead, he looked away, nodded at her to continue. She smiled and went on.

"There is only one true *failing* of democracy: the fact that it allows tyranny over a group of people to persist, only so long as an adequate amount of the voting population is willing to go along with it. And if the ruling class manages to keep its voting population small—as in the days of legal enslavement during the Antebellum South—you can effectively terrorize large swaths of the population with the simple mathematics of minority rule."

"Now wait just a minute!" Williams interrupted. He slid his feet off the floor and crashed them to the ground, grabbed at his screen and pointed at Jazz. "You're not allowed to just say things like that. Allegations against the Founders have to be backed up by evidence—"

"But Mr. Williams, I just happen to have that evidence right here," Jazz said smoothly, and she swiped a slide over to the display for all of us to see. "For instance, in 1800, democracy's most famous plantation owner, Thomas Jefferson, became President of the United States by winning a total of around 50,000 popular votes. This in contrast to something like 30,000 for the loser, John Adams." The class began to buzz just a little; I heard more than a couple low-key exclamations. Williams was muttering to himself, frantically swiping at his own screen, pushing her data off the display. Jazz went on, undeterred. "The population of America, on the other hand, was over five million people at that point. Meaning that Jefferson became slave-driver-in-chief with less than one percent of the population voting in favor of his ascendancy."

She paused, waited for Williams to look up at her. Then she extended her arms slightly to draw taut the chain connecting them, sliding it back and forth through the u-bolt and making a horrific grinding noise. "Not incidentally," she said, raising her voice to rise over the sound, "there were somewhere close to a million enslaved persons held in lawful bondage in America that year. Again, I repeat, this is the one true *failing* of democracy: that 50,000 voters could legally trap twenty times their number in captivity, held as property, in perpetuity."

The class exploded. Jazz stopped grinding that chain, but amidst the mixture of laughter, catcalls, and boos, I could scarcely even hear Williams calling out for quiet. At first only a couple of kids paid him any mind—it felt like a celebration in the room, a victory lap for Jazz—but the second he stood up and flashed his scanner we all went dead silent. His finger hovered just over the panic button as he glared at us, moving his gaze around the room as if hoping for a reason. For a long moment he didn't say a word, only stood there and scowled.

The only person who hadn't made a sound during the celebration was Jazz. She sat there silently watching Williams and that button, hands again flat on the table, a picture of calm.

Finally, Williams returned his scanner to his pocket and stalked back to his desk. "The highest grade possible for that presentation will be a B+, on account of the full letter grade docked for tardiness of the rough draft." He looked at Jazz and went on. "I will need to verify the potentially misleading information you have posed to the class, and after that I will be able to judge a final grade."

Jazz smiled and nodded. There was no way that B+ was going to stand—Williams would find some small, unimportant little thing wrong with what someone had said in order to lower their score. Jazz, though, didn't care about her grades at all. The fact that Williams couldn't immediately go off on her presentation was more than enough of a win.

Williams recovered quickly, jumped back to his usual arrogant self almost as if nothing had happened. He ripped David and Carlos's group apart from the jump, gave them poor marks for what he called their "shoddy research." By the end of class, things felt normal again. Meaning, if my mind wasn't buzzing with Jazz's presentation I would have been halfway depressed walking to lunch, thinking about the waste of brain space that was Williams's class.

But I couldn't stop thinking about what Jazz had said. And I knew I wasn't alone. We may have looked like we were dragging our way to the cafeteria—the Algorithm may not have been able to quantify any difference in our attitude through the halls. There were things the Globes couldn't see, however. The memory of Williams's bluster in face of Jazz's facts was one of them.

———————————

I was busting to get to the lunch table and talk about what had just happened in Williams's class, but, again, Admin had other plans for our meal. There were at least twice the number of Associates in the cafeteria—most of them actively patrolling. Four of them, however, were posted up directly along the length of our table, facing us and blatantly recording. There were even a couple of Drones floating laps around us, weaving in and out of the Associates, whirring their weird little noises and spinning their primary eyes around. I glanced across the chain link and noticed that Orion and the rest of the Peeks from our class were dealing with the exact same situation. It was like what they did to us this morning, but worse. This time everyone else in the room was talking. Our class was the only one eating in silence.

Halfway through lunch Randall caught my eye and grinned. He balled a piece of paper up and tossed it nonchalantly toward his tray, missed and watched it skitter toward me. After a minute of flicking my eyes from Associate to Associate and registering no response, I casually picked it up. It appeared to be half a page from some long-forgotten math assignment—most of it blazingly incorrect, I quickly noticed—but at the bottom were some pencil marks scrawled in a slightly lighter shade.

Yo this is crazy man! You think they're going to come into the dorms with us tonight so we don't talk? Or are they just playing damage control right now, trying to keep Jazz's presentation from getting around to the rest of school right away?

After the note was an arrow that curled around itself in spirals and led to the edge of the paper. I flipped it over to the other side and the arrow continued in lazy circles around the page, ending at two words: *You suck, Ben.*

I looked over at Randall and he shook his head in mock sadness, mouthing the words, *I'm sorry but it's true. You do suck.* I laughed and balled the paper up again, small enough to stuff inside my empty milk carton.

On the way out of the cafeteria Liam sidled up next to me. Once we cleared the looming Associates and our silence was broken by the noise of the rest of the Guests, he said to me in a low voice, "You think it's true? What Jazz said?"

"Look at you, man!" I replied. "You've already learned how to keep these conversations quiet!" I looked around just to make double sure we were safe to talk, then glanced away, kept my eyes forward. "You bet your ass it's true. If Jazz said it in front of Williams? She knows how to find things on the Stream—even the stuff they don't want us to be able to find. There's no way she said something unless she was one hundred percent sure it was right."

Liam let out a low whistle. "I didn't know all that. Not just about how few people voted back then, I mean. But, also, I didn't know…you know, about…" He paused.

"About that crazy number of slaves?" I said, stopping to look him in the eyes. He looked relieved that I had said it out loud. "Nah, me neither. It's some kind of bullshit, though."

We rounded the corner to Mason's room. The hallway was clearing out as kids from other Blocks went to their afternoon classes. Somebody had spilled coffee on the ground, and we followed the flow of students seamlessly around it, keeping it off our sneakers. They'd be back to clean it up or Admin would get the Globe footage, pull them right out of class and make them clean the whole hall. Kiki pushed past us during the last stretch.

"Ya'll taking forever!" she said. I hustled to keep up, determined not to be the last one into the room today. We made it inside just in time to hear Mason starting class a few minutes early. The Peeks were all in their seats today, books out, ready for a do-over on yesterday's conversation.

I paused in the doorway and looked at Jazz. She was in her seat, still in handcuffs, still shackled to the desk. She flicked her eyes in my direction, but for some reason I panicked and looked away.

CHAPTER 7

FRANKENSTEIN

"Frankenstein, or The Modern Prometheus," Mason was saying as I entered. "A remarkable novel by a fascinating young woman named Mary Shelley." Kiki, Liam, and I quietly took our seats as the last couple of kids snuck in; I had to dodge carefully around Mason as he was pacing down my aisle. "Let me repeat our guiding question from yesterday, let it lead us where it may. Why does this book continue to exist? Why are we still reading it almost two hundred and fifty years after it was written?

In stark contrast to Williams's class, there was no gap between Mason's question and a response from the class. David raised his hand and, without waiting for acknowledgment, began speaking at the same time. "Well, Mr. Mason, sir, obviously the book just continues to affect us generation after generation. Probably because of the abundant parallels between Dr. Frankenstein and the mythological character Prometheus. These are both stories, at their root, about technology, specifically the rapid advancement of—"

Mason cut him off. "Yes, David, that is true. The parallels between the fire, brought to the ancient Greeks by Prometheus, and the life, created ex nihilo by our new friend Victor—they are a rich metaphorical playground. One worthy of writing a semester paper upon." I saw David smile and make a note in his book. Mason was still pacing around, peering at us over his glasses. "I wonder what else we could say, however? Maybe something that doesn't just slap us in the face from the subtitle?"

"Ah, Mason, what the hell with this book?" Orion cut in. "I just don't understand why you're having us to read some story that goes so slow!" He waved his hand in the air as he was talking, back and forth, nodding his head to the rhythm. He gradually slowed to a stop and froze into place, shutting his eyes at the last moment and faking as if he was asleep. The class busted out laughing and he popped his eyes open, looking around in faux confusion as if newly awake.

Mason smiled, stopped in place, looked through his glasses at Orion. "Say more about that, young man. Talk about the speed of the book." He began pacing again as Orion went on.

"I don't know, Mason, it's just, why does it take so long for the actual story to get going? In the first place, they make us get through all this lame-ass North Pole stuff, and then right about the time the monster actually comes to life? Like something cool is finally going to pop off? Nah. Then this monster just runs off into the mountains. It's like a hundred pages before anything even close to exciting happens!"

Maddy cut in. "But, Orion, you remember all those old horror movies we used to watch on the Stream, right?" He turned to look at her and I expected him to be angry at being interrupted. Instead, he just nodded and gestured as if the floor was hers. She swiped at her bangs and went on in a rush. "Remember how it always took forever for the killer or whatever to appear? How they'd show little glimpses of the monster, but we wouldn't actually see him until near the end?"

"And then it was never as scary on the display as it was in your head," Diana added. "Half the time I would see those monsters and couldn't stop laughing at how corny they looked."

"Not Chucky," one of the Peeks said. "That little freak puppet was the scariest thing I ever saw in my life." The class broke out into a general chorus of agreement, several kids raising pencils in the air, stabbing them downward as if they were Chucky's knife.

Mason brought the room back together. "What you're all noticing is a typical device of the fictional story, be it in a novel or a film," he said. "Typically, the more detail that the audience provides from their own imaginations, the more effective a piece of fiction can be at evoking a feeling. So that by the time we meet the monster at the end of the first half of *Frankenstein*? We have already found him, perhaps, haunting the imagination of our dreams."

"Ah, Mason," Orion said, "it's still just so boring. Get him out there earlier? Give me a legit haunting? Then we can talk about this being a great book. As it is?" He paused for dramatic effect, then dropped the judgement bomb. "It feels a little bit glitchy."

Mason laughed. "Duly noted, Orion. I will try to choose a more immediately action-packed work for our next foray into the world of horror literature." He leaned forward to look at us over his glasses. "Anyone else have an observation? Perhaps one of you has a thought that can take us in a different direction."

Randall spoke up. "Mason, my big problem is what a piece of shit baby this scientist is." Mason turned and pointed at Randall to continue. "I mean, first he spends all this time to build the whole Frankenstein monster—"

"Technically, Randall, Frankenstein is the name of the scientist," I interrupted. "The monster is just called 'the monster' in the book."

Randall reached his middle finger over to me without even looking my way. "Shut up, Ben, I know that. Like I was saying, finally Frankenstein makes the monster, brings it to life or whatever, and what's the first thing he does? Like Orion said, this guy runs away screaming. He spends the rest of the book complaining and lying to everybody.

Meanwhile, the monster is killing folks right and left—including Frankenstein's own family—and all this guy can do is run his mouth and cry about everything."

"And you think that makes him…?" Mason asked.

"A piece of shit," Randall replied. "All this is his fault, and he doesn't do anything about it but complain about how hard his life is."

"It raises the question," Mason said, "of whether Frankenstein is actually the protagonist of this eponymous novel." He looked around. "After all, as Mary Wollstonecraft, the rather famous mother of Mary Shelly, once wrote, *The same energy which renders a man a villain would have rendered him useful in society, had that society been well organized.*"

Mason kept walking for what felt like at least a minute as we all sat with that. He knew there was zero chance any of us had ever heard that quote before, and we needed space so we didn't screw up our response. Finally Liam spoke. "You mean you think that the monster is the hero here?"

"Do I?" Mason stopped and swept his eyes around the room. "I appreciate your contribution, Liam, on only your second day of class. But it matters little what I think. The better question is, do any of you think the monster is the hero?"

"There's a way to argue that none of this is his fault, right?" I cut in. I could admit that I hadn't loved this book all that much, was even a little confused about why Mason had assigned it. But something resonated here with what Mason was asking. "I mean, like Randall said about the scientist, he can't be the hero."

"He's a piece of shit!" Randall hollered across the room.

Mason caught Randall's eye and flicked a finger at the Globe, shook his head ever so slightly. There were limits even to what he was allowed to tolerate in here. Randall nodded, held up two fingers in the peace sign. I went on.

"So the monster is abandoned by the guy who created him. Alone in this world, trying to figure everything out. And everybody hates him! I mean, it's not right what he did, killing all those people. But there's something understandable about it, right? What else was he supposed to do? He just did what he had to do to survive, right?" The class broke out into low conversation, arguing back and forth about which was the hero—the spurned murderer or the scientist who created him. Mason kept pacing, clearly reveling in the cross-currents of dialogue.

"Y'all missing the main point of this book," a soft voice cut across the room. Everyone went silent immediately. It was Jazz. She had been quiet thus far in class; she looked uncomfortable sitting in that desk still shackled with those heavy chains. Someone new to the room, like Liam, might have assumed she was having a hard time paying attention.

Mason knew better, of course, and came near to look at her through his glasses. "And what, Jazz, might you consider the point of this book to be?" His tone was rushed and, again, Liam might think he was mad. The rest of us were ready, though, for Jazz to drop something on us, something that would make Mason do that little happy teacher dance. He waited, not for the first time ceding control of the room fully to her.

"The thing about this book is that it's not Frankenstein's story. It's not the monster's story, either," Jazz said. "I mean, Frankenstein is relaying the information, but what we're reading is actually a letter from this guy Captain Walton, written to his sister. Captain Walton is the narrator. We may not even remember who this guy is, but it's actually his story." She paused and looked up at Mason, a rare moment of seeking affirmation. He nodded, and she went on.

"So think about it. Most of this book is some monster telling a story to Frankenstein who's telling it to this guy Captain Walton who's telling it to his sister, right? It's like one of those Russian Dolls or whatever—stories stacked inside of more stories. But when you think about it, the story isn't really about any of these people. It's about the person on the outside of all the dolls. The real outside, I mean—the person who's actually telling the story to us. There is no Captain Walton. Y'all forgetting all about Mary Shelley."

"What about Mary Shelley, Jazz?" Mason asked. He was bouncing back and forth again. She was clearly onto something.

"All y'all reading this book like a bunch of men. Or, let's be real here, like a bunch of boys," she said, glancing around the room to make sure we all caught her shade. There was a little bit of rustle, but nobody had the guts to clap back. Not with her on a roll like this. "The story might be about a monster and some ship travelling to the North Pole, but that's just a small part of what this book's really saying. The real story is about creation and control. Loss of control, really." She paused again. "This book is about a woman who's afraid she might be pregnant." She turned to look at Mason. "Didn't you say she was only 18 years old when she started writing it?"

"In fact, I did," Mason said. "And, germane to your thesis, Shelley was not only pregnant for much of the time she wrote *Frankenstein*, but also she had recently given birth to a premature baby, when she was 17. That baby died."

Jazz smiled. "I know. I looked it up. I just wanted them to hear you to say it."

Kiki laughed and said, "You mean this book is about being pregnant?"

"Sort of," Jazz said. "I think, more to the point, this book is about the feeling you get when there is something outside yourself, something that has control of your body and soul. For Mary Shelley, that was her fear of pregnancy—what it had already done to her and might one day do again. But nobody back then wanted to read a book about some woman being pregnant. So she wrote about something people did want to read about. A crazy scientist and his fear of the monster he'd made."

"But what should we be afraid of?" Orion said. "If it's our story, too?" He waved his hand pointedly around the Peek side of the room. Everyone had been buzzing just moments before, alive with the rush of considering something that felt dangerous and new. Suddenly, we all went dead.

"Yes," Jazz said, turning to look at the door that led back to their Zone. "That is an excellent question, Orion. What is it that might have control over us? What does this book have to do with our bodies? Our souls?"

Mason stepped quickly into the middle of the room, waving his hands around wildly overhead as if he were suddenly super excited about something. Liam probably though he was crazy, but I knew exactly what he was doing. He was making sure that the Algorithm took its eye off the Peeks and started watching him instead.

"This is nothing short of a fascinating conversation," he said loudly, still waving his arms. "But I wonder if we have lost the true intention of our friend Frankenstein in the midst of all this wild conjecture?" Liam and a couple other Guests still looked confused, but most of us settled back into our seats; we knew that Jazz and Orion had crossed a line in there somewhere. Mason finally came to a stop directly under the Globe, briefly invisible to its observation. He rotated slowly to face the room, his lips soundlessly working the words, *no more today, sorry.* One by one, we all looked away.

I opened my book and randomly flipped through it, unable to get Jazz's words out of my head: *something outside yourself that has control.* It definitely resonated with me—being here could be suffocating even on the best of days. Trying to imagine how it felt to Jazz, though, or to Orion and the rest of the Peeks? Just like the book, maybe there were no villains in this room, either.

Mason was back at the front talking about the essays we were going to write when the Globe began blinking its angry red color again. The siren wailed and the voice rang out: "CODE RED. CODE RED. PLEASE FOLLOW PROTOCOLS AND ASSUME THE POSITION FOR YOUR OWN SAFETY. CODE RED."

The room burst into life with scraping chairs and squeaking shoes. Guests and Peeks hit the ground, started arranging bodies, and Mason sprinted straight for Jazz. The Code Red automatically authorized his scanner to let her loose; I'm not sure what the Associates would do if they came in today and she was stuck in her seat. Before moving, I turned instinctively to check on Liam, but he was already crawling under his desk. A little over 24 hours at 231 and he was sheltering in place like a pro. In spite of the circumstances, I smiled.

After getting myself settled I turned back to look at Jazz again, the view between us through the chaos of the room somehow unimpeded. I had expected to see her hunched up under her desk by this point, trying to avoid a repeat of yesterday. For whatever reason, however, she was still standing up in the aisle, completely motionless, watching the door to the Guest hallway. I kept my eyes on her as we waited.

All of a sudden she turned to look at Mason, who was still running around the room making sure that everyone was safely in place on the ground. After passing by and giving me a thumbs up he stopped in front of Jazz, and I watched him angle his body to slide between her and the Globe. She looked up at him and said something I couldn't catch—the siren was wailing and her lips were turned away from me just askance enough that I couldn't read them. For a moment it seemed like they were arguing about something, and then I saw Mason shake his head and point at her, two quick jabbing motions with his finger. She took one last look at the door and then back to him, nodded curtly.

He waved his arms again in those big sweeping motions, presumably for the Globe, as she crawled under her desk. While she was scrunching her legs up under her body she happened to look over and catch me watching her. My ears burned, but this time I didn't turn away. At first she just froze and stared me down, but then suddenly her face broke out into a smile. The rest of the room faded into the background as she pointed her fingers at her eyes, made pantomime binoculars with her hands like a little kid and held them up to her face. Then she lowered them slowly, never breaking eye contact. She shook her head quickly back and forth.

The message was clear: *you didn't see a thing.*

The siren blared as we watched each other across the room. My head felt thick. I only vaguely noted that Mason had crawled under his desk, and then the sudden clanging of the door sounded as if all of us were underwater. The Globe turned purple when the Associates came in, four of them this time. Two made straight for Jazz, one for Mason, the other taking stock of the rest of the room in a big, sweeping arc.

It seemed as if I could hear disappointment in the metallic voice when it crackled through the radios, "Zone K-7. Clear!"

CHAPTER 8
BASKETBALL

Over a week went by before Jazz came back out onto the court for Recks. I don't know if she was still nursing some injury from the Infraction, or if she just had something more important to do than play basketball. Either way, her absence left a huge hole in our only chunk of what passed for recreation here at 231.

We had the run of a handful of places during Recks—the indoor gym, the outdoor field, the weight room, the library. In addition, it was the only time of day you could be in canteen without convincing someone to authorize your Credentials. It stayed pretty busy with kids getting snacks or just hanging out at one of the tables that crowded around the room. Most nights we found our way there at some point, but usually the kids from our Block just picked up supplies and headed to the basketball court.

We didn't have anything like official sports teams here at 231. I'd heard that back at the beginning of Federal Sites they tried to keep a league running between buildings, but the logistics had quickly proved too daunting. A rash of fights and a couple of attempted breakouts and that was the end of that—no more sports. Now we were stuck scrimmaging each other in an ad hoc system of football and basketball games. Seasons ran for most of the year, and some kids would try to play on both teams. The best, though, stuck with one or the other, hoping to make their way out of here on a scholarship someday.

I didn't play, but Randall did—he was the unofficial captain of the Guest first basketball team. Jazz and Orion both played on the Peek first team—she was unequivocally in charge—and so our Block had a lot riding on the rivalry in the gym. There were five different levels, but only seven players could carry on each team; students from all the Blocks and Zones played mixed up across every level. There were no tryouts, nothing like a delineated path to move from team to team. If you did well playing a team ahead of yours, you might get moved up a level; but you might not. If you played badly you would almost certainly get relegated, even if the team didn't move someone up to replace you right away. It was exciting to watch, and K Block was here for all of it.

With Jazz gone, though, the first teams hadn't played each other in almost two weeks, so Liam hadn't been able to see anything like a real game. The first night she was gone I'd given him a quick tour of the limits of our freedom—from the library to canteen and back—and for the most part since we'd followed that same pattern of walking and talking. We sat down in the gym once to watch the Peek second team play the Guest third; a couple of times we stopped to check in on Randall running drills with his guys on the first team. Madison stayed to watch him regardless of how boring it was, so we would bring her a snack most nights and catch up on anything we might have missed. The rest of the time, however, we walked, eventually convincing Kiki and Carlos to walk with us. The Globes were evenly spaced along the entire route, of course, and nobody was foolish enough to say much of anything important out loud. But even the limited freedom of being able to choose where to be—the gym or canteen, the library or the field—it was intoxicating in its own small way.

When the word broke that Jazz was back, we were in canteen, grabbing some snacks. While Liam and I stood in line Kiki held forth in the corner, telling stories to a mixture of Guests from across Blocks. It was crowded, even though Peeks weren't allowed inside the canteen proper. There was a pick-up window where they could order, looking out over a small hallway that ran a circuitous route back to their dorms. Usually, the Associates were lax about Guests hanging out by the window to talk, and so Peeks were able to linger for just a minute after ordering and engage in something like normal conversation. All of this noise made it loud in here every night, but doubly so once Kiki got her audience going. The room smelled like coffee, chocolate, and hot chips. I'd heard Associates and Admin complain about the food and the mess, but to us it felt a little bit like the outside.

"—and that's when this girl looked up and I was all DAMN I guess I need new shoes!" Kiki was saying, and then a couple of kids close to the Peek window just up and walked out. She looked around, confused—in general nobody was foolish enough to abandon a Kiki story partway—but then we all heard some kid in the corner say something about Jazz.

"Time to go, Liam!" I said, grabbing him by the arm. He spilled some of his monstrous mixture of decaf coffee and powdered hot chocolate and gave me a wounded look. "You'll thank me, friend. We need to get back to the gym ASAP."

Kiki was right behind us as we made our way down the crowded Guests-only hallway. Normally even a top-notch basketball game wouldn't cause this much commotion, but by this point everyone in the school had heard the story of her Infraction a dozen times over. Seeing her back on the court was something like high drama for 231 tonight.

We got to the bleachers just in time to see Jazz and Randall vie for first ball. As always, they settled it with a match of rock-paper-scissors, best five out of seven. For a couple of seconds their hands were a blur—nobody else could have followed the action—and then Jazz turned around and walked away, laughing. Randall smiled, said something to her that I couldn't catch. Then he started giving instructions to his guys. The game was on.

Jazz took the ball, dropped quick behind the baseline, passed it in to Orion. He gave it right back to her as she danced inbounds, and then he sprinted down to the other side, pointing and shouting to his teammates. She dribbled up the court slowly, our whole team back in our key setting up on defense. Just before she crossed over the half-court line she paused and hit the ball on the ground with a monster dribble. While it was bouncing up and down, but before it slowed completely, she pulled a sweatband out of her pocket and put it around her forehead, making a big show of fixing her hair just right. When Randall came to the top of the three-point arc, making as if he were going to take a run at her, she snatched the ball back into her control and glared at him.

The crowd erupted in cheers. Jazz was back.

She was about halfway to the arc when Randall came at her for real, but instead of moving forward she stopped in her tracks. Still dribbling, she pulled up to her full height and waited. She was a couple of inches shorter than me, maybe 5'6" or so—fully 8 inches shorter than Randall. The closer he got to her the higher she inclined her chin, keeping her eyes locked on him as she kept the ball in a calm, tight bounce. He stepped up to her in a graceful crouch, reached out one of his long arms, trying to sneak into her orbit. Immediately she spun the other way, dribbled through her legs and around him, passed the ball to some guy on the left side who sent it to Orion who bounced it right back to her. She ducked under one of our guys and dished a layup in for the first score. All told it was maybe a two-second play.

Randall was still back outside the arc; there wasn't even time for him to turn around and move to the basket. He had probably hoped she was a little rusty after a week off, but that notion was off the table now. The whole gym went wild, Guests and Peeks alike. We had been so hungry for this—finally, something in this place worth watching.

Pretty much the same thing happened a couple more times—once Orion took the shot himself; once Jazz passed to a kid named Que as an outlet so they could reset. After Jazz scored her fourth layup of the game, Liam glanced back over his shoulder at us. The bleachers were all packed tonight, kids laughing and talking everywhere, but he was sitting on the front row, watching intently; I could see his whole body moving back and forth to track the motion of the ball. "She's amazing," he said. "Does she always dominate like that?"

Kiki laughed. "Uh, yeah. You didn't believe us?" On the court Randall had called a quick huddle; we were down 14-6 already and I knew he wouldn't be taking it well. I could see him cursing out loud to himself as the rest of the team gathered up.

Liam turned all the way around now that the action had paused. "No. Wait—I mean, yes, I believed you," he fumbled over himself. "I just didn't know she'd be that much better than everyone else. Watching her out there—it's insane."

"Now you see why we haven't been here much, with her taking time off and all," I said. "No disrespect to Randall or anything," I added quickly, cutting a glance to Maddy. Fortunately, she wasn't paying us any attention, her eyes riveted on the court.

"No, Ben, definite disrespect to Randall, for sure," Carlos said, and he mimed the lurching look Randall just had when Jazz went around him for the fourth time. Kiki laughed again as we watched the huddle break up.

Jazz called out from her defensive spot at the top of the key. "Hey Randall, you might need this!" She threw the ball over his head, just barely tipping it off the ends of his fingers when he jumped. She laughed and slapped hands with all her teammates. Understandably, their energy was on tilt.

The ball rolled over to where we were sitting, bumped up against the side of Liam's foot. He picked it up and started dribbling—quickly at first from his sitting position, but then he stood up and dropped the speed in half. His entire countenance changed instantly. Rather than some awkward, gangly kid sitting there in his huge shoes, he looked something like graceful. He sent the ball back and forth to himself a couple of times through his legs, bobbing his body side to side as if to some internal music.

Randall jogged up and held out his hands for the ball. He looked frustrated—not at Liam exactly, but this delay certainly wasn't improving his mood. Liam faked a pass to him, but flipped the ball expertly back into his own hands, kept the dribble up without missing a beat. Randall tried to smile, but I knew it was only goodwill that kept him from snapping. He wanted desperately to get back to the game.

"Hey, rookie, gimmee that," he said, moving up on Liam and snatching at the ball. Liam turned to face him as if he were going to give it up peacefully, still dribbling, but at the last second he moved it away from Randall's reach. The ball slid smoothly behind his back to his other hand, stayed there dribbling without so much as the slightest break in its rhythm.

Randall stopped, stood still, watched Liam for a long moment. He turned to look at Jazz and the Peeks—still laughing and talking—then back to Liam. "Get past me," he said to him, dropping down to a defensive stance. Liam grinned. For a moment, only his hand moved as it kept the ball in a lazy kind of bounce. Then he turned to look at me and shrugged, feinted left and went right when Randall lurched for the empty air.

Liam turned around and flipped the ball to Randall, who passed it right back. He turned around and hollered out, "Sub!" Pointing at some kid on the far side he flicked his fingers to the sidelines, then turned back to Liam. "You're running point, rookie. Try not to screw this up for us."

Jazz called out from across the court, "Randall! We beating y'all so bad as all that? You pressed enough to bring in the new kid?" She barked that little laugh and the Peek side lit up, hollering out to Liam and each other. Orion ran around in a couple of tight little circles, then fell down theatrically and lay there laughing. Que came over and offered him a hand, then faked a fall himself when Orion reached for it. For a moment it was chaos on the floor as they rolled around, cracking themselves up.

For his part, though, Liam didn't blink. The rest of our team was giving Randall anguished looks, but Liam just stood there waiting calmly while Orion and Que climbed slowly back to their feet, breathing big in exaggerated exhaustion. He checked the ball in to get the point started again, and began to move forward with that same lazy dribble he had showed out on the sideline. The Peeks let him cross half-court and all the way to the key before finally someone approached him. Orion stepped forward and smirked as the rest of the players ran patterns, and Liam stood still for just an instant as they stared each other down. Then he feinted left and went right, the same way he had just done to Randall. The difference this time, though, was that when Orion fell for the trap and went for that empty space, Liam pulled up smoothly and shot a perfect jumper from just inside the 3-point arc.

The energy of the crowd flip-flopped in an instant. The Peeks went quiet and our side rose up in our seats. "Liam!" I shouted, slapping at Kiki's hand. She was pointing and laughing at Orion, watching Jazz holler at him from across the court.

After the inbounds pass she got the ball again and drove down, dribbled through a couple of defenders, then spun and took the outlet to Que. He shot and scored, easy as that. She gave Liam a look as Randall picked up the ball, took it out of bounds, and put it right back in to him.

This time Orion was there from the jump. He put his shoulder into Liam, running right up alongside him, trying to slap the ball away as he pushed his way up the court. Liam just kept switching directions, stopping and starting, moving the ball from left hand to right as he angled his body. For all of Orion's efforts, eventually they found themselves back at the top of the key. It was almost as if Orion hadn't been playing defense at all.

"You watching this, Kiki?" I said, grabbing her arm and shaking it for attention.

"Ben, you'd have to be an idiot not to be watching this," she said, her eyes locked on the court as she knocked my hand away.

Liam paused, looked to a couple of his teammates, then made for the same feint-left but go-right move he tried last time. Or, at least, that's what it looked like to me, but when Orion smoothly went to defend the spot where Liam had shot the time before, there was again only open air. After leading Orion into that position, Liam had crossed the ball back up, hard and fast, and moved to the left after all. He stepped cleanly past Orion, took a second step before pulling up, and easily drained another jump shot. The gym went crazy again. Even the Associates were starting to pay attention, and typically they watched the crowd way more than they watched the game.

About a minute later, after Liam showed off yet another move and scored for the third time, Jazz sprinted over from the baseline. "Orion!" she called, "take a breather, man." She came up close to him and grabbed his shoulder. "Go take Randall. I got this new kid." The crowd was so loud by this point that I couldn't hear a word she said; she just happened to be facing me, allowing me to read her lips. Orion backed away, anger all over his face. He jogged across the court to Randall, who immediately started moving his mouth a mile a minute—talking trash at this crazy turn of events.

Jazz waited just a moment after the inbounds, took the pass cleanly as she looked across the gym at the defense. Then she suddenly blazed the ball downcourt. She skipped straight past a flailing Randall and two other defenders, looking like in her frustration she was going to take it all the way to the basket. At the last second, though, she stopped on a dime and spun around, kicking it back out to Orion on the 3-point line. He was wide open and drained an easy shot. The crowd seemed disappointed at Jazz's decision, but it was the right call—a quick three versus a risky inside move. And Jazz almost never made mistakes.

Randall grabbed the ball, put it inbounds to Liam, took off down the court. Orion met him halfway and checked him up, completely refocused. I wondered briefly if that was why Jazz had given him the shot after all. Liam followed behind them in their wake; he was entirely unguarded. Jazz was standing at the top of the arc, watching him, waiting to see which way he would drift. She seemed unconcerned, almost bored.

One of our words from the Testing came to mind: she looked desultory.

The next couple of minutes were like a master class in basketball defense. Liam tried all the moves he had used to get past Orion; he tried several we hadn't seen yet. Every time, Jazz either knocked the ball out of his hands or stayed in his lane and forced him to pass away. I could see Liam growing more and more frustrated—he began making mistakes, risking angles that were clearly unwise. Given that Jazz had shut down his A-game, these backup plans didn't go well. He went scoreless the rest of the game. Afterwards he drifted over to us, forlorn, his shirt dripping with sweat. Across the gym I could see that Jazz was barely breathing hard.

The mood on our side, however, was ebullient. With Randall free from the grip of Jazz he was able to score far more points than he usually did—Orion could keep up with him for the most part but not completely. The Peeks ended up winning 41-37, but the first teams hadn't been within fifteen points at all this year. Suddenly, the Guests maybe winning a game didn't seem outside the realm of possibility. Liam was down on himself, totally frustrated, but he didn't know he'd changed the course of this entire bootleg league.

Randall was bursting when he ran over. "Did you see that? Did you see my guy?" He slapped Liam on the back, bumped up into him and shook his shoulders like an affectionate big brother. "That was amazing! I've never seen Jazz have to guard anyone like that! You kept her stuck to you the whole time!"

"Yeah," said Liam, "but she shut me all the way down! I couldn't get anything past her—and I tried everything I know!"

Randall laughed in his face, still on eleven. "My man, you don't even know what you're talking about," he said. "Most of the time she doesn't even waste her time to cover any one person—they just leave the slowest guy on the court open and she runs like hell the whole time, helps double team whoever has the ball and takes us all down in turn. The guy they leave unguarded usually doesn't score any more than the rest of us. With her focused on you we were finally able to put up some serious points!"

We started out of the gym, Randall still bumping up against Liam in his excitement, the rest of us floating around answering his questions. *Did you see when I crossed Orion up? Did you see when Jazz missed that shot? Did you see me drain that three?* He was bouncing with excitement; I'm not sure I'd ever seen him so happy.

On the far side of the court, by the door to our hallway, the Peeks were shooting around under the basket. They were laughing and appeared to be just having fun, though as we got closer I could see that Jazz was imitating Liam's moves with Orion. She had her hand on his chest, pushing him this way and that, talking through some defensive pointers.

We crossed paths with them near the key at about the same moment as this kid named Colin. He was on the second team for the Guests, a lanky sophomore who almost certainly would be playing first by next year. Randall didn't much like him, but he had undeniable skills. He slowed down, veered unnecessarily near Orion and Jazz, and said, "Better watch out, Peeks. We'll be coming for you next game."

Orion turned, picked the ball up off the dribble and held it still. For a moment he just stared at Colin, but then he busted out laughing. *"We?"* he said, flicking the ball to Jazz as he turned away. "Go on with all that, son," he hit back over his shoulder, "I didn't see no *we* out on this court tonight."

Orion went back to guarding Jazz's imitation of the triple feint, and for a second I thought Colin was going to keep walking. Suddenly, though, he reached out and slapped the ball out of Jazz's hand, reaching around her from behind and bumping her forward into Orion. The ball bounced away and Colin laughed. "Yeah, I guess there's no *we* outside this school building, either. There's just *me*. And you two losers will be stuck in here playing ball with each other for what? Ten to twenty? If you get good behavior?" He looked pointedly at Jazz and added, "Well, we all know that's not exactly likely, now is it?"

He said it just quiet enough that the Associates guarding the court couldn't hear him, but everyone in the nearby vicinity froze. Randall instinctively started to step toward Colin, but Madison put a hand on his arm and he stopped, waited to see what would happen next. For his part, Orion made a show of watching the ball roll to a stop across the court, taking a long moment before turning around to face Colin. He moved around Jazz in a series of slow, deliberate steps, got within inches of Colin before stopping to speak through an exaggerated smile. "Jazz, I could have sworn I heard this little bit of noise from over here." He looked around comically, left and right and up and down, finally landing his gaze dead into Colin's eyes. "But, Jazz? Ain't no man over here to speak. Just some little old mouse."

He crouched down to brush the dust off his shoes, deliberately bumping his shoulder square into Colin's chest. Colin fell back a step, grunting, and Orion looked over at Randall. "You might want to get your pet mouse out of here, my man," he said. "Sometimes little critters that squeak too much can get into an awful lot of trouble. Sometimes they get themselves stepped on."

Orion stood back up, looked directly at Colin, waited. Then it happened: Colin spit straight in his face.

The scene—breathless and still just a moment before—burst all at once into motion and noise. Orion went straight for Colin, ready to throw hands, but somehow Jazz got up into his face before he could swing. She buried her shoulder into his ribcage, knocking him off balance and keeping his fist from connecting with Colin's face. At the same time, Randall grabbed Colin by the shoulders and yanked him backwards; they were about the same height, but Randall outweighed him by a good twenty pounds, mostly muscle. A group of Associates began a lazy walk over to us—flare-ups weren't uncommon on the court or the field, and the adults were rarely in a hurry to break them up.

All I could hear was Orion and Randall, both screaming at Colin at the top of their lungs. Jazz was holding Orion tight in a bear hug, whispering up into his ear. He was struggling to get free, but it was all theater. It would have been nothing for him to actually throw Jazz off, but he trusted her enough to let her protect him from an even larger disturbance. In contrast, Colin wasn't even pretending to try to get away from Randall. He knew that he could only end up on the losing end of any further interaction with Orion.

Instead, he just laughed. "Yeah, you best pay attention to your little girlfriend, Orion!" he called out over all the noise. Randall was holding him from behind; he thought he was safe to throw shots at the Peeks. The Associates were closing in, but in all the chaos they weren't close enough to pick up his next two words on their mics. He grinned in a wicked sort of way and spat out, "Fucking pick."

For just a moment it felt like someone had hit pause on the whole thing, like time was actually standing still, like we might still be able to rewind and all walk away. Then, somehow, over the noise of the scrum, I heard Kiki curse.

Everything happened in maybe three seconds, but I saw it all as if it were in slow motion. Randall shook his head, let go of Colin, and gave him just the slightest of shoves forward. Because Colin had been leaning away from Randall, he stumbled a bit with the change in inertia; it looked as if he were lunging at the Peeks. At the same time, Jazz took her hands off Orion, pushed sideways as she spun around into Colin's space. The Associates finally closed in but were too late to stop her—she punched him three times in the face, quick little rabbit throws, like a featherweight working a sparring partner way outside her class. His nose exploded in blood, and then his head hit the ground as she swept his legs out from under him. It was only then that the Associates were able to grab her, stop her from leaping onto his chest and continuing to pound on him. Two of them got her from behind to keep her from Colin, another slammed his truncheon into her stomach and doubled her over.

"What the fuck are you doing?" Orion screamed at the Associates, recovering his footing from Jazz's shove. He lurched forward as if he was going to interfere, but Randall grabbed him and held him back. For just a second I thought Orion was going to break away and make things worse—he was trying for real this time—but Randall was able to hold him up. The Associate with the truncheon turned around and pointed it at Orion, like a gun, made the little upward motion with his hand as if the gun had discharged.

Suddenly, Orion seemed to remember where he was. He froze.

The Associate turned back to look at Jazz, who was thrashing wildly around in a vain effort to escape. "You want to get tased again, little girl?" he said, pulling in close and getting right up into her face. His gas mask was swinging wildly as he hovered over her; his voice shredding as he shouted over the chaos. He pulled his taser out of his holster, backed up and pointed it at her chest.

She stopped struggling immediately, blinking up at him for a second, then hung her head to stare at the ground. The scene went from sixty to zero in an instant, like the momentary calm right after a car crash. In the stillness that followed, I could hear Orion's ragged breathing, Colin's muted groans. Madison was whispering something under her breath; Liam was fidgeting his legs so hard they sounded almost like Morse Code. Then the radios crackled to life, breaking the spell—the Algorithm had contacted Admin, they were wondering what was going on in the gym. The Associate grabbed for the mic with his free hand and said, "Just having a little problem with Jazz Lewis over here."

I didn't catch what Admin said back. But then, even though she wasn't resisting at all, the Associate tased her anyway.

The darts stuck into the sweat right under her throat. She shook violently for a long, terrible moment, and then the Associates dropped her and hovered overhead, waiting. When her body finally went still they went to their knees and rolled her over on her stomach, right into a pool of Colin's blood. Moments later she was cuffed and they were dragging her backwards out of the room, wires from the taser still trailing wickedly behind. She was definitely unconscious; her head lolled to the side, drool spilling out of her mouth all over her chest. A trail of blood followed her for twenty feet or so, streaking away into nothing as it left the court.

Most of the gym had cleared out; there were maybe twenty people in the room to witness what had happened. Every single one of us was dead quiet as the Associates hauled her away. Everyone, that is, except for Orion. He was crying, great huge sobs wracking his body, forcing him to his knees. He was making such a ruckus that one of the Associates—the one who had tased her, I think—turned back.

He pointed his truncheon at Orion. "You good, boy?" he asked, the only voice in the gym rising up out of the sounds of the bodies in agony. When Orion didn't answer he turned to Randall, a couple of feet away. "Well?" he asked again.

Randall had fire in his eyes, but he managed deference and the briefest of nods.

"Someone get that one to the infirmary," the Associate said, indicating Colin. "You two boys, though, report to your Admins. Immediately." He aimed his truncheon again at Randall and Orion in turn. "They're going to need answers about why Lewis suddenly felt the need to assault an innocent Guest."

With that he turned on his heels and walked away.

The rest of the gym cleared out, the joy from just a moment ago having dissipated all to hell. Some kid from Colin's Block came over and helped him to his feet, walked him off the floor. I stood there, helpless. Randall was my best friend, but I still had no idea how to help.

I had never felt like more of an outsider. Waiting alone, I watched

Randall kneeling down next to Orion, whispering at him and holding his shoulders to keep him from falling apart.

PART TWO

TWO ROADS

There are no magics or elves
Or timely godmothers to guide us. We are lost, must
Wizard a track through our own screaming weed.

- GWENDOLYN BROOKS

CHAPTER 9
AFTER THE STORM

The next day, atypically, the Head ran the Meeting from start to finish.

It wasn't like this had never happened before, but it was unusual enough to charge the room with something like electricity. Typically, Admin stayed pretty militant about putting a parade of students on stage, rotating different G.A.s through their one small chance to be in charge. It always felt like part of some scheme to try to prove how each and every one of us mattered here at 231, that we were all important. All the Guests, at least; Peeks were never allowed on stage. This morning, in stark contrast, it was crystal clear whose voice really mattered. Unequivocally, the Head was in command.

"We would like to begin today's Meeting," the Head said, his voice steely, "by acknowledging the eight thousand, four hundred and thirty-eighth day of the Braswell Administration. We also gratefully acknowledge the peace and prosperity that our President has wisely brought to this great nation."

He gave only the briefest of pauses before going on. I noticed that he didn't so much as glance at the sheet of paper taped to the lectern. "For our non-denominational moment of silence today we remember those who have gone before us. We know that it is only our actions that determine our character, and it is only our character that determines our place in the world." Here he looked up and over at the Peeks, and I could just catch the flash of a smile across his face. "We pause, also, to consider those who will one day come after us. May their burdens be lighter by virtue of our days of refinement."

"Always," he said. He managed to make it sound something like a threat.

I had said the words here hundreds of times—it was all muscle memory at this point—but for some reason I froze. Whatever solemnity they pretended to put into the moment of silence had always felt forced, but today the Head was bringing a new level of hypocrisy to the exchange. I barely managed to choke out, with everyone else, "We remember."

The Head replied, a little too quickly, "We remember."

"Always," we finished, though I only mouthed the word this time.

He went on, barreling through the announcements at what felt like warp speed. It got hard to listen here—the announcements basically stayed the same every day, tempting you to tune them out like the rest of the Meeting. And yet, every couple of days something new would drop into the list, and if you didn't hear it you might be admonished later for missing out on what they called "necessary information." Today, though, was pretty much all about the Testing—starting as planned in a couple of days—and the stolen contraband, still as yet unrecovered. We had heard this every day, in the exact same order, for over a week now.

Some movement against the side walls of the room distracted me, and I risked a glance over to see Associates moving silently down each of the aisles. Every ten feet or so one of them would halt and post up, and the rest would file right past to positions closer and closer to the stage. I fought against the urge to turn around and scan the entire auditorium. There were always Associates around the room in an all-school gathering like this, but never to this extent—I wondered how many were in here altogether. It was unsettling; doubly so because I had no real idea of what was going on behind me.

We were almost to the end of the Meeting. Coming out of the announcements, the Head went right into a long, rambling speech about how important it was for us to beat last year's performance on the upcoming Testing—do your best, show the world what we are made of here at 231, that kind of stuff—when he suddenly stopped cold. I thought he was simply balking a bit at the transition to the Pledge, that he'd lost the plot of the Meeting during his attempt to motivate us, but I quickly realized that he was waiting for something. He was staring over his shoulder at the display, tapping his foot. Clearly frustrated, he turned to glare out over the audience at the poor G.A. in the control room, running the display in such a delinquent fashion. Then, finally, it happened.

A massive picture of Jazz blinked onto the display.

The room broke out into a low gasp that dampened immediately into a slowly decaying hum. The first thing I noticed was that it was obviously not the intake picture linked to her Credentials—the background was different, and the proportions were zoomed in far too tight. The extreme close-up brought immediate attention to what was wrong with her face, though, like one of those "spot the differences" games we played when we were kids. Several of her braids had come completely undone; they were curling up, jutting out of the frame of the camera. Her jaw was swollen on the side, near her ear, giving her whole face an eerie, lopsided look. She had a nasty cut above her eye, also swollen, already turned a violent purple—she seemed barely able to keep that eye open. The whole vibe would have been one of menace if you hadn't known that she was just sixteen years old, basically still a kid. I could hardly look at the photo; it made me feel uneasy in a way

I couldn't quite explain.

I signaled to Randall, *She didn't get those bruises during the game, right?*

Without a pause to think twice, he shook his head and signaled back, *Nope.*

And Colin? I asked.

Randall snorted. *He couldn't land a punch on her. No way. Had to be Associates.*

The Head stared at the picture looming over him, letting the voices taper slowly away, then tapped just one time on the mic. The Globes flashed blue and the room immediately went dead silent again.

He cleared his throat and said, "The events of last night's Recks have caused some not inconsiderable consternation among the Admin." He was reading from a paper for the first time today; it almost felt like a press release or something the way he was handling it. "The Admin are very displeased with the dangerous behavior manifested by certain students, chief among them Ms. Jazzlyn Lewis. As the Head of this Federal Site, I am particularly concerned for the safety of Ms. Lewis, given her recent inability to maintain adequate control of her emotions. As such, we have remanded her to In-School Suspension for an unspecified period of disciplinary correction."

A murmur fluttered quickly around the room. We didn't often hear about folks being sent to In-School. Sometimes certain kids would go missing for a couple of days at a time, maybe a week. We all knew what that meant, but nobody ever talked about it out in the open like this.

"In addition," he went on, "in light of recent events, the Admin now have enough information to name a suspect in the case of the missing contraband." He looked over his shoulder at Jazz, then back toward us. "Anyone known to be colluding with Ms. Lewis, willingly or unwillingly, will now be considered to be complicit to her crimes and subject to punishment once proof is provided as to her guilt."

The room roared dully to life again. It felt like I could hear a collective "what the hell?" bouncing out of every corner. The Head did that small smile again and spoke over the noise.

"At the moment we are unsure as to where your classmate—this Jazzlyn Lewis—has managed to stow the delinquent supplies. Again, the Admin would like to stress that any information offered regarding Ms. Lewis's recent malfeasant behavior will be rewarded commensurate to the value of said information. We would also like to stress that any information being withheld will be considered a punishable offense, tantamount to collusion." He nodded and pocketed the paper. He was speaking to a silent room again. "Now stand for the Pledge of Allegiance."

The picture of Jazz disappeared, replaced by the giant flag fluttering in the wind. In the noise of the clattering seats Randall cleared his throat and I looked over at him. He signaled to me, *What you know about any of this, son?*

I closed my eyes for a moment and pictured Jazz sitting under that desk in Mason's room, saw her making the binoculars with her hands and shaking her head at me. I said the Pledge by rote for probably the two thousandth time in my life. Afterwards, I looked at him and shrugged lightly, tapping back, *Nothing at all. But I think it's time for me to find something out.*

———————

The night before in the common room, everyone had been in a miserable state. Randall was gone all through the News and right up until lights dim; the Z.A. had sent him and Orion straight to the control offices for questioning. We figured he was going to be okay—he would probably be able to say that Colin broke free all on his own strength, and the cameras were too spotty out there on the floor to contradict him. We all knew the truth, though. Randall had to let Colin go; he did Orion a favor after Colin said that word. There was no way he could have done anything different.

It took a while to explain to Liam how an insult that meant nothing on the outside could mean so much here at 231. Part of the problem was that, as far as we knew, there wasn't really any one story to tell about that word. Or, if there was, it was just another one of those things lost to the history of this place. But each of us learned it at one point or another: inside the walls of this building, you did not, under any circumstances, ever call anyone a "pick."

"It's not the word. It has nothing to do with the word," Carlos interrupted the flow of conversation. "It's the power of these guys being able to say something insulting, and yet they can't be blamed for it." He had been silent up to now, diligently working on his homework. Kiki had been doing the major lifting in the explanations, and she looked relived to pass the mic to someone else.

He went on. "I mean, it's obvious that it's kind of like a shortened version of a pejorative for people that look like me." He spread his hands out in a slight presentation of himself. "And if you add an -er to it? Well, then it just happens to sound vaguely like another word, one that doubles as an insult for people who look like you." He waved at Kiki, who gave a curt nod in return. "And then there's the trifecta—it sounds like you were trying to say 'Peek,' but you're talking in some kind of foreign accent. These people can say it, and it's like they're making fun of someone for not being American enough or something."

He took a breath, paused, then went on, "But as legit as all that is, it's not really the whole story."

The room had gone completely quiet—not that anyone was talking all that much to begin with or anything. But everyone had dropped whatever they were doing to dial into what Carlos was saying about that word. I'd never heard anybody get this deep into it before.

"The real draw, though," he said, "is that if you say it right, Admin can't catch you doing it. So long as they don't have a mic pointed at you or anything, the Algorithm can't tell the two words apart when it tries to read your lips off the Globe footage. All it can see you saying is 'Peek.' It's like that makes these assholes want to say it all the more—if they can say the word just right, they can go on and pretend it never even happened. So Jazz gets blamed for hauling off and whaling on Colin. But Colin gets away scot-free for insulting Orion in the first place."

"That doesn't make any sense," Liam said. "It's still just a made up, nonsense word. I mean, who cares? If I called you a *blurgendorf*, and then went off and pretended it never happened? Well, it's a nothing word. So, basically, it really is like nothing even happened at all!"

"Easy for you to say," Carlos muttered, but Kiki cut in.

"No, Liam, think about it," she said. "It's about having power over someone else. You ever steal something from a store when you were little? Something small that you didn't even need, but that you thought no one there would ever miss? Just to see if you could put one over on them?"

Liam shook his head, and for a second I thought the conversation had run out of steam. Then Madison spoke up. "I did," she said quietly.

Everyone turned immediately to face her. She was sitting small in the corner of the couch, knees scrunched up to her chin, half of her face hidden behind her legs. She hadn't spoken since they took Randall away. "I was about eight," she said, "and me and my dad were wandering through this hardware store, looking for the right drill bit or something like that. And I saw one of those sets of tiny screwdrivers, like the ones you use on glasses? I didn't even wear glasses—I was never going to use them. But I took them anyways."

She broke off, sat for a moment staring at her shoes. Her hair hung into her face, masking the fact that she was crying. Nobody said a word until she continued. "I just put them in my pocket, tried not to think about it, you know? Then I walked out with my Dad after he paid for his stuff. It was this total thrill, but when I got home? I was so ashamed that I had to bury them in the back of my desk. They're probably still there, just lost." She paused again. "I never told anyone about it until right now."

With Randall out of the room, it was on me to reach out my hand and place it on Maddy's knee, briefly, pulling it back into my own space after only a moment. Carlos pointed at her and said, gently, "See? It's the same thing." She looked up and smiled at him, and his voice rose a little as he turned away from her. "Don't get me wrong—Colin, and everybody else who uses that word? They're real pricks. He got his little feelings hurt and wanted to get back at Orion, and he knew for sure that a Peek would get into way more trouble than him even if the whole thing led to a fight. I mean, it worked, right? All I'm saying is that the reason this word has stuck around is because it gives assholes like Colin a secret little thrill, knowing they can't caught saying it. He knows that it will look like he got hit for no reason. They can't prove he said anything other than 'Peek,' not from looking at the camera footage."

"Randall will tell them, though," Liam asked, looking around. Kiki laughed. "I mean, right?" Liam added, lamely.

Carlos said, "I guarantee you that he will not. Jazz won't either. And neither will Orion. No way any of them are going to say a thing to Admin about that word. It's not worth their time trying to speak about something Admin wants to pretend doesn't exist."

"Wait, what?" Liam asked. "What are they pretending about?"

"Racism," Carlos said, looking him hard, straight in the eyes. "They don't want to hear a word about it here." When Liam didn't respond, he went back to his homework. The conversation was over.

"Well, that's our City News for tonight," Donna said.

"Keep in mind, City, that it is our solemn duty to eliminate the darkness," Dan added.

"—but never forget to praise the progress of lights," Donna finished, with a smile.

Randall came back after the News, just minutes before lights dim, and he confirmed Carlos's words. He and Orion had sat in interrogation together for over an hour, a couple of G.A.s making them go over every detail of the video from the fight, frame by frame. They had to work out a script verifying every word of dialogue, and before they were allowed to leave they each signed a form saying that, as the key witnesses to the altercation, they were able to authenticate the events with all accuracy. Without so much as a word passing between them, they had each agreed with what the Globe footage showed: Colin had called Orion a Peek, and then for no real reason Jazz had pushed off from Orion and instigated the fight. Once their signed statements were in order they were told to return to the dorms.

Jazz, on the other hand, was to be held indefinitely.

Admin may have known better, but now the official record was securely locked into place. The entire argument was only a matter of a couple of kids talking trash about a basketball game.

———————

CHAPTER IO
THE TESTING

Four times a year, the school shut down completely so we could sit for the Testing.

It went down just like clockwork: the second week of school, the last week of school, the beginning of October, and the end of February. The day-to-day schedule at 231 was always subject to sudden change, of course. An unexpected Meeting, a Code Red that ran too long, an absent teacher that led to a double block in another teacher's class—any given hour, things might run differently than they had the day before. But not the Testing. The date was set by whoever it was the Head eventually reported to, and that was that. It was as reliable as the seasons. More so, maybe, given how little of the outside we were allowed to see around here.

Just a few days after the fight, the rhythms of the year took over and classes got ugly. For at least a couple of weeks leading up to the Testing teachers would cancel our regular lessons and only run review. Whatever small breath of creativity we might see in here—and there wasn't all too much of that to begin with—would gutter out as we faced front and answered question after question, any one of which might show up during the Testing to come. Even Mason couldn't resist the pull of this gravity; he held out longer than the others, but still spent a full week ahead of time cramming us full of facts that he thought might prove useful. Homework doubled in all our classes, and it wouldn't have mattered even if Jazz was released from In-School—there was no freedom during Recks in the week leading up to the Testing. We were prohibited from being anywhere save for the library and our common rooms, could send someone on a snack run only with our Credentials authorized.

It was as close to permanent lockdown as it got here at 231. We all hated it.

"Is it always like this?" Liam asked one night during one of our endless study sessions. We were working on a batch of five hundred flash cards for Mason, split up amongst our group. Most of us handled prep for the Testing like this, treated it as a giant group project that just needed to get done. We were hanging out in the common room with one other group, loosely negotiating the available space with them. Pretty much everybody else was holed up together in the library. David refused to work with anyone, though, so he sat in the corner alone. He said that he got better grades without all the extraneous input.

Carlos sighed and turned to Liam. "Rookie, I've been here for six years now, and the Testing has changed not even one little bit." He squinted at a smudge on his flash card, frowned and balled it up, started another. "It's the same thing every couple of months—they somehow make school extra miserable and even more boring than usual. We all sit around and work our asses off and complain, and eventually it's over and we get a couple of months off until the next round."

"Just wait until next week," Madison said. "You think this is bad…." She trailed off without even looking up from her work.

Liam watched her, waiting for her to go on. When she didn't, he turned back to the group and said, "But why? What do they do with all this data? At my old school we only did this at the end of the year." He looked around and a couple of folks just laughed.

"They don't do anything except rank us, extra hard," Randall said. "Big old lists, printed out and posted all in public just to let you know exactly who's smart and who's dumb." He smiled and added conspiratorially, "But don't worry about anything, Liam. You just happen to be sitting with the third highest-ranked member of the entire junior class. At least, according to October's Testing. We'll just see how your guy does next week."

Liam looked at Randall, clearly impressed, and Kiki lost it laughing. "Liam!" she said. "You can't think he's talking about himself? High ranking my ass!" She fell on the floor, rolled around laughing, scattered flash cards everywhere. Carlos poked her with his foot, sighed dramatically, and started cleaning them up.

Randall feigned indignation. "Kiandria!" he scowled. "Are you insinuating that I don't have the…the…the intellectual acumen to succeed as highly as our good friend Ben here? Are you in some way calling me deficient?"

Maddy quickly rooted around in her stack of cards, came up holding one with the word "ACUMEN" written on it. Glancing at the back, she beamed at Randall. "Well done, sir. If that word shows up on the Testing, you will indeed be sufficient."

Liam turned to me. "Ben? You're third?"

I did my best to follow Randall's lead and act affronted. "You're surprised? You think I don't have the acumen?" The group laughed and I shrugged. "Right up behind Jazz and that kid from C Block whose name I never can remember."

"He is a boring fellow," Randall said. "It's probably his own fault you can't remember his name. If only he had a bit more untoward, am I right?" Maddy shook her head and mouthed, *so close.*

Kiki smacked her teeth and waved her hand in the air, pushing my words to the side. "Whatever, Ben. You know those tests are dumb as hell. They just prove you're good at taking tests. Not how smart you are."

"Whatever they prove," Carlos said, glaring at the rest of us, "they're going to be my ticket out of here someday. And I need y'all to shut up so I can get mine, you hear?" Grudgingly, everyone went back to work.

I got distracted, though, tired of all this unnecessary labor. I mean, it made sense that we needed the Testing our senior year, so the Scouts could figure out which of us might be able to cut it in college or whatever. But we had been doing this every year for as long as I could remember, for what? And why four times a year? My old school was just like Liam's—we didn't have all this extra drama every three months. Everyone here just kind of went along with it, because it was the way things had always been done; that doesn't mean it made a whole lot of sense. Especially not now, with Jazz gone and Admin acting completely extra.

Kiki snapped her fingers in front of my face, breaking my reverie. She grinned at me and pointed at my stack of unfinished cards. I blinked, shook my head, and started up with the writing again.

———————

We spent the entire week of the Testing stuck in Williams's class. Five hours a day with only one break for the bathroom and another to eat a junky bag lunch. The Meeting ran at least double long every morning—the first day they pushed reminders about test-taking strategies, and the rest of the week they gave extensive updates about preliminary data returns. In the end, we would just skip first period and go straight to whatever class came right before lunch. In our case, unfortunately, this happened to be Williams.

Every day we had to be in place by 10:30, a full thirty minutes ahead of the mandated start time. Williams had a special scanner, a device we only saw during the Testing, and he spent some of that time linking each of our Credentials to our test computers. We weren't allowed to use our regular screens during the Testing—too much danger of somebody cheating, I suppose—and so they would distribute a class set of ancient tablet computers to every room. These devices must have been thirty years old; I had never even used a tablet before coming to 231. They were wiped clean of everything, only able to open the protocols for the Testing once our thumbprints were synced and our retinas scanned for vitals. We had to stay in complete silence during this authorization process—even though nothing official had yet occurred, Williams didn't play around with conversation during the Testing. After getting our tablets hooked up to the Algorithm, he came around for our blood samples. Without a word we would extend our hands as he pricked them with his device. It was an old machine; it hurt like hell.

"Good morning, students of Federal Education Site 231," he said, finally, after the DNA match was official. It was precisely 11:00. "Today we will commence the first day of our February Testing. Over the next five days you will be rigorously examined in order to determine your knowledge and growth in the four core subjects: mathematics, science, reading, and Nation. Each day will be comprised of seven 35-minute test sections, with five-minute breaks between sections. The exception to this will be your lunch break, which will be fifteen minutes in between sections three and four."

He droned on like this for a good ten minutes, details about how many questions were in each section or how many points each question would count toward the overall score. Today wouldn't be that bad; science and Nation were just a bunch of facts they had instructed us to spit back out on command, like a bunch of trained dogs. I was a good memorizer—that's why I scored so high on the Testing. Tuesday and Wednesday were reading, which was for the most part fine. They didn't always choose the most interesting things to read, but Mason had us more than ready. The end of the week was math, though, which most of us were dreading. Question after question about triangles and equations, lists of numbers that couldn't be further from real life? It was exhausting, even if you were good at it.

Williams stopped talking for a moment, which snapped me from my thoughts. I looked at him and saw him casting his eyes around the room. I had to believe that teachers loved the Testing. They just got to sit around for five hours while we suffered—it felt like I could see Williams gleaming, eager to get into it.

"Finally, students," he went on, landing the plane on the instructions, "be reminded that no breaches of protocol will be tolerated in the slightest. There will be no bathroom breaks outside of the allotted time between sections. No food or water is permitted in the room. If you finish early, you may not read or draw on your scratch paper; you will put your pencil down and wait. You will not speak. You will not stand up. If you have a problem or a question you may raise your hand—that is the only change in your behavior that will be permitted."

He swiped at his screen. The display turned into a giant clock, showing a countdown timer that gave us thirty-five minutes. Williams looked up at the display and then back at us, his faced splayed with a wicked grin.

"Good luck, students of 231," he said. His voice was laced with sarcasm; it felt like he was bubbling with something like glee. "Your time starts now."

I wondered whether Jazz was doing a special session of the Testing by herself. Last year they had hauled a Peek from Zone 7 up out of the infirmary and made him answer questions all week—he was sick as a dog, could barely stay upright in his seat he was so woozy. He kept falling asleep and our teacher kept waking him up; sleeping was, of course, prohibited. I had a hard time believing that they were going to give Jazz a pass on this just because she happened to be stuck in In-School.

On the fourth day of the Testing, I was staring at the countdown timer, watching the seconds tick by and trying hard to get my pulse down to 40 beats per minute. I had finished the sixth math section super fast—it happened to be heavy on stuff we had learned recently in class—and I was trying desperately to entertain myself. No reading, no writing, no drawing, no sleeping; there weren't a lot of options. I'd heard it said that they deliberately kept us bored in order to encourage us to check and re-check our answers and look for mistakes, but I was exhausted of the Testing in general and math in specific. I had no appetite to go back over answers I was pretty sure were correct.

It was at that moment that the Code Red sounded.

We had only five minutes left to go in the section, and I had been working extra hard to get my pulse down. I had relaxed my body, slowed my breathing, and timed it out to just 42 beats per minute. My last thought before the Code Red was that I might see the upper 30s for the first time, but then the Globe turned to fire and the siren sounded, ruining my chance. My pulse shot up immediately, and out of curiosity I stayed still for a few extra seconds in order to monitor it. I couldn't help but wonder how bad all of this was for our bodies—my pulse jumped from 40 to 100 in only an instant, all because of the Globes.

When I finally looked away from the countdown I was surprised to see that everyone was still frozen in their seats, staring at Williams. He was at the front of the room, frantically flipping through the huge instruction manual that was issued to him at the start of the week, and it hit me: this was a no-win situation for all of us. Jumping up from our seats would be a serious violation of Testing protocol; I'd heard of people getting Infractions for way less. Similarly, not being underneath the desk by the time the Associates came through? Unthinkable. Williams was understandably terrified to make a mistake—he would for sure be blamed for any irregularities either way—and he was looking for guidance. Given his frantic flipping, it seems obvious that he wasn't finding any. It would have been funny if I hadn't been able to picture the consequences.

Mercifully, an announcement issued forth from the Globe, somehow rising above the repeated declaration that we were in a Code Red and needed to assume the position for our own safety. "STUDENTS OF FEDERAL EDUCATION SITE 231. CLOSE YOUR TESTING TABLETS IMMEDIATELY AND ASSUME THE STANDARD POSITION FOR A SCHOOLWIDE CODE RED. REPEAT, CLOSE YOUR TABLETS IMMEDIATELY AND ASSUME THE STANDARD POSITION FOR A SCHOOLWIDE CODE RED. PROCTORS, YOU MAY PAUSE YOUR TIMERS NOW."

For just a moment Williams showed enough humanity to look relieved at the directions, but then he went and ruined it by screaming at us, "You heard it! Get under the desks, you lot! Now!" With a clatter of smacking plastic, we closed the covers on our tablets and scrambled under our desks. Last thing before I hit the ground I glanced over at the abandoned desk where Jazz wasn't, imagined the ghost of her laughing at Williams as she climbed down to the floor. By the time I got myself crammed into position I couldn't quite see through the bodies to her empty spot, but I could feel her absence all the same.

This was maybe our eighth Code Red in just the couple of weeks since Liam had enrolled. A few nights back we had got to arguing, basically skipped an hour of study time trying to determine if we were having a normal amount of Code Reds or not. Everyone was scouring their messages and notes, trying to figure out which one happened on what day—we all had strong memories of certain lockdowns. Madison remembered the one in math class because it happened in the middle of a problem she didn't understand; Carlos remembered one from when Williams was teaching about World War 2 because the siren locked in a weird image of Williams goose-stepping around in a German military uniform. Whether or not we tracked them all down, the consensus was clear—we had been having something like three Code Reds a week lately, and that was way higher than normal.

I shifted my body under the desk so I could look at Liam. He flashed me nine fingers, shrugged his shoulders in a questioning sort of why. More than any of us, he was definitely keeping track.

We had been sitting on the ground long enough that I was starting to cramp up. I started counting my pulse again, trying to distract myself by pushing the flashing light and the blaring voice into the background. I didn't have a clock to time my hearbeat out, but I could definitely feel it slowing down. For a while I tried to count out Mississippis in order to judge, but once my pulse dropped below 60 I gave up and just counted heartbeats for fun. When I passed two hundred I realized that we had been sitting in this Code Red for far longer than usual. Something weird was going on.

Finally the Guest door buzzed and crashed open. The room turned to violet and exploded with bodies; it felt like there were Associates everywhere, spilling into the rows, poking under every desk. One of them crouched down and got right into my face, pointed a taser straight at my chest. His gas mask and goggles were engaged in place on his helmet; it was like looking into the face of some crazed robot. He stared at me long enough that I began to think he was going to say something. Then I heard someone shout out from across the room.

"I got him!"

The Associate jumped up, shoving my desk sideways in the process and giving me a slightly better view of the others. I turned in time to see two of them hauling Orion past Williams's desk, headed for the open door to the Guest hallway.

"Hey, what the hell—oohm!" he yelled, his protest dissolving into a breathless grunt. One of them had smashed a truncheon into his stomach, doubling him over as they dragged him forward—they had him one on each arm with a third shoving at him from behind. A Drone was hovering in the doorway, revolving its primary eye around to take some sort of scan of Orion and the room. It floated out the door in front of him and the Associates, and for just a moment I was shocked to get a glimpse into the hallway.

The Head was standing there, waiting. His three-piece suit was a bizarre sight amidst the sea of riot gear.

"Zone K-7—clear!" the last Associate in the room shouted into his microphone, and I could hear a cacophonous echo of his words spilling in from the hallway. There must have been more than twenty radios out there. The Code Red stopped flashing immediately; we had been the last room in the entire school to get cleared. In the relative quiet, just before Williams clambered out from under his desk and resumed the Testing, I was able to hear a couple of words from outside in the hall. They had all been shouting at each other just a moment before in order to be heard over the Globe, and their voices carried perfectly into our room.

"...isolated the suspect..." one of the Associates hollered.

"...in league with her..." yelled another.

"...run his Credentials first..." screamed a third.

"...put him against the wall..." brayed a fourth.

Then the door shut, clicked, whirred to a lock. The door was utterly soundproof—it could have been chaos still on the other side and we would never know. I wasn't alone in continuing to stare at it, though; half the class was paying more attention to what we couldn't hear outside in the hall than to Williams's flustered reboot of the Testing. Soon the Globe called out that we were to begin again, adding ninety seconds to the timers. Williams regained authority and began ordering us about. Everything returned to what qualified as normal around here.

I pulled my gaze away from the door and back to my computer, but my thoughts were out in the hallway with Orion. Whatever Jazz was up to, they thought Orion was mixed up in it, too—pulling a student out of the Testing was no small thing. And what was the Head doing on a routine sweep? Williams began our timer again, and I was grateful to have a couple of minutes remaining in the section I had already finished.

It gave me time to sit in silence and think about Jazz.

CHAPTER II
THE OTHER DOOR

Next week, in the cafeteria, I spent the entirety of my lunch periods watching Orion like a hawk.

They had kept him out for the last day and a half of the Testing, but he showed back up unceremoniously on Monday morning. No word crossed the chain link about where he was or whether they had him complete his final sections, but I suspected not. The results for the Testing had been posted Friday night, and Jazz's name was nowhere to be found. Wherever they were holding her, she didn't seem to be doing her tests. It went against all precedent, but there was no reason to think that Orion had done them, either.

Her absence had moved me up to 2nd place, a fact which caused a stir in K Block even if it didn't really change all that much for me. I was pleased, of course; like most of the Guests here, my big hope was to get a scholarship out of this place at the end of next year. In that sense the results definitely mattered to me, even if I tried not to get too hung up on them. I knew my parents would be pleased when they got the report, but this was both good and bad, its own extra level of annoying. The Testing would be all that they would want to talk about at Visitation next month.

"Wait, you're not going to eat that at all?" Randall reached across me for Carlos's lunch. It was less of a question and more of an accusation—pizza was a hot-button issue at 231. You either loved it or you hated it, and Randall happened to love it.

"Um, do you want it, Randall?" Carlos asked, blinking slowly and giving his voice an inquisitive upspeak. He moved his tray just out of Randall's first grab for the food. "I don't want my pizza? But you might?"

Randall made his move and snatched the pizza off Carlos's plate. "There is something wrong with you, son. It's just facts that they make a fine slice up here." He took a big bite and mock bowed to Carlos, who stopped blinking suddenly and rolled his eyes.

"There is a lot to admire about you, Randall," he said. "But your opinion about the quality of pizza is not one of them. I don't understand how you eat that shit."

I was on day three of staring through the chain link at Orion, blindly eating lunch while trying not to get food all over myself. Jazz still wasn't back, and their table was unusually subdued—it was easy to keep on eye on him when they were all sitting so quietly. Monday he didn't go to the coffee station at all. Tuesday there were a couple of folks from each side already there by the time he went over, so I stayed put. By Wednesday I was getting restless, only half paying attention to Randall and Carlos argue about pizza. I didn't want to miss my chance to talk to Orion when it came—if he went for caffeine, I needed to be sure to get there first.

He stood up three times while I was watching him, and each time I started immediately for the chain link fence. The first two he sat back down—only stretching his legs or telling a story—and I had to get stupidly back in my seat, try to act for the Associates like I was doing something more legitimate than stalking a Peek on the other side. The third time, though, he slapped a couple of palms and then turned toward the empty coffee station. By the time he arrived I was already there, making a big show of deciding whether I was going to use a mug or a paper cup for my beverage.

"You again, huh, Ben?" he said, not looking directly at me. Instead, he seemed to be having a lot of trouble opening a cardboard sleeve for his cup; all his attention was focused forward toward the station. I was nervous, wishing he would have said something more encouraging, and so I was a little slow on the uptake—he was on his third try before I realized that his actions were belying his words. He was stalling for time because it wasn't just me that was looking for this conversation.

He wanted to talk to me, too.

"Yeah, me again," I said cautiously. Just because Orion might be willing to stop and speak didn't mean I could get away with saying any old thing. Too late it occurred to me that I'd been so focused on the timing of meeting him over here that I hadn't really put enough thought into exactly how I was going to phrase what I wanted to say. "So, how are things going over there?" I followed up, lamely.

He looked sideways at me, and I knew instantly that I'd said the wrong thing. For a second I thought he was going to tell me to just fuck off, but instead he laughed. "You mean, with my side of the chain link taking heat for all the things that are wrong with this crazy place? Or do you mean how are all the Peeks feel about Jazz taking the fall for some shit going on with the Globes? Or are you asking how I feel about being dragged into this whole mess during a random Code Red? Pulled out of my seat for no good reason other than Testing while Black?" He was finally able to attach a sleeve to a cup, and had moved on to making some very slow choices about what to pour inside.

Afraid of saying something stupid, I just kept picking up random carafes and examining them carefully in turn. I even stuck my nose over a couple and inhaled deeply, as if I had any idea what I was doing. If I was honest, they all just smelled like burnt shoe to me, and I reflexively made a face. Orion broke off his speech and laughed again.

"Ben, I know you must be cool because Randall rolls with you," he said, and he reached through the gap in the chain link, took the carafe out of my hand. "But you look dumb as hell over here pretending you old enough to handle this grown folks drink." He poured some coffee into his cup.

Just then I noticed an Associate headed our way, drifting over from the Peek side of the chain link. It was that white guy, the one Orion knew by name. Cursing my luck, I shut my mouth tight and decided to fumble for the sugar instead. Hopefully it would look like I was doing something legit.

The Associate stopped a few yards away and let his hand fall lightly to his truncheon. "Y'all good over here?" he asked, cutting his eyes back and forth between me and Orion.

Orion smiled, turned, spread out his hands in front of him. I wondered briefly if that was his natural way of talking or if it was learned behavior when communicating here in this building. "Yes, sir, Derek," he said. "We're just going over some of yesterday's notes from Mr. Williams's class. Really excited to be done with all that Testing, you know?"

Derek took his hand off his truncheon and stared hard at me. I blinked, nervous, but then he looked back over at Orion, who nodded in the slightest possible way. Derek held Orion's gaze for just a moment and then, without even a backwards glance at me, he spun around and went back to his station, just outside of microphone range. Orion turned away from him and faced forward again, started the process of finding the perfect top for his coffee. "Talk fast, Ben, we probably don't have long here at this point. What do you want?"

I glanced briefly over at Derek and wondered what had just happened, but there was no time to ask about that right now. Instead, I swallowed hard and went for my original question. I wasn't going to articulate it well, however hard I tried, so I just started talking. "Orion, the other day in Mason's class, the day we talked about *Frankenstein* and had the Code Red? While the rest of us were under our desks, but before the Associates got there, I saw Mason talking to Jazz, angled away from the Globes. Like, they were angled on purpose so they could talk, something secret or whatever." I paused for a second but Orion didn't give me anything. I went on. "She saw me watching them. She knows that I know. But, Orion? I don't know what exactly I know."

I paused again, running out of steam, and then asked, "I guess I'm just wondering if you know what I know? And, maybe, could you tell me what that is exactly?" I noticed that he had finished fixing his coffee. He turned to face me square for the first time, stared at me over the station as he picked up his cup. He was five inches taller than me. I had to crane my neck to look him in the eye.

"If I ever see her again, I'll tell Jazz you asked about her," he said. He waited a moment and I nodded. The conversation was definitely over. I picked up my own cup.

"See you in Mason's class, Orion," I said, raising my coffee in a weak salute. "Thanks for that talk." I turned away from the chain link and went back to the lunch table.

———————

Several more days went by, but Jazz still hadn't returned. It had been two weeks now, and there was no word on why they were holding her so long or when she would get to come back. If not for the fact that they showed her face every day in the Meeting—still the picture with the nasty cuts and bruises from right after the game—I might have doubted what I'd seen that day under the desk. Her face convinced me beyond a doubt that something was going on, however, even if I didn't know what it was.

We were in Mason's class one day, starting work on the essays that would close out our study of *Frankenstein*. I hadn't talked to Orion since the cafeteria, and nothing had changed about our interaction in class. Meaning, he and all the other Peeks stayed huddled up on their side of the room, keeping to themselves while they worked. I tried to catch his eye every once in a while, hoping for some of the solidarity I felt in the cafeteria, but to no avail. Except for Jazz's empty desk, everything about school was completely routine.

I was huddled over Madison's screen, trying in vain to figure out why her opening paragraph was so much better than mine, when I saw Mason at the class phone. He spoke in low tones for a minute and, after he hung up, called my name. "Ben, come up here for just a moment, please."

One thing about a Federal Site that was entirely consistent with my life on the outside: it was a rule that when a teacher called you to the front of the room for no obvious reason, the rest of the kids just had to make some noise about it. I walked up to Mason's desk, basking in the attention, as the whole room let out a low "ooooooo!" Guests and Peeks alike came together for this time-honored ritual, and even Mason had to crack a smile about it.

"Yes, Mason?" I asked, and he held out a batch of papers, leaning backwards in his chair so he could look up at me through the lenses of his glasses.

"I need you to take this work to Jazz at In-School Suspension, please," he said, and the room, still rumbling with laughter, instantly went still. I reflexively looked to Orion, but he was assiduously avoiding my gaze, apparently hard at work on his screen. I quickly turned back to the front.

"No problem, Mason," I said, pulling my eyes back to the front and taking the papers. I paused and asked, "Um, how do I get to In-School Suspension, exactly?" Not only had I never been there, but up until this current situation with Jazz, I had never even heard of someone spending this much time at In-School.

Mason picked up his magazine and nodded toward the Peek door. "I'm not quite sure how they'll take you there, Ben. The Z.A. will be here shortly to escort."

Whispers and murmurs fluttered to life, and I turned to Randall with wide eyes. He signaled to me, *You made it, Ben. Going through the Peek door.* He grinned as I looked back to Mason, but he had already returned to his reading.

I headed back to my desk, but before I could sit down the buzzer clanged and the intercom crackled. "Here to pick up your runner, Mr. Mason," the voice said. Mason stood up, made as if to walk over to the retinal scanner, but suddenly the door buzzed again and swung open. The entire room stopped and stared; we knew what it meant when the door opened without a teacher's permission. In walked one of the G.A.s.

Mason balked for just a moment. He always acted as if he out-ranked the Z.A.s, but a G.A. visiting a classroom was something like a power move. He recovered smoothly, however—the G.A. might not even have noticed his hesitation as he bowed slightly and said, "Well, good afternoon, sir. I was expecting one of the Zones." An Associate posted himself up in the doorway behind the G.A., though he didn't step inside the room.

The G.A. nodded and gave Mason a stony-faced look. "Yes, well, the Head wants to make sure that Ms. Lewis receives the utmost atten-tion. Her assignments are of paramount important to Admin. Nobody wants to see her…left behind." He paused awkwardly, turned to look at me, beckoned with his hand. "Is it you, young man?" he said. "Come quickly, I haven't all day." I stepped over quickly, clutching the papers that Mason had passed me, both hands tight. Something weird was going on here, and I needed to be cool and not mess it up.

The Associate slid sideways for me to pass out into the Peek hall, but before I could leave Mason called out, "Ben." The G.A. and I both turned around; I could see that he was annoyed at the delay. Mason was back at his desk, leaning casually against the top, looking at us over his lenses. "Please tell Ms. Lewis that I expect her extra credit packet on Robert Frost directly upon her return. Tell her that her op-tions are extremely limited at this point. This is extremely important for her to hear, Ben. Make sure she knows that her options are limited."

He kept his eyes on me for an extra beat and I nodded before turning back to the G.A. He had moved past me to the other side of the door; I could see him checking his watch, obviously bothered by this entire errand. Crossing the room to follow, I risked one last look over my shoulder, somehow catching Liam's eye. He was not the person I was looking for, but he smiled and waved before blithely turning back to his screen—unaware of how utterly unprecedented this situation was. I didn't know a single Guest who had ever stepped across the threshold into the Peek hallway.

And yet, here I was, making that move into the unknown.

The Associate followed me out of the room to stand at attention right outside the door, pulling it shut behind him first. The click sounded different out here, echoing oddly off the bare cinder block. The G.A. held out his hand, clearly looking for my Credentials; I fumbled my wrist and held it out for him to scan. At the same time the Associate all but snatched Jazz's papers from me, leafing idly through them while the G.A. scanned me in. He pulled a reader out of his pocket and pointed it at my card—I noticed that his was different from the standard Associate issue. There was a small beep and then he put his hand to his ear, listening to his earpiece reading off my details. While they were checking me out, I quickly took stock of the hallway.

It was smaller than ours in width, maybe only by a couple of feet, but it seemed super cramped with the three of us standing so close together. I couldn't even imagine what a long line of students and Associates would feel like. Turning to the left I saw the end of the hall a couple hundred feet away, past all the doors to our classrooms, turning right back toward the cafeteria— I more or less knew this section of the hall. Just like their side of the chain link on our common walk, there were no windows here, nothing but Globes and unpainted cinder block down the entire stretch. The sight was so long, straight, narrow, and grey that it made me slightly dizzy just trying to keep my eyes trained in that direction. Blinking, I turned the other way and looked past the handful of classrooms remaining on the hall. As I expected, it turned to the left toward what I could only assume were the Peek dorms.

The G.A. dropped his hand from his ear and said to me, "So, Mr. Walker, I wonder how you are finding the quality of your academics this year." It wasn't really a question, just a command for me to talk. For someone who worked in a school, he seemed strangely uncomfortable speaking to me.

I fidgeted a little, twisting my Credentials on my wrist. "Yes, sir, very good, sir," I managed to get out. I had never talked to a G.A. before. "Mr. Mason is just the best. The best teacher I've ever had, I mean. We're learning so much in there and everyone loves it."

The G.A. cleared his throat. "Yes, I've heard that from many students in my years serving here at 231." He cut his eyes to the door for a moment, lost in thought. The Associate was still flipping through Jazz's papers. After a long moment the G.A. turned back to me and said, "I see that your grades put you in the top ten percent in your class, Mr. Walker. And second place in the recent Testing? Congratulations. Your father must be very proud."

He paused and stared at me, looking for an answer to his unspoken question. Meanwhile, the Associate finally finished with the papers and handed them back. I made a show of taking them and straightening them out—like Dan from the News, I couldn't help but think—trying to stall out my response to the G.A. After a beat, he motioned down the hallway, away from the cafeteria. Then he began walking toward the dorms. He didn't even bother to look back to see if I was following.

"I wonder at your presence here, Mr. Walker," he said over his shoulder as I hustled to keep pace behind him, the Associate slow-walking behind the both of us. "It would seem to me that someone with your father's...position...might be able to find more suitable schooling for you...elsewhere."

I flinched. My parents weren't rich, and any money they might have had at one point had been used to get my older siblings into college. But my dad had spent his whole life working at City Hall, and a couple of years back his boss's boss was elected Mayor. He wasn't the most important person in her office, not even close, but he was plenty high up the chain of command that he could pull some strings to get me out of here. If he wanted to.

"Yes sir, I guess so, sir," I said. I had no desire to explain my father's career decisions to this G.A. That was assuming I even understood them myself. The G.A. let it drop and I tried to push thoughts of my dad from my mind.

We got to the end of the hallway, about thirty feet or so past the last classroom door. I almost walked right past the G.A., heading into the turn toward the dorms, but at the last moment I caught myself. Both the Associate and the G.A. had stopped at the dead end and, instead of turning left, had turned right. It wasn't until I was right up next to them that I finally noticed it. There was an elevator door inconspicuously tucked into the wall here at the corner.

I had no idea there were elevators anywhere in this place. The only thing resembling a second story I had ever seen were the guard towers ringing the edges of the Recks field. Aside from a couple of underground tunnels traveling from one Zone to another, I had always assumed the whole building was one sprawling ground floor. The G.A. pulled out his Credentials, swiped them in front of a panel set into the wall, and put his eye up to a retinal scanner placed in the center of the door itself. Instantly it whooshed open. They stepped inside and I quickly followed.

I turned around to face the door, expecting to see a bank of buttons. Instead, I just saw one switch, a clean stem of metal stuck out from the wall next to the door. It was clicked into the up position, and the Associate leaned over and cranked it down.

The intercom flared to life. "Voice access requested," it said in a flat, robotic voice. The G.A. glanced up at the Globe overhead.

"It's me," he said, and the elevator lurched to life. It took me a moment to realize that we weren't going upward. Rather, we were moving down.

For a long minute the elevator hummed as we left the classrooms behind. We weren't moving too quickly, but it was a steady drop. Unlike a regular elevator, there was nothing to watch, no lights flashing to tell me how far we'd come or how far we still had to go. There was only the thrumming sound of this little compartment sliding down the shaft and that vague, queasy feeling in my stomach associated with rapid vertical movement. The Associate stared straight ahead at the door. Neither he nor the G.A. said a word.

When we finally came to a stop I had no way of estimating how far we had come. One thing was for sure, though—it felt like we'd gone far below the level of a typical basement. It felt more like we had dropped down into a dungeon.

CHAPTER 12

IN-SCHOOL SUSPENSION

The door opened with a clatter, and even from the back of the elevator I could see that we were headed straight into a huge room. There were people everywhere—Associates, Admin, regular-looking folks dressed in street clothes. One entire wall was filled with a bank of displays, two or three people positioned at every station, watching. Some of the footage appeared to be live, but I could tell that several people were scanning through old nighttime scenes, searching for something. A dozen or more hallways branched off from the other two walls; bodies were coming and going, pushing hand trucks loaded down with boxes and five-gallon buckets. The middle of the room was dominated by a massive table, covered in random bits of Associate gear as well as what looked like the insides of some sort of engine. Most of the people in street clothes were here, busy working at the machinery—handing tools back and forth, passing parts around. Everyone was talking in hushed tones, their words mixed up into something sounding like the rustle of wings.

As the Associate ushered me out of the elevator I immediately noticed the height of the ceiling—the room was easily taller than the cafeteria or the auditorium. A catwalk ran around two walls, doors and windows leading from it into who knows where. "How far down are we?" I asked, involuntarily. I didn't expect an answer, but the G.A. turned back at my words. For a moment he seemed almost surprised to see me, as if he had forgotten that it was his job to bring me here.

"This room, Mr. Walker, is the reason why Federal Education Site 231 was built upon this specific place in the southwest part of our great City." He trained his eyes upward, speaking with something almost like reverence. He seemed weirdly proud of the cavernous space. "Many years ago, this room was a nuclear bunker, built to withstand an attack from our Russian allies. This was long before the Great Treaty, of course, before we realized just how much the economic interests of our Nation coincided with theirs." He smiled, almost wistfully, and turned away. I noticed that he didn't actually answer my question.

A door banged open from the catwalk. I looked up to see the Head looming over us, aides following him out and spilling to his sides along the narrow path. He didn't say a word—none of them did—rather he merely leaned onto the railing and watched the three of us walk across the room. He was so tall that, from my vantage on the ground, it seemed as if he could lose his center of gravity and tip forward at any moment. The G.A. saluted and the Head nodded back curtly. I was desperate to know what was going on down here—Admin took over an entire wing of the campus up above, dorms and offices and meeting areas, and I had assumed the Head spent most of his time working there. What could be so important to compel him to choose to be down here, deep underground?

It occurred to me that I had gone almost three years at 231 without seeing the Head anywhere except for the Meeting. And yet, for the second time in less than a week, here we were, together because of Jazz. I watched him up there for as long as I could, until it would have been obvious that I was staring. When the Associate steered me left around the giant table I broke my gaze away.

The last thing I saw before we veered toward one of the unmarked hallways was an unobstructed view of the street-clothes folks at the table. They were working on a couple of disassembled Drones. Wires and gears were spilled out all over everywhere, insides on the outside like a haphazard kind of surgery. At first I flinched when the angle of our walk took us through the sightline of a primary eye, but I reassured myself that the Drones must be deactivated. And, anyway, I had every reason to be here with all these Admin; I was authorized. For a moment I wondered who else at 231 had seen what I was seeing, if I was the first Guest to be down in this room.

The G.A. picked up his pace as soon as we entered the hallway, and I had to walk double time to keep up, the Associate clomping along behind me. The walls were brick, old-timey masonry type things; they stretched out in front of us into the darkness. It felt like we were walking forever, straight into nowhere, though it was hard to tell. There were no doors, no signs, no marks, just us headed away from the receding light of the great room and toward a tiny light at the distant end of the hallway. The space felt uncomfortable, claustrophobic; I couldn't shake the thought that we were separated from daylight by an immense amount of earth and rock. At some point I realized that the darkness itself was unsettling in its own way. I wasn't used to it at all—anywhere I was authorized to be inside 231 was lit up by the Globes.

Except here. For whatever reason, this hallway was devoid of surveillance. The sudden freedom left me a little uneasy.

Abandon all hope, ye who enter here, I thought suddenly. Mason would be proud of the reference. I'm not sure this is what Dante had in mind when he thought about hell, but it was definitely getting warmer the further we walked into the bowels of the school.

The light at the end of the tunnel grew steadily bigger and eventually dropped us straight out into a small, square room, lit only by a single Globe in the center of the regular-height ceiling. Directly across from us was a door, clearly leading into a small office. Next to it was a barred window through which I could see an Associate and another of those guys in street clothes. They glanced up at us, nonplussed—they obviously knew we were coming, despite the lack of Globes, and they didn't even bother to ask for Credentials. I suppose no one made it this far into the pit without being properly authorized. The G.A. never broke stride as he crossed to the office and barged right in. I reflexively made to follow him, but our Associate put a heavy hand on my shoulder, keeping me firmly in place.

I looked to the right and saw a couple of shadowy doorways, separated from the rest of the room by thick metal bars. I squinted into the darkness, wondering where they went, but it was impossible to see past the threshold from where we were standing. They seemed like old access tunnels, used to maintain airflow or to run supplies. Turning around to the left I saw another pair of doorways. At first I assumed these were more of the same, inked as they were by shadows, but then a rustle of movement through the one on the left grabbed my attention and made me look again. I caught my breath. There was a glimmer of light back there, enough for me to see that these weren't tunnels or hallways. I was peering into a tiny little room, nothing more than a cell.

Inside, lit only by the reflection of a weak flashlight bouncing off the pages of a book, I saw Jazz, reading.

The G.A. crashed out from the office, the door extra loud in this small, still room. I turned to him, for some reason startled by his presence; seeing Jazz behind bars had unnerved me. "Welcome," he smiled, waving his hands around in what he probably supposed was a grand fashion, "to In-School Suspension."

The next few minutes passed by in a blur of activity. The Associate from inside the office brought me a chair, dropping it on the floor in front of Jazz's cell. What I was starting to think of as "my" Associate signed some papers in the office, passed over the work from Mason. The street clothes guy gave it all a long look, going so far as to scan several of the documents with some device I had never seen before. Meanwhile the G.A. filled every moment with a long speech, nattering on about the exceptionally humane treatment each and every student received at 231, even students who might not deserve the myriad benefits accorded by the recent innovation of In-School Suspension.

"In the past, Mr. Walker," he said, "a student such as Ms. Lewis would not have been able to take advantage of any educational opportunities after such an unfortunate outburst as she recently demonstrated on the basketball court. She would have been remanded immediately to a high-security facility located within the region, one concurrent to her Federal Site. The location of this facility would also have been determined by her status and jurisdiction, of course." He paused and a sort of smile passed across his face. "Now, though, after our relentless work developing an In-School Suspension onsite, she is able to continue her education here at 231, in our Educational Annex."

I kept my eyes on Jazz, even as the G.A. wouldn't stop talking about their amazing work here in the "Educational Annex." In the dim light reflected by her flashlight I was able to see the chair she was sitting on—metal, a twin to the one the Associate grabbed for me—and a freestanding cot pushed against the wall of her cell. A metal chest with the lid wrenched off sat at the foot of her cot, presumably to serve as storage for her things. I wasn't really sure what personal effects Peeks were allowed upstairs, and I could only imagine that she must have brought almost nothing to this place. She was wearing their standard issue jumpsuit with the legs rolled up past her knees; it was sweltering down here. I was shocked but not surprised to see an open toilet in the far corner of her space. She had yet to even so much as glance up at us, despite the ample distraction provided by our arrival. Somehow, in all this, she appeared to be reading peacefully.

The G.A. finally drew his speech to a close and sighed. He looked around with obvious pride on his face, and, without a word, spun on his heels and went back down the long tunnel toward the central room. I stood there sweating for a minute while his footsteps faded away, then my Associate turned to me and pointed at the chair. "You have fifteen minutes to talk to Lewis about her schoolwork," he said, "and then we're going back topside. Do not ask for even one minute more." Then he, too, withdrew into the almost-certainly air-conditioned comfort of the office.

The whir of the locking door echoed weirdly around the room, bouncing back and forth between ceiling and floor, and then I was left in nearly complete silence. It was so quiet I could hear the tiny buzz of the Globe overhead, Jazz breathing, my own pulse beating up into my ears. I walked over to the chair placed haphazardly in front of the bars, straightened it up and sat down. Jazz held a finger up to me—*wait*—and continued to read. For a long couple of minutes I simply watched her as she read, completely still, before she carefully dog-eared her page—from the bottom, I noticed—stood up, and dragged her chair over to sit across from me. The sound of the metal scraping against the floor reverberated out from her cell and felt like a jolt of lightning in my brain. When she sat down, it was the closest we had ever been, probably five feet apart, the only thing between us being those ancient iron bars.

"Benjamin Walker," she said, her face devoid of expression. Her eyes flitted from my face to my shoes and back again. "So, Mason sent you all the way down here just to tutor me, did he? Learn me some literature?"

"Hey, Jazz," I said, my voice cracking just a little—it had been at least five minutes since I'd spoken to anyone and my body was drying up in this sweat box. I tried to cover by clearing my throat, hoping Jazz hadn't heard it, but I saw her smile.

"So, what'd I miss?" she asked, a little more warmth to her voice than before. "That new guy y'all got, your little rookie—has Randall been cleaning up the court with him out there and me gone?" She leaned back in her chair, popped it up on two legs and kicked her feet against the bars for balance. I noticed that her shoes were uncharacteristically dirty. She was still holding her book, cradling it carefully in her lap, like she might pick it back up at any moment and start reading again.

"Um, yeah," I said, trying to relax into my own chair. Then I shook my head. "I mean, no, not at all. Randall won't even play without you there. He just runs up and down the sidelines and coaches the rest of the team. He keeps telling me that you're going to be so pissed when you hear—Orion still can't stop Liam for shit."

"Truth," Jazz laughed, "those boys are pretty hopeless without me. I'm impressed with your rookie, though. Can't wait to come out and shut his ass right down again." She gestured toward the papers clutched in my hand. "What did Mason send down with you, anyways? They're only going to give us a few minutes before they banish you back to the daylight."

I passed the work through the bars. She flipped through it quickly, eyes skittering back and forth over the pages, and then dropped the whole lot on the ground under her chair. "Is that it? Y'all don't get much done in class without me, either, do you?"

I changed the subject quickly before I lost my nerve; we both knew she didn't need my help with schoolwork. "Jazz, why are they keeping you in here so long? When are you coming back?" I don't know what I expected her to say; we both knew that the Globe was picking up every word of our conversation. Even still, I broke down into something like a whisper. It just felt like a private moment, even in this place that didn't respect our privacy in the least.

She looked at me with something like curiosity. Leaning further back in her chair and holding her arms out, she pulled her feet away from the bars. Seeming to float, she managed to keep the chair balanced on just two legs for an impressively long time. It was only after she lost her center of gravity and the chair clattered back to earth that she broke eye contact with me, staring over my shoulder at the window through to the office.

"Once upon a time, Ben," she began, "long ago and far away, there was a rabbi who told a strange kind of story." She leaned forward to get closer, and I instinctively followed suit. She went on, barely more than a couple of feet from me. "There was this man, put in prison for something he didn't do. Unjustified incarceration, we would call it today, but back then they just called it bad luck. This poor guy spends years in jail, you know? And some of those days he would sit in his cell and think about his enemies, what he would do to them if he ever got out of his cell. Revenge, am I right? It's that tale as old as time. But, on other days, he might fill the space lost in his memories, living in the past, wondering what he could have done different in life, how he could have avoided his fate if only he'd done this or that. He regretted his choices and invented alternatives that might have been. If only, Ben, if only."

I nodded throughout to let her know I was tracking. Her voice was low and level, enchanting even in this terrible place. I couldn't tell if she was reciting something or if she was making the story up on the spot. She never looked away from my eyes as she continued.

"When the man died he ended up meeting God, because that's how these stories go, right? And damn was this man furious. *Where were you?* he asked God, tilting and railing. *Where were you all those years when I suffered in prison alone?* And God smiled, sadly, and told the man that he had visited his cell every day, but the man was never there. He was always gone. Visiting the past or the future, off on a flight of imagination, always somewhere else. But he never took the opportunity to meet God in the present." She paused here, looked pointedly at the Globe and then over to a stack of books piled up beside her bed. "I don't know much for sure about this God, Ben. But if he's out there, somewhere? I'm sure as hell not taking a risk on missing him. I'm going to meet God right here in the present."

She stood up suddenly, stretched, smiled. "I think we're done here,

Ben Walker. I really appreciate you coming, but I'm pretty sure I've got everything I need."

I pulled back from the bars, hot with embarrassment at being so summarily dismissed. I didn't know what I expected, but I had built this conversation up in my head somehow, and it wasn't supposed to go like this. There was no reason for me to feel this way—Jazz and I weren't friends. Aside from Randall and Orion, there really weren't any friendships across the chain link in our class.

I hastily stood up, trying to prove that I was fine with this sudden turn of events, but then I remembered Mason's final bit of business. "Wait, I forgot," I said, hoping I didn't sound too pitiful. "Mason said to tell you that he needs your extra credit work, the Robert Frost thing or whatever, right away when you get back. He said that your options were limited at this point."

Jazz froze. She had begun rooting through her trunk, all but ignoring me, but now she turned her head slowly in my direction. "He said that my options were limited? He used those exact words?"

"Yeah, that's what he said." I shrugged. "He might have said extremely limited? I don't know." I watched her standing there, and was shocked to realize that for maybe the first time ever she seemed a little behind the eight ball. She put down a book she was holding, picked up another at random, made a stack of several and then shuffled the order. Eventually she turned to face me, started walking my way but paused, went back to the trunk and picked one of the books back up again. She stuck a slip of paper in between the leaves and then brought the entire stack to me at the bars. She stared at me for a long moment, then seemed to come to some sort of decision before she spoke.

"These belong to Mason," she said, handing me the books. "Please make sure he gets them. Let him know that I'm unsure about one of them, but I trust him."

I nodded, bewildered. She was acting so weird, and I had no idea how to respond. Was she trying to low-key tell me something or just ready to get rid of me?

"Do you know Robert Frost's most famous poem, Ben?" she asked. Her voice had softened to a soothing pitch. She was standing just inches away from me, still looking intently into my face as if trying to divine something. Her hands had begun to toy with her flashlight, flicking it on and off and spinning it around. The effect was mesmerizing, and it took me a second to think about what she was saying.

"Yeah, I guess," I said. "The one about the two roads, right?" We hadn't studied Robert Frost in any of my classes at 231, but this was the only poem of his I knew.

Without breaking eye contact, still spinning that light, Jazz began to speak.

"Two roads diverged in a yellow wood,
And sorry I could not travel both
And be one traveler, long I stood
And looked down one as far as I could
To where it bent in the undergrowth;"

It was a sing-song, rocking kind of poem, and for a second I was so caught up in the words and the light that I almost missed what she was doing with her hands. She had been playing with the flashlight just long enough that I had stopped paying attention to its random flight around the room. When it suddenly paused on the side wall, however, the jolt grabbed my attention and, almost instinctively, I happened to glance over at it. There I saw the shadow of her left hand, splayed sideways out across the brick, making shapes. I almost gasped, but at the last second managed to keep control of myself, tried my best to be cool.

The shadows showing against the wall were forming signals. Signals that Randall and I had come up with together, signals I thought only we understood. Jazz was talking to me with her hands.

Ben. We don't have much time, she signed. Then she signed it again, three times while I stared.

The shapes were huge, two-dimensional, slanted from the angle of the flashlight beam. But they were also unmistakable. Randall and I had invented a secret language, and somehow Jazz was speaking it to me out of the depths of this dungeon.

All along she kept talking out loud, reciting the poem in that slow, stately voice. I realized that the Globe couldn't see onto the side wall of her cell. All it could see was her, fidgeting with a flashlight and having an innocent conversation about Mason's schoolwork.

"Then took the other, as just as fair,
And having perhaps the better claim,
Because it was grassy and wanted wear;
Though as for that the passing there
Had worn them really about the same,"

Ben! The hell? Are you listening to me? I realized that in my shock I hadn't responded to her, terrified as I was at being spotted by the Algorithm. But with the Globe behind me, I knew I could risk a curt reply. I moved my right hand in front of my chest and signaled, *yes, I'm here, sorry.*

"And both that morning equally lay
In leaves no step had trodden black.
Oh, I kept the first for another day!
Yet knowing how way leads on to way,
I doubted if I should ever come back."

Be ready and listen to this please, she said. Her signals weren't perfect, but I couldn't tell if that was because she didn't know exactly what she was doing or if she wasn't able to do it one-handed while also keeping the flashlight trained properly. I understood well enough, though, even if this entire situation was completely insane. She paused for a moment and then went on in a burst.

Hands up don't shoot. Hands up don't shoot. Hands up don't shoot.

I stared at the shadow of her hand, bewildered. What in the world?

"I shall be telling this with a sigh
Somewhere ages and ages hence:
Two roads diverged in a wood, and I—
I took the one less traveled by,
And that has made all the difference."

She stopped and slowly let her hand drop to her side. "All the difference," she repeated, boring the words into my mind with her eyes.

Hands up? Don't shoot? What on earth was she talking about? She smiled at me and nodded, looking at me in an entirely different way than she had just a few minutes ago, a kind of stillness spread across her face. For just a moment we stood, staring at each other through the bars. Suddenly she pointed over my shoulder, and the spell was broken.

"Time's up, Walker!" cried a rough voice, as the Associates tumbled together out of the office door. One of them grabbed my chair, the other snatched the small pile of books Jazz had handed me. The flashlight winked off and Jazz turned back to her trunk.

Our interview was over.

CHAPTER 13
THE MESSAGE

In short order I found myself right back in Mason's empty room. Class was over already—I was going to be late to Chemistry for sure—but they brought me here to pick up my stuff. The G.A. had kept up a steady stream of chitchat our entire trip back, asking me questions about the most recent round of Testing and the rigors of junior year, wondering about my high results and my thoughts for the future. Largely, though, it just seemed like he needed me as a landing place for his own voice. He seemed in a good mood, which gave me hope that Jazz's communication to me had actually remained secret. There was no doubt the G.A. had watched every minute of our conversation through the Globe.

Mason was at his desk, feet kicked up and reading as usual. He looked over as we entered but didn't stand, glancing at me only cursorily before addressing the G.A. "Is everything well with Ms. Lewis?" he asked. The G.A. shrugged.

"She is doing as well as her unfortunate station would predict, Mr. Mason," he replied. "You worry yourself too much about some of these more...troubled...students. Sometimes the best thing we can do for certain children is simply to help guide them down the path that they have previously chosen."

"You mean give up on them?" Mason asked with a sigh, closing his magazine and looking up. For a second I thought he was staring at the Globe.

The G.A. gave a thin little smile. "I prefer to think of it as the most expedient of mercies, Mr. Mason." He snapped his fingers at the Associate, still lingering by the door, who brought over Jazz's books. He had carried them back from the cell, lazily skimming through the tables of contents. No flags, presumably, and he was clear to return them to their proper owner.

Mason gestured at a small blank spot on his over-crowded desk and the Associate put them down. The G.A. pointed at my belongings, still sitting at my own seat, and said, "Time to get on to your next class, Mr. Walker." He clearly was not going to leave me alone with Mason for even a moment. Not that I even knew what to say to Mason, or even if I should be saying anything at all.

The Associate had gone back over to wait by the Peek exit, but the G.A. crossed the classroom, opened my door to the Guest hall, and waited for me. I grabbed my bag and turned to maybe risk a goodbye to Mason, but he still hadn't looked in my direction; he was preoccupied by Jazz's stack of books. Then, however, when I was halfway out the door and into the hall he called out to me. "Ben, one moment." I turned around and stuck my head back in, noting that the G.A. seemed completely exasperated. Mason was holding out one of the books. "This isn't mine. You must have mixed one of your own books in with the ones Jazz was returning."

For just an instant I froze. I knew full well that wasn't my book—I hadn't carried anything but the papers down with me, and I hadn't been near his desk since picking up my bag—but I also knew that if the G.A. put those facts together he would snatch the book up and stow it away in an office somewhere. Probably Jazz just returned the book on accident; no reason to let her personal property get lost in the depths of 231.

"Yes, sir, Mr. Mason," I said, going over to his desk and reaching out for the proffered book. When my hand closed over it, however, he held onto it for just a moment longer, giving me the slightest of resistance when I tried to pull it away. I looked at him, confused, and he held my gaze without blinking.

"In the future, Ben, please be more careful with your personal belongings. Tending to your property is an essential skill in a setting such as this." It wasn't super obvious, but he hit the word "your" in such a way that I realized something was up, something more than just Jazz misplacing some reading material. In a flash I knew that she wanted me to have this particular book for some reason, and also that Mason was on the inside of the situation, at least enough to make sure I got my hands on it. I thought back to that day of the Code Red again, saw Jazz saying something to Mason, remembered her under the desk shaking her head at me. What was happening here?

And, most importantly, what did Jazz mean? *Hands up don't shoot?*

Thinking about Jazz made me remember something. "Mason? I forgot to tell you that Jazz said she wasn't sure about one of your books. But that she trusted you. Or something like that."

A flicker of a smile shot through Mason's eyes as he let go of the book. He nodded, and I quickly turned around only to see the G.A. looking at something on his screen. If he had noticed anything in Mason's manner he was a tremendous actor. The Associate was waiting in the hallway; the door was open so he might have heard, but he hadn't seen a thing. I hustled past the G.A. and turned left toward Chemistry.

"Goodbye, Mr. Walker," the G.A. said from the doorway. "It has been most delightful to spend this time with you, even if the errand itself was less than essential." I turned around to reply, but he shut the door on me before I could even think of anthing to say.

Then, and only then, did I dare to take a look at the mysterious book Jazz had expertly managed to get into my hands.

It was definitely old, considerably well-worn—the dust jacket was missing and all the words rubbed off the spine even. The cover gave a slight creak as I turned to the title page: *The Autobiography of Malcolm X.* I checked the copyright; it wasn't as ancient as *Frankenstein* but it was close enough—something like a hundred years old. I skimmed the table of contents, turned it over a couple of times, rifled quickly through the yellowing pages. From somewhere near the middle a piece of paper fell out and fluttered to the floor. I crouched down to get it, examined it on the floor for just a moment before picking it up. *Like a piece of evidence,* I thought. It appeared to be a bookmark of some kind, about the size of an index card, smeared in three broad stripes of color.

I stood up, baffled. Jazz wanted me to have this book and, I was equally sure, this piece of paper. But I had no idea why.

Later that night we were huddled up in the corner of the common room, staring at the colored bookmark.

The rest of the day had flown by in a blur. Everyone wanted to know about what it had been like to visit In-School; I gave a shortened version of my trip down there at least five times. They wanted to hear all about Jazz, too, but I was nervous to talk all that much about her, though, even in the cafeteria. For some reason it just didn't feel safe, even when I could see full well that there were no Associates or Drones within mic range. At any rate, the only person I really wanted to talk to studiously avoided my gaze. Several times I caught myself watching Orion, wishing we could get a moment alone together, running through the questions I would ask him about Jazz and Mason. At dinner, though, he didn't get anywhere near the coffee station, and at Recks it would have been too obvious for me to break in on basketball just to speak to him.

Some of us ended up leaving the court early, heading back to the common room and taking over the small table furthest from the door—me, Kiki, Maddy, and Carlos. The room was empty; Randall and Liam had stayed in the gym to practice and the rest of the Block was still wandering around. I took advantage of the opportunity to speak completely undisturbed and, putting my back to the Globe, just in case, told the whole story of the trip to In-School. The bunker-turned-dungeon, the research they were doing on the Drones, Jazz's cell, *hands up don't shoot,* and Mason so clearly passing me back this old book with the colored paper stuck inside of it.

Everybody listened with rapt attention—the Algorithm probably thought I was reading them a story or something for how hard they were looking at me. The second I finished Kiki exclaimed, "Damn that girl is smart! I've been watching you and Randall for months, sitting right up next to you, and I haven't been able to figure out but a couple of phrases of y'all's little language! How the hell did she do all that from across the room?"

"Well," Carlos said, "she is one of the two reasons that Ben can't come out on top in the Testing. The other one, of course, is the simple fact of his unfortunately thick skull." He held up his hand for a dap and Kiki happily obliged.

"I think you're making too much of this," Madison said, picking the bookmark up and turning it over in her hand. "I mean, it's probably just something she left behind or whatever. Maybe Mason? I wouldn't pay it any attention." She handed it back to me and I examined it for what felt like the hundredth time already. It appeared to be a section of a piece of notebook paper—you could still see the blue lines rising up faintly through the color—about the same size as if it had been folded in half three times and then ripped into pieces from there. There were three colors in roughly equal sizes running across it lengthwise: a green stripe at the top, a yellow one in the middle, and a brownish one at the bottom. The stripes bled into each other, however, blurring the borders between them in an odd way. It was surprisingly beautiful.

"Are you kidding?" Kiki said. "We just proved once and for all that Jazz is too smart for all that. The paper means something for sure, and I'm betting that this has got to mean something, too." She grabbed the book from Carlos as she was talking and flipped through the pages. I knew exactly what she was looking for—underlining or markings of some kind—but I'd already searched it thoroughly, twice. Nothing.

"You going to read it?" Carlos asked.

I nodded, even though that felt like looking for a needle in a haystack—it was a lot of words to work through with absolutely no guidance. He tapped his finger twice on the table and I placed the paper between us. We all leaned over to stare at it.

"Is it bars maybe?" Maddy asked. "You said Jazz was in a straight-up cell, right? And wasn't this guy Malcom in prison in one of these pictures in the book? Maybe it's got something to do with being locked up." We had all been looking at the paper with the stripes going left to right, but she picked it up and rotated it so that they ran vertically.

"Maybe?" I said. "But what good does that do? I mean, I guess I could read the book and look extra carefully at the prison scenes?"

"Six and half years," Carlos said, looking up from his screen. "That's how long Malcolm X spent in prison. Later he said that it was where he got his education." He paused for a second and added, quietly, "Just like Jazz."

I sighed, feeling hopeless. "But none of this gets us any closer to the only thing she actually said to me, to *hands up don't shoot.* Does that mean anything to anybody?" I looked around at everyone. Maddy and Kiki shook their heads while Carlos started tapping at his screen. He looked up and shook his head.

"Nothing," he said. "I mean, it'll pull hits where the words are used, but nothing where they're used all in a row. It doesn't mean anything at all, at least according to the Stream."

Just then the door burst open and the rest of the Block spilled into the room. I checked the time and we were closing in on the News. Randall and Liam made their way back to us, talking and laughing about something. For just a second I felt a small pang of jealousy—was Randall leaving me for Liam just because I couldn't handle a basketball? Then I felt ashamed of myself, in both directions. Randall had never been anything but loyal to me, and Liam was a good kid. I should be glad that he was fitting in so well here at 231. The alternative would be to have a depressed loner on our Block, and nobody wanted to go through that again. We all remembered how it had gone down last time.

Randall bounced over to us at the table and drew himself up. "Why the sad faces, friends?" he asked in mock formality. Then he looked down at the table and saw the piece of paper. In science class I'd used our signals to tell him about the book, but we hadn't gotten so far as the paper yet; he didn't even know it existed. "And what's the deal with the African flag? Y'all doing some extra credit for Williams or something? Let me get in on that!"

We all looked up at him, stunned. I was the first one to recover, and, after a beat, I managed to ask, "What did you say? African flag?"

He leaned over the table and turned the paper so that the green side was running across the top from his point of view. "I mean, that stripe at the bottom is supposed to be red, and it looks a little brownish. But with the art supplies they usually give us around this place, it's not half bad. My mom would be proud, I think."

He looked up and around at the rest of us. "What's with the looks, y'all?"

We used our final free minutes to quickly trade information with each other. Apparently the African flag had been banned nationwide some years back, something about Greater Europe moving into the continent for diamonds and cobalt. Randall only knew about it because his mother had made it a point to always have these colors showing somewhere in their house. On his part, he wanted to hear more about the bunker, and he was especially interested in how good Jazz's signals were. I rushed parts of the story, though, in order to beat the clock. Skipping the part where we had almost convinced ourselves that the flag was meant to represent jail bars, I managed to get to the question I had now convinced myself he could answer.

"So, what does *hands up don't shoot* mean? Why would Jazz say that to me?"

He was leafing idly through the book. I think he was hoping that he would be the one to find the secret marks that the rest of us had missed. He picked up the paper, slid it back at random somewhere in the middle, and shook his head.

"No idea, Ben. It doesn't mean anything to me at all."

"Well, that's our City News for tonight," Donna said.

"Keep in mind, City, that it is our solemn duty to eliminate the darkness," Dan added.

"—but never forget to praise the progress of lights," Donna finished, with a smile.

Just like always, I couldn't fall asleep that night. For the first time, however, it didn't bother me at all. My brain was buzzing, my thoughts full of books and paintings and Jazz's hands projected out against the wall of a tiny jail cell. The extra time alone gave me plenty of space to think.

I had started reading *The Autobiography of Malcolm X* right after the News, so I had a good forty-five minutes before lights dim to really get into the book. By the time the Globes cut to that sleepy golden glow, I was pretty sure I knew at least part of what Jazz was saying, even if I didn't know what it all meant. We were in prison; Malcolm X was in prison. Jazz and most of the Peeks were Black; Malcolm X was Black. The flag that used to be a symbol of African solidarity was an obvious signal that I was supposed to be paying attention to all these things. I just didn't know what I was supposed to do with what I was seeing. There was something more for me to understand, something to do with *hands up don't shoot*. I needed to figure out what that something was.

Jazz had been on the News again. Dan seemed simultaneously disappointed and thrilled to bring us information about the ongoing investigation at "one of our City's most dangerous Federal Sites." Being an actual student at 231, of course, I could tell that the segment was all bluster. They couldn't actually connect Jazz to the stolen contraband in any way, and it wasn't Jazz that made this place dangerous. But I could see how those on the outside might be afraid of the "terrorist" in our midst here. I wondered briefly what my parents thought about it all. I would know soon enough, assuming they came to Visitation.

Thoughts of my parents pushed Jazz from my mind. I wondered if my dad had any idea what it was really like here at 231, the fear and control and violence. It was so important to him that I go here, to attend what he called a "real school"—but did he have any idea about the ways Admin flexed their authority over the "real kids" that went to school with me? Worse, I thought, maybe he did know, and he just didn't care. I quickly pushed that thought away.

I was no Malcolm X. I wasn't even officially locked up in this place; I could leave at whatever point my parents chose to pay for a better option. But, in that way, I was stuck just the same.

The thought of home, even the messed up place I came from, finally brought me to tears, and I fell asleep.

CHAPTER 14

SNACKS

The next night I was sitting in the common room with Liam and Kiki, working on their signals.

Randall and I had talked it over and decided, now that the cat was out of the bag, that it was time to bring more people in on our secret language. It was a tricky business, though. We couldn't do anything like holding tutorial for the whole dorm—if the Algorithm grabbed ahold of a couple of lessons it would crack the code for sure, even faster than Jazz. We had to start small, just a couple of people sitting around a table covered in books, occasionally tapping on our screens in order to look like we were studying. Kiki was an obvious choice for the first class; she was fired up about Jazz stealing our signs and wanted in. We took a low-key survey of a couple of other folks on the Block and Liam quickly volunteered, too. So here I was, working my best Mason vibe, trying to teach them the basics of a completely made-up bunch of hand signals.

Hello, Kiki. Hello, Liam. How are you doing? I signed slowly with my left hand, trying to hold *The Autobiography of Malcolm X* with the other. I figured if Jazz could recite a poem and sign with her hands at the same time, I could at least pretend to read a book while running through these basic signals.

Kiki had her screen in front of her, but I could see her putting all her attention into her signs. She was watching her hands closely as they made the motions, *Hello, Ben. I am good.* She looked up and grinned. "I still can't believe y'all invented a whole-ass symbol just for my name. I feel so special!" She flashed the *Kiki* symbol with both hands and waved them in front of her face.

Liam's turn, and he slowly signaled, *Hello, Ben. I am snacks.* He looked at me hopefully and I busted out laughing. The sign for *snacks* was like an inversion of the sign for *hungry*—he was obviously feeling a certain kind of way about how terrible dinner had been and was mixing up his signs. For just a second he got a hurt look on his face, but then I saw realization dawn and he started laughing, too.

"What? What happened?" Kiki asked. "Why y'all laughing about poor little Liam being hungry?" She had misread his jacked-up sign and inadvertently corrected his mistake, like two wrongs making a right. "I could get behind some food, though. Let's send someone for snacks before canteen closes." She clutched her hands over her stomach and twisted her face into a cartoonish look of concern.

I was still laughing too hard to explain what had happened with the signals, and now the mention of snacks was making me feel like I wasn't going to last until breakfast without a little something extra to eat. "Yeah," I said, pulling myself together. "Let's send someone for snacks."

"Did somebody say snacks?" Randall roared from the other side of the room. He and Maddy had been sitting together, about as close as they dared while also at least pretending to study, but the promise of decent food proved too much temptation even for that little situation. He jumped up and immediately volunteered to go. Liam and I agreed to make the run, too; class was just going to have to wait. We shopped around for orders from the others.

"Jon!" David called out. "Remember that you owe me ten dollars from that pizza!"

"No, I don't," Jon shot back. "I bought Ellie chips and a drink last time, and you owed her eight dollars. So now she owes you the other two."

"Wait, what? I bought Ellie chips and a drink, too!" David argued. They both turned to Ellie, who smiled and shrugged.

The whole dorm broke out in a similar vein. It was chaos, but after a few minutes of back-and-forth about who owed how much money to whom, we managed to settle on everyone's orders. Fortunately, Carlos kept assiduous records of all our previous snack runs, and he was able to step in and settle the inevitable disagreements.

"Nobody's going to cheat me out of so much as a single chip, rookie," he said when Liam asked why he did it. "The only way to make sure I get mine is to make sure that none of y'all are getting more than yours."

"Rookie! Ben! Let's go!" Randall called, halfway out the door already. I grinned and grabbed Liam's arm, pulled him away from Carlos and hustled to catch up. We only had about forty-five minutes until the News.

It was a long hike from our dorm to canteen when the gym was closed. First we had to head back toward the main class hallway before cutting left, then switching back after a hundred feet or so and scanning through a couple of access doors. Another minute or so and the route straightened out, quickly sloping downwards into something more like a tunnel.

"What is this place?" Liam asked, looking around. It occurred to me that he'd only ever been back and forth to canteen from the gym—now that he was playing basketball he spent almost all of Recks there every night.

"It's an old service tunnel, we think?" Randall said. We had sloped gently downhill for a while before levelling off; now the tunnel was straight cinder block in all directions. There was nothing to see but the evenly spaced Globes.

"We're going right under the gym, as best we can figure," I said, pointing upward. "Canteen is on the other side from the dorms—so if the gym is still open, cutting through is the best way to get there. Walking around the gym takes forever, though. Only the kids who get claustrophobic ever go that way."

"And so, us? We go underneath!" Randall shouted, taking off into a run. "But y'all can't keep up with my flow, so I'll see you there!"

The run back up the slope took it out of me, and by the time I puffed into canteen—well behind Randall but ahead of Liam, I noticed with pride—I was done. Impressively, Randall was already standing in front of the drink cooler, totally relaxed, acting as if the sprint had been nothing at all.

"Rookie! You finally showed!" he called out as Liam stumbled in. "You got that list?" We quickly filled up a couple of those small baskets with drinks and chips. I added a few things that hadn't made the list but that I knew would be appreciated—Kiki was obsessed with peppermint chocolate—and then we headed straight for the front. Only a few minutes remained until canteen closed for the night; we had made it right under the wire.

"What is this shit right here?" Randall asked, grabbing a bag of red hot chips out of the basket and waving it around. "Who put this here?"

"Carlos told me he wanted them?" Liam said.

"Carlos only eats blue hot chips. He won't touch this stuff." Randall scoffed. He looked hard at Liam. "Are you planning on eating these?" Liam quickly shook his head, and I did my best not to laugh. Randall knew as well as I did that Liam wasn't going to get within ten feet of one of those hot chips.

"They didn't have any of the blue left on the shelf, but I didn't know there was a difference," Liam said. "It's the same brand and the same size and everything!" He turned to me for help, but I shook my head and grinned. He was on his own with this one.

Randall gave Liam one more good stare, and then turned to the clerk. He leaned on the counter and his entire demeanor changed. "Hey there. Thanks for putting up with my friend here. Rookies, am I right?" he smiled, smooth as he possibly could. "As if we could possibly break this kind of bread together. Just wondering, though if y'all got any blue hot chips back in the stock room?"

The clerk looked up at us, somehow managed to grin and roll her eyes at the same time. She was a senior working for next to no money, but there weren't a lot of opportunities to make extra cash here— counter clerk was a job coveted by all the upperclassmen, and only the highest-ranked students got hired. She smacked her gum and shrugged, then said, "Maybe? I don't mind going to check. But you'll need to get authorized to stay in here because it's going to take me a couple of minutes." She jerked a thumb at the clock behind her as she nodded her head toward the Associate guarding the door. It was 8:53 right now, and a five-minute walk back to the dorm. There was no way we would make it back by 9:00 with that math working against us.

Randall turned to us. "You know there's zero chance he'll authorize Credentials for all three of us." He looked at me and said, "Ben, you head back to the dorm and Liam can wait here with me. Let me go get my Credentials scanned for the both of us."

He turned to go, but Liam shook his head. "No, I want to run back and get a little bit of work done before the News starts. I'll see you guys there." Randall shrugged, ran outside to talk to the Associate and ask for a favor. Liam and I split the snacks up real quick so he could carry as much food back as possible. He paid—in the process making a huge mess of the careful accounting Carlos made of all our overlapping debts to each other—and then he took off right at 8:55. He was going to have to hustle, but he would make it back just in time.

Meanwhile, Randall came back, flashing his wrist over mine to get my Credentials authorized. Then we waited. It was weird being alone in canteen like this—the counter clerk was in the stock room until after 9:00, and the Associate disappeared as soon as the Algorithm time-locked the door from the outside. It was just us and the Globes and the hundreds of thousands of calories of delicious snacks. It went without saying that we weren't going to talk; even hand signs felt risky in such an exposed moment. The Algorithm was probably paying extra attention to us right now anyway—two teenagers in the face of all this food? Thinking back to Madison's little screwdriver set made me laugh; you'd have to be an idiot to so much as step toward the food in this situation.

The counter clerk came back with a triumphant look on her face and a bag of blue hot chips in her hand. "Found 'em!" she crowed, and we gave a little cheer. Carlos would be thrilled. And, in addition, we were going to get to roast Liam in front of everyone for thinking that all the colors would taste the same. All in all, the night was shaping up to be a win for everyone.

We left canteen, heard the door whirr shut behind us. The hallway was dark now, lit only by the occasional Globe. It was after 9:00, and in all likelihood we were the only students still out of the dorms. We made straight for the turn off toward our tunnel, but before we got there we were startled by a pair of Drones coming out of the darkness from the gym. They hovered smoothly across the floor, just the slightest of wobble in their glide as they came to a stop in front of us. The primary eye on top of each machine flashed the briefest of reds, and that creepy, robotic voice emanated from them both at the same time: "Credentials, please, students of 231." I ran my wrist under one while Randall ran his under the other, and immediately the primary eyes gave off a longer flash, but this time of purple. "Thank you, students," they said at the same time. "Return to your dorm in peace. Be quick, but do not run."

"I hate those things," Randall said after we made the turn and started sloping downward under the gym. "They just really freak me out, all talking together like that." He glanced back over his shoulder as if they might be following us, and I tried to do my best imitation of the primary eye swiveling back and forth, staring him down. All I got for my efforts was a punch in the chest.

The Globes seemed brighter down here, reflecting wildly off the whitewashed walls of the tunnel. Once we hit the bottom of the slope I expected to be able to see straight for what felt like forever, just a line of Globes guiding us home. I was surprised, though, to notice a pair of Associates at about the halfway point. They seemed to be searching the corridor for something, waving handheld sensors back and forth over the join of wall and floor. As we got closer the beeping and squawking from the sensors got louder and louder; I couldn't make out anything the Associates were saying over the noise. It wasn't hard to tell that something was wrong, though—their gas masks were engaged and their goggles snapped into place. I could understand enough to know that they seemed on edge.

As we drew near Randall twisted his wrist to loosen his Credentials, and I followed suit. We were almost right up on the Associates before they noticed us—the racket from their sensors had totally masked our approach. They were cut off in mid-conversation, and even without being able to see their faces I could tell from their body language that they were annoyed to see us; they stared just a beat too long before speaking.

"Hold on there just a minute. Where did you lot come from?" one of them finally asked. The metallic grind of his voice turned the question into a vague kind of threat.

I stopped and turned around, noticed that Randall had frozen in place a few steps behind me. He was awkwardly holding his arm out in front of him, putting his Credentials about as far from his body as he could reach. "We're just coming from canteen, headed back to Zone 7," I said, holding up the bag of snacks with one hand and my Credentials with the other. "Study fuel, you know how it is."

"Canteen closed seven minutes ago," the other Associate said, checking the time on his comm. "Why has it taken you so long to get back to your dorm?"

I shrugged. "Something we wanted was in the storage room. The counter clerk went to get it for us, but it took her a few minutes. We have passes authorized by the Associate on duty, though." I paused a moment, waiting for them to check our Credentials, but they just stood in place, seemed to be waiting on something. After what felt like forever I asked, "So, can we get back to the dorm now? The News is in twenty minutes and you know we're not authorized to miss that."

One of the Associates turned away from me and looked over my shoulder. "What about you, son?" he said, handing his sensor to his partner. He pushed past me, roughly brushing me back against the wall as he approached Randall. "You don't have much to say."

Randall swallowed and shook his head. He was still holding his wrist out for the approaching Associate to run Credentials. "Um, no sir. Just...I was...we both were, I mean...we both were at canteen. We were getting snacks for the dorm." I noticed that he was hunching down, almost as if he was trying to make himself shorter; had he stood up straight he would have been several inches taller than the Associate. For a moment he took advantage of this level and tried to look the Associate in the eye, but the goggles made that impossible. Randall hung his head and stared at the floor, bent over even more in an effort to make himself small. His arm fell limp at his side.

By this point he was so short that the Associate had to lean down in order to get back into in his line of sight, snapping his fingers a couple of times right in Randall's face. "What's going on, son? You seem pretty nervous. I can't think of any legitimate reason you would have to be so nervous. Can you?" He disengaged his gasmask mid-sentence, giving his words a startling lurch, and then he stepped a little closer, slapping Randall's Credentials aside. "You're a little too quiet, boy. I wonder why you don't have anything to say for yourself?" Somehow his voice was even more disturbing now than it had been filtered through the gas mask. Randall looked at me one more time. All I could see in his eyes was panic.

The Associate turned around, stared right past me to his partner. For a moment we all stood there, frozen in place, waiting, and then the partner gave the slightest of nods. At the same time, he took a couple of steps backwards down the tunnel and took some device from his belt. I thought I was familiar with all of their gear at this point, but this object was new to me: it was about the size of one of those old school credit cards, but triangular, tapered at one point so as to be slightly oblong. He twisted the longer end, and even from a few yards away I could hear a loud click.

Instantly, the globes overhead blazed out with a sickly green light. I looked up, startled; I hadn't even know that they could turn that color. At the same time the Associate up in Randall's face pulled off his helmet altogether, tossed it on the ground, and turned back to him, grabbing him by the collar and shoving him against the wall. I cried out and instinctively tried to move forward, but the partner laid hands on me from behind and spun the both of us around, like some perverse dance move. Now his body was between me and Randall. His truncheon was out of his holster and against my chest before I even fully caught on to what was going down.

"You think you're too good to talk to me, boy?" the Associate said, getting a little bit louder with every word. He was rocking Randall back and forth against the wall, shoving his shoulders against the cinder block; I could hear his head hitting the bricks.

"What the fuck?!" I yelled. "Stop! Stop! Stop!" I tried to push my way past my Associate, but he kept his hands braced on the sides of his truncheon and shoved it hard against me, at the same time sweeping the back of my legs with his foot. I flailed backwards, tripped up and sprawled onto the ground. Snacks flew everywhere as my head rocked back against the floor, and my vision went sideways for a second in a flash of pain. In that moment he moved onto me, faster than I expected, and put his boot square into my chest. I'm not sure he was using enough force to actually hold me down, but his truncheon swinging around over the front of my face was enough to scare me into lying still.

I was able to turn my pounding head and see that Randall was also on the ground. He wasn't nearly as lucky as me—his Associate was kicking him in the stomach, over and over, now screaming at him. I couldn't even make out what the man was saying because he was so out of control; every couple of kicks he added a knock of his fist against Randall's head. Randall was curled into a ball, trying to protect his face but otherwise staying completely inert. After what felt like dozens of kicks the Associate suddenly stopped, leaned against the wall, breathing heavy. He pulled his truncheon from his belt, extending it at the same time in one smooth motion, a series of sharp clicks rising up over the ragged sound of all our lungs. Kneeling down, he poked Randall in the chest, whispered a few soft words to him that I couldn't quite catch. Randall didn't respond. His face a mask of sweat and blood, he stayed perfectly still as the Associate patted him down.

He was looking for something. Why he thought Randall might have it, I had no idea.

After what felt like forever the Associate stood up, paused for a moment, looked at his partner and shook his head. He tapped Randall gently on the neck with the truncheon, then leaned down and picked up his helmet, fixing it on his head as he clicked the gasmask and goggles back into place. He used his boot to push Randall's outstretched arm back toward his prone body.

"You just keep all this in mind next time you're out of area, son," he said, turning away to square up on me and his partner. For a moment he just stared at us, as if considering something, then he nodded. The boot came off my chest, but I stayed on the ground, watching the two Associates move away from us. They were headed back in the direction of canteen, again sweeping the area with their sensors.

I waited for them to get a couple of Globes away, the beeps and squawks receding up the green tunnel, and then rolled over and stood up, moved quickly to where Randall lay. "Are you okay?" I asked, reaching out my hand to help him get off the ground. He groaned and gripped his stomach as I helped him to sit up.

"Those fuckers," he gasped, looking their direction. We could still hear the racket of their sensors, but because of the uphill cast of the tunnel we couldn't see them any longer. I wondered if they were headed to canteen to run Globe footage, checking up on our story, or if they were just going to keep on about their business of searching the halls. I turned to stare up at the Globe overhead.

"What is with that green light?" I asked, squinting into its one-way glass as if I could see through it by sheer force of willpower. "Have you ever seen it do that before?"

Randall coughed and spit up what felt like an insane amount of blood. The light made it look strangely yellow, almost like vomit. He leaned back against the wall, felt around at his ribs. I saw him wince sharply at several of them. "No," he said, closing his eyes and taking a couple of slow, shallow breaths. "Someone told me they saw a corridor lit up this way once, but I never believed it."

I looked both directions down the tunnel, uphill to the dorm and back the other way to canteen. Both ways had Globes lit with the same sick green glow, but outside that halo I could see the normal light peeking through on the other side. "Whatever it means can't be good." I said. "They obviously wanted the Algorithm to pay special attention to us. But why?" I stopped, shook my head, shut my mouth and looked away. That was a stupid move on my part, saying so much right underneath a Globe in an empty hallway. I quickly gathered our snacks and turned back toward Randall. "Come on, man, let's get out of here and go talk to the Z.A."

Randall took my hand, pulled himself to a standing position, attempted to straighten his clothes. I could see his eye swelling up already—he had tried to keep his face from getting hit, but it was going to be a nasty bruise. His lip was bleeding, too, dripping on the floor in rivulets with each ragged breath. "Why?" he asked, giving up the ghost with his shirt and using it to clean off the worst of the blood. It turned instantly yellow in the ghostly green light.

"We need to get you to the infirmary," I said, "obviously. And we've got to go report those Associates right away. I think we'll be forgiven for missing the News on account of this shit."

Randall coughed again, spasming into a laugh devoid of anything like joy. "First of all, Ben, I'm fine." He wiped blood from his face as he said it and flashed a weak smile. "Nothing that won't heal up in a couple of days. And second off, there is no way in hell we are talking to anybody outside the dorm about those assholes."

He put his arm over my shoulder and we started walking toward the dorm. Whatever flex he was putting up about how he felt, he was struggling even to walk straight. "What are you talking about?" I said. "Of course we have to report them. The Z.A. needs to know what those guys are doing out here in the halls."

Randall laughed again and winced, gripping at his ribs. Blood was running down his shoulder onto mine. "Ben, the Z.A. knows exactly what goes down out here, on both sides of the chain link." I made to interrupt but he managed to cut me off. "Let's just get the hell out of here, okay? All I want is to get these snacks back to the dorm, watch the News, and go to bed." He flicked his eyes up at the next Globe and I nodded.

We made it about halfway up the tunnel and paused. In front of us Globes were lit normally, the white fluorescence strangely comforting after what we had just been through. I turned around to face the green Globes strung out as far as the eye could see; the other side was now lost to the slant of the tunnel. In that moment, though, they suddenly cut out, a line of five or six clicking back all at once to their normal color. If not for Randall's full weight leaning against me and the blood seeping through our clothes, the last five minutes might almost have been some trick of my imagination.

CHAPTER 15

THE Z.A.

Several hours later, after everyone else was asleep, I got out of bed, slipped my shoes on, and quietly left the dorm. Whether Randall wanted to be in on the conversation or not, I had decided that I needed to talk to the Z.A.

We had made it back to the dorm just in time to see the News, straggled in right as everyone was bustling around and arranging seats. The room exploded when we entered. At first we were hit with a mass of shade about the tardiness of the snacks, but as soon as everyone got a good look at Randall the mood quickly turned to dismay. We had to wave the questions away and sit down immediately, though, Randall on the couch sunk down deep between me and Maddy—the story would just have to wait. Donna and Dan had never felt so pointless.

In the few minutes we had after the News, Carlos and Maddy helped wrap a couple of old flannel shirts around Randall's midsection, compressing his ribs, and I explained what had happened. The others either did exercises or moved furniture around aimlessly—we had to keep the Algorithm watching something other than Randall. Everyone was all over the map in the conversation: Kiki had heard the same rumor about the strange green Globes; Carlos was in full support of the decision not to go to the Z.A.; Liam sat quietly in the corner, clearly in something like shock. The remainder of the reactions ran the gamut from tears to rage-cursing. Pretty quickly, though, Randall called it a night, and the rest of us followed to bed.

I tried to read *The Autobiography of Malcolm X* for a few minutes before lights dim, but I just couldn't focus. Instead, I ended up simply staring at the slip of paper with the African flag, turning it over with my fingers, thinking about Jazz and the Peeks. I wondered what they would say about what had happened to Randall, if shit like that went down all the time on their side of the chain link. I felt guilty for getting out of it with nothing more than a small bump on the head. After lights dim, when everyone began dropping off to sleep, I kept glancing over to look at the Globe, imagining the room suffused with that sickly green light. After what felt like an hour I gave up on sleep altogether, and decided that Randall and Carlos were wrong—the Z.A. needed to know what had happened. If I got to see some video tape of that green color again, all the better.

Ten minutes later I was padding down the hall, holding my Credentials up at every Globe so I wouldn't raise any alarms with my passage.

Halfway to the Z.A.'s office a Drone met me. I rounded a corner and its head—or whatever you called it—swiveled in place and pointed its primary eye straight at my face. By this point I knew the Z.A. would be expecting me; the Algorithm would have alerted him the moment I first left the dorm. Still, though, it was unnerving to have to scan my Credentials with the Drone, to walk the last couple of turns with it trailing along behind me in that humming sort of way. I was totally on board with Randall: these things freaked me out. Not that

I had anything like warm feelings toward the Associates at this moment, but still—being forced to interact with the Algorithm's robot lackeys was terrible in a totally different way.

The Drone drifted ahead of me into the Admin wing, posted itself up outside the Z.A.'s office with a soft whirr. The door buzzed open as I approached, and I walked inside. The Z.A. was sitting on a couch watching the Stream—some kind of crazy game show, one where teams battled it out tooth and nail against each other under the instruction of some smarmy smiling host. I had watched the guy on the Stream before, but the whole thing seemed extra foolish to me now. The display was huge, taking up almost the entire wall of the small apartment that the Z.A. called office and home. I could see into his tiny bedroom from here; for some reason the fact that his bed was unmade felt sad to me.

He looked over at me, hit the mute button on the remote. "What can I do for you, Ben?" he said, glancing at his screen. He would have been using it to watch me the entire time I was out of the dorm; I didn't flatter myself that the night-shift Z.A. actually knew my name.

"Sorry to bother you so late, sir," I said. "But it's important."

"Not at all, Ben," he said. "It is quite literally my job to assist students in Zones Seven through Nine with both their personal and academic needs." He was a young guy, maybe in his twenties. I had heard he was an Associate for only a couple of years before getting promoted to Admin. "So which is it here? Personal? Or academic?"

I was just a breath away from laying out the whole story for him— the trip to canteen and the authorized passes, meeting the Associates in that strange green light, Randall's injuries and our helpless frustration—when I completely panicked. What if Randall and Carlos were right? What if this guy didn't believe me, and my explanations only made things worse? I thought of the African flag marking my page back in Jazz's book. I remembered the way the Associates had treated Randall; I felt another wave of shame about the way they had let me off the hook. I looked at the Z.A. and suddenly wondered why it was that

I trusted him so much when Randall and Carlos didn't.

"Ben?" he said. I was waiting too long. "Is there something I can help you with, or...?" He gestured back toward the display. There was nothing obviously unkind about him, but suddenly I didn't have any faith that he would listen to my story.

"Yes sir," I stalled, trying to think of a reason I would be out in the middle of the night, requesting to look at Globe footage. I settled on the only thing that I thought might buy me a quick look. "This is stupid, but I got back to my room for the News and couldn't find an important homework assignment. I think I dropped it back in the hallways somewhere?" I tried to give my voice a lilt of insecurity, hoping he would read it as something like innocence. "Anyways, my friends told me to just go look for it in the morning, so I went to bed. But I'm kind of freaking out. I can't sleep because I'm so worried about it. I was hoping we could check the Globes real quick?" More worry in my voice, and I crossed my fingers in my mind.

The Z.A. sighed and smiled, grabbing his screen. "A lot going on junior year, huh, Ben?" Again with him using information from my Credentials, acting as if he knew me. For some reason this obvious subterfuge was really getting on my nerves. "I get it. You don't get ranked so high in the Testing without working extra hard on your homework. And you guys in Block 7 have a lot on your mind, especially with all this nonsense about that pick, Jazz."

The word set off a blood rush in my ears.

It felt like I had been punched in the gut, woozy, like I might fall down. I'd never heard an adult use that word; for all I knew they weren't even aware it existed. For just a moment it was as if all the air had been let out of the room, and then I managed to pull myself together and blurt out, "Sir, we don't use that word about our classmates. Sir. It's rude. Sir." I trailed off lamely.

For a long moment he stared at me. Then he put his finger to his nose, pointed at me and laughed. "Of course, Ben. Of course. We would never use that word." He kept laughing as he began tapping at his screen. "Where do you think you dropped your work, son?"

It was clear he thought we were in on the same joke, and I had only a moment to decide what to do. Argue with him and probably get myself tossed out, maybe get sent up to see a G.A. tomorrow? Or let it go and maybe get him to show me the footage? One thing was for sure: Randall had been right. It's a good thing I didn't try to tell this guy the real story from the jump. He'd have to see it first to believe.

I swallowed my anger for Jazz and the rest of the Peeks and said, instead, "Yes, sir, thank you, sir. I think I dropped it in that access tunnel from canteen to the Guest dorms. We were walking through there a little after 9:00."

He raised his eyebrows at that, and I told him the truth about the first part of our story—the blue hot chips and the authorized Credentials—circling back to the thought that all I was hoping to see was me dropping some papers in that tunnel.

It took him only a moment to find the footage and swipe it to the display on the wall. He got all the Globes from the tunnel and the one from the gym entrance up there at once, synced them up to 9:00 and put them on fast forward. For a moment there was nothing, then the Associates came sweeping through with their sensors; they looked like they were doing some bizarre dance, raising and lowering their arms in double time to a hidden beat. At 9:05 Randall and I came speed-walking down the hall, flashed our Credentials at the Drones who appeared as if from nowhere, and then we entered the tunnel. Any second now the Z.A. would see what his colleagues had done to Randall. I held my breath and waited for it to drop.

At that point all four of us disappeared.

I turned to look at the Z.A., stunned, but he just watched the display and tapped his feet. He looked bored. The footage ran all the way until 9:15, but none of us ever showed back up. No motion in the tunnel at all. Just blank cinder block lit by completely normal fluorescent Globes.

The Z.A. turned to me. "Tough break, Ben! The Algorithm must have pruned that footage."

"What?" I asked. *Pruned?* What did that mean?

He shrugged. "It's just what it does every once in a while. Usually late at night in areas where there isn't likely to be anything of note to record. It powers down and runs diagnostic tests, dumps excess data in order to maximize long-term storage. It's pretty random—every once in a while you'll look for some footage and it just won't be there. They call it 'pruning,' like a tree."

Again, it was like getting punched in the gut. No way was I buying this story. My best friend gets jumped by a couple of Associates for absolutely no reason, and it just so happens that the Algorithm chooses that exact moment to prune itself? Obviously, whatever else the green light meant, it meant this: there was no proof of what had happened to Randall. It was our word against theirs, and we all knew exactly what would happen if we tried to accuse them of any kind of wrongdoing. Nothing. Randall and Carlos were totally right—telling the Z.A. would have been a disaster.

It was curious, however, that he seemed to genuinely believe his explanation. It wasn't clear to me that he knew anything about the little device and the green light.

Regardless, it was past time for me to get out of there. I thanked him profusely, played up a little extra worry about my homework, and went back to bed. He was watching his game show again before I even made it out the door. The Drone followed me the entire way back to the dorm, hovering along behind me, whirring and clicking. It might have been coincidence, but it felt as if someone was going out of their way to keep an eye on me.

———————

We spent the rest of the week glued to the table in the common room. Randall was nowhere close to being up for basketball—he was breathing easier, but Maddy was pretty sure at least two of his ribs were cracked—and so, with him and Jazz both gone, the first teams melted away into the seconds and ran a series of friendly scrimmages. Liam played a couple of nights, passing Randall's instructions along to the rest of the team, and once Randall went down there to speak to some of the younger players. Neither of them felt much like missing the action in the common room, though—between Jazz, the book, and that dangerous green light, we had a lot to talk about. Even if we weren't really accomplishing much of anything, it felt like at any moment something might break loose in the conversation, and it would all somehow start to make sense.

"Was the footage that the Z.A. showed you green?" Liam asked one night. I had explained my little trip to the office in several different waves, starting with Randall. I knew I owed him a major apology for not respecting his pessimism—I should have trusted him from the jump and steered clear of the Z.A.'s office altogether. He was mad for a good minute, but the story of the missing Globe footage was more than enough to bring him back, especially since I'd had the last-second sense not to give any actual information away. Liam had missed the first couple rounds of the story and was just now catching up on the details.

"No, it was just blank," I replied. "I mean, not blank. It was, like, gone or missing or whatever. Blank, like it looked as if we never walked down that section of the hallway at all. It was just empty cinder block."

"Not even the Associates?" he asked. I shook my head. "Nope. They just disappeared."

"The question," said Kiki, not looking up from her screen, "is whether the story the Z.A. told you is total bullshit, or was it at least partly true." Tonight, like every other night, we were all trying to look busy on various homework projects while at the same time furiously researching Malcolm X and the African flag and that vexing phrase *hands up don't shoot*. Everyone was certain there was a connection buried in there somewhere, one that we were right on the verge of discovering.

"What do you mean?" Randall asked, annoyed. Once I told him the part about the Z.A. calling Jazz a "pick," he'd had zero tolerance for any talk of Admin. He didn't trust anything at all that came out of their mouths.

I stopped staring at the paper with the African flag long enough to see Kiki shrug and say, "I mean, it seemed to Ben like he really didn't know that it was the Associates that made the video snap back to that resting shot. With their special toy, or whatever. Let's give him that, maybe. But is he right about the pruning? Is the footage gone? Did the Algorithm actually dump it for good or maybe just hide it away?" She looked up at us. "I'm thinking it's out there somewhere."

"Snap back," I repeated, turning to Randall. "That's exactly what it felt like. As if the Associate twisted that little device and somehow rewound the whole time code back on the Globe footage. Made what they did to you just disappear—" I snapped my fingers in the air as I said it and Randall winced.

"I wish I could lay hands on a snapback," Kiki said. "Feels like we could get away with some major shenanigans if we had one."

Liam cut in awkwardly. "Well, guys, I learned that if you want something? Well, then, you had better make some noise." We all turned his way, confusion all over our faces. He held up *The Autobiography of Malcom X* and looked sheepish. "It's one of the quotes I remember seeing somewhere at some point. It maybe felt appropriate here."

"Make some noise, shit," Randall said, waving his hands away. "They'll just snap back and kick you in the ribs until you can't breathe." He gave a grim laugh, but nobody else joined in.

Jazz came back the next day. There was nothing ceremonious about her return; we just looked up during breakfast and saw that she was in her usual spot next to Orion. I had been keeping an eye on him all week, waiting for him to get a cup of coffee, but he never went over to the station. Half a dozen times I made a slow show of stopping there, dawdling as long as possible to choose my drink. I hoped that he could come give me some more information about what was going on with

Jazz, wanted to ask what he knew about that green light. In the end it was just a lot of wasted coffee. He never showed.

I felt like my heart stopped when I saw her sitting there that morning, and instantly I convinced myself that today was the day. I played it cool as possible during breakfast, stayed away from the coffee station even as I was ready to jump if she headed that direction. She didn't. Neither did she give me even so much as a passing glance during class. I spent the entire time watching her, but she completely ignored me. If I didn't know any better, I would say she was entirely unaware of my existence.

She had sent me that message, though—that had happened for sure. But what did it actually mean?

I was struggling to pay attention in all of my classes at this point, the return of Jazz notwithstanding. We had just come out of the Testing, which meant that most teachers were ramping back up with new material. Even still, it all just felt so boring. I had hoped that Jazz being back might precipitate a basketball game, but Randall was unsure about when he could get back on the court. So, again, we found ourselves around the table the night of Jazz's return, staring at the African flag while flipping through *The Autobiography of Malcolm X*. We were still getting nowhere.

"Hands up don't shoot," Randall said, to no one in particular. "Hands up. Don't shoot… Hands up don't. Shoot…Hands. Up don't. Shoot." He looked around at the rest of us, hoping his change of rhythm might trigger some kind of memory, but nobody responded. There was nothing to say; the words were inscrutable to us, and repetition wasn't helping.

"Hands. Up. Don't. Shoot," he said again, one word at a time.

Still, nothing.

———————————

A couple more days went by—more than a week after the crazy

moment with the snapback. Randall was feeling good enough to start some light jogging, though he said he was a good ways from shooting a ball; raising his arms up above his head still made him wince, even with nothing in his hands. Jazz had been back for three days and hadn't looked in my direction even once. Liam had returned to the court full time and, under Randall's guidance, taken proxy control of the second team. Apparently they were dominating. Orion passed word across the chain link that Jazz wouldn't play again until Randall was ready. Williams was insufferable. Even Mason seemed bored.

Then, finally, something happened.

At lunch, more out of habit than anything else, I was looking across the chain link at the Peek side. I had pretty much given up on Jazz—she wasn't giving me any indication of what I was supposed to do with all the strange information she and Mason had sent my way. Even still, I couldn't turn away from watching her. It was kind of pathetic and I knew it; day after day with her showing me not the slightest bit of attention, and me still just hoping for something. But then one day, midway through my sandwich, Orion stood up and stretched, took three steps toward the coffee station and suddenly stopped.

He was looking right at me.

I completely froze. Even though I had been hoping for something like this pretty much every minute of the past week, now that I actually had some contact with the Peeks I panicked. Here was Jazz's best friend—if anyone knew anything about all this mess with Mason, it was Orion. I didn't want to screw this chance up; was he really wanting to talk to me?

Then he smiled and signaled at me in hand signs: *you want coffee, Ben?*

I probably should have been expecting it, but I was still too surprised to reply. He kept grinning at me for a moment, then turned and made for the coffee station without so much as another glance in my direction. Incredulous, I turned to look at Randall, but his only contribution was to laugh, shake his head, and point toward the coffee.

Quickly, I jumped up and followed Orion.

We got to the station at the exact same time. If anyone had noticed that this was our third coincidental meeting for coffee in the past couple of weeks, they didn't seem to care. The Associates were posted up in their normal places, just outside of mic range. A couple of Drones hovered nearby, but not too close. I went about the now-familiar routine of agonizing over my choice of beverage.

"Hey, Orion," I said, trying to gather my thoughts. It felt like there were a thousand things on my mind and I didn't even know where to start.

Fortunately, he didn't seem to be looking for my input. "Ben, Jazz wants to talk," he said, pouring coffee, reaching for the cream. This was going to be a short conversation, apparently.

I caught my breath. All I had wanted for the past week was to talk to Jazz, and here was my shot. "Now?" I asked, nervous, fighting the urge to turn around and look at her.

Orion laughed. "Come on, man. That would be way too obvious." He snapped a lid onto the top of his coffee and looked directly at me. "Tomorrow. Exactly thirty minutes into the start of your breakfast period. Right here." He turned and walked away without waiting for a reply. It was all I could do to go through the charade of preparing a cup of coffee that I was going to dump out at the earliest possible convenience.

Dodging a series of Drones, I went back to my table on cloud nine. Pretty much everyone was watching me when I sat down, so I signaled, *tomorrow I'll talk to Jazz.* Randall grinned and Kiki nodded. Liam furrowed his brow for a moment, thinking. Carlos rolled his eyes; Madison mouthed to me, *not all of us speak hands, Ben.*

Liam looked around suddenly, obviously panicked, and then he whispered to me, "Why would you fight with Jazz tomorrow?"

It was just the reaction I needed; it had been a long week. I lost it laughing.

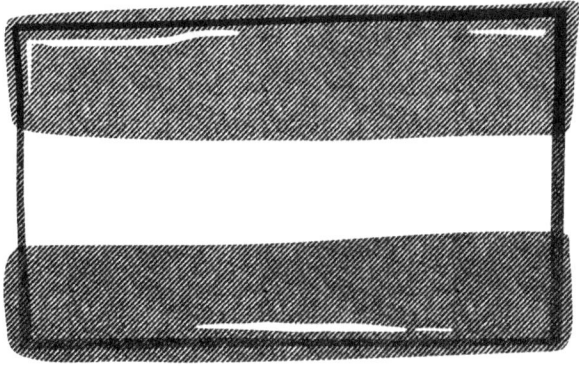

CHAPTER 16

HANDS UP DON'T SHOOT

The next morning, for maybe the first time in my days at 231, I woke up before the end of lights dim. The room was quiet but for the sound of my roommates breathing. Another aspect of learning to sleep here was getting used to the absolutely soundproof nature of the dorm; even in a storm you could see the lightning but not hear the thunder through the reinforced glass of the skylights. It was weird—no noises at all from heating or plumbing or just people moving around like back at home. No birds, no crickets, no wind. All you could hear was the sound of people sleeping.

I was exhausted still, but as soon as I rolled over I knew I was never going to fall back asleep. It was like a weird kind of Christmas morning vibe—and I was always the kid in the family who woke up crazy early and lay in bed until I was allowed to get my brothers and sister up. Whatever was going on around here, Jazz was for sure the key. Today was the day I was finally going to be able to ask her some questions.

The Meeting skipped along in a monotonous blur. With Jazz finally out of In-School, they had removed her picture from the display and stopped calling for informants to step forward. Though the News continued to update us as to the "ongoing investigation into a known terrorist," everything about the Meeting had gone back to whatever qualified as normal. Meaning, I only had to give Admin about half of my attention, and I could depend on my friends to fill me in if anything important got announced.

Orion had given me half an hour to eat, but after only about ten minutes I was completely done with the small breakfast I forced myself to choke down—I was too nervous to eat much more. From that point on I was just bouncing in place at the table. I tried not to stare across the chain link at Jazz, but I was terrified at the thought of missing her movement toward the coffee station. Randall was on the lookout with me—a task he accomplished while also using raisins to detail some complicated new basketball play to Liam. Maddy and Kiki were starting work on this new assignment for Williams, something about America's decision to retreat from the War for Central Europe. I hadn't been paying any attention in his class lately; it was going to take some hustle for me to catch up after a week of them covering for me.

"That's never going to work," Kiki said, looking up from her screen and pointing at the raisins spread out in front of Liam's tray.

"What? Why not?" Randall said, staring at the play. He'd smushed three raisins together to represent each of the players, sticking orange seeds into the ones that stood for our team. He and Liam looked pretty ridiculous sitting there arguing, moving the little raisin balls around the table.

Kiki rolled her eyes. "Which one of these is Jazz?" she asked.

"It doesn't matter," Randall said, waving her away. "This play is going to be Jazz-proof. That's the point! Now that we've got Liam I've finally figured out a way to do it."

Maddy laughed. "Jazz-proof? What does that even mean?" She

leaned over with her straw and began pushing at the raisin-Peeks on the table, moving them into positions that bore no resemblance to an actual basketball game. It was a testament to how Randall felt about her that he didn't lose his mind complaining at the interference.

"Hey, now I'm open!" Carlos said, leaning over and swatting Maddy's straw away with his own. "Randall! Pass to me, quick!" The ball was a straw wrapper, rolled up tight, and Carlos started moving it around the table.

Randall, fed up, started to come back with something but suddenly stopped, punched me in the arm. "Ben, she's moving. She's moving." He was staring at Jazz through the chain link. She was, in fact, finally standing up and walking toward the coffee station.

Raisins were completely forgotten as I jumped up to meet her, trying desperately to look nonchalant on the walk over. Just another guy looking for caffeine here on this fine morning, I hoped.

Despite my best efforts at playing it cool, I beat her to the station by a good ten seconds. Wary of looking around and tipping my hand about the plan, I again went back to studying the beverage options. I wondered if maybe I should take tiny sips of different brews and look like I was comparing their tastes, then decided that this might draw more attention than just moving slow.

Jazz slid up next to me on her side of the chain link as I poured a small amount of the darker roast into a ceramic mug. I saw her out of the corner of my eye and eagerly turned to face her, burning with questions. "Jazz, please tell me—" I was saying as I looked her way, but immediately swallowed the words into the back of my throat. Floating behind her, mere feet away from the two of us, was a Drone. Its primary eye was aimed right at her.

She smiled at me and winked, her face pointing in my direction and away from the Drone. "Damn, Ben!" she said. "Please tell you the homework assignment for Williams from last night? I know he's boring as hell, but don't you pay any attention in that man's class?" She smacked her teeth and shook her head at me as she began to tear open a packet of hot chocolate.

I panicked and turned back to my coffee. What were we going to do? The Drones must be following her around, recording her whenever she's out of direct Globe observation. I should have seen this coming, but I despaired—there was no way we could talk openly in front of this Drone.

"Ben," Jazz said sweetly. "Any chance you know whether this is decaf or full strength?" The tone of her voice caught me off guard, and I turned to look at her holding up a carafe of coffee. My eyes flew instantly to her empty hand—flooded with relief, I saw her signal. *Ben, we don't have much time.*

I turned away to face forward and awkwardly signaled back with my right hand, *Jazz! What is going on? What is with this flag you gave me?* My left hand would have been more graceful, but it was on the far side of her.

Her hand froze for a beat, and then she flahsed back, a little too quickly, *flag? I don't understand.*

I cursed silently. This was going to be more difficult than I had hoped; Jazz obviously didn't know all the signals yet. *Forget it,* I signed. *Just tell me what to do.* I cut my eyes at her and tapped again, *Tell me what to do, Jazz. Please. I'm so confused, I just need help.*

Green trees, Ben. Green trees. No one can tell you what to do. Green trees.

Green trees? I had to stop myself from saying it out loud. What was she talking about? Feeling like a little kid playing at being a spy, I stirred sugar in with my left hand while I signaled back with the right, *What is green trees? What are you talking about?*

Mason would love this, I thought suddenly: one of his favorite sayings is something about not letting the left hand know what the right hand is doing. I wondered if I would ever get the chance to talk to him without the Globes and Drones, tell him I finally understood what he meant.

I risked a more direct look at her. The cut over her eye was healing up, though you could still see a faint halo of purple rung around the side of her face. Her hair no longer looked anything like that picture from the Meeting; the braids were out, and it was pulled up in short little semi-twists instead. She looked at me with kind of a half-smile, a curious expression on her face, and for just a second I lost my train of thought, struck suddenly by the ridiculousness of the scene. The Drone was still hovering in place over her right shoulder, its primary eye toggling back and forth between us. She was angling her body to completely shield both of our hands; we could have talked here all day if they would just give us the time. It was clear that we were running out, though—I noticed that Jazz had already popped the top onto her cup. She was working a cardboard sleeve out of the holder, and it seemed like her curiosity was giving way to concern. Her eyes scrunched up as she continued to look at me, her head titled just a little, as if in thought.

*Green…trees…*she tapped, slower, as if I didn't understand. Then, as if in answer to my unasked question, *hands…up…don't…shoot.*

My heart leapt into my throat. I watched her slide the sleeve over her cup and turn to me. "Well, Ben," she said, "It looks like you're going to be on your own in class today. You'll have to make a decision about what to do all by yourself. All by yourself." She repeated the last phrase as her free hand slid down near the middle of her stomach and flashed several times in a row, rapidly, *hands up don't shoot hands up don't shoot hands up don't shoot.*

Jazz! I signaled back, switching to my left hand just in case that was part of our miscommunication. *What is hands up don't shoot? Don't leave! Tell me!*

She smiled and winked again. "See you round, Ben." She held my gaze for just a moment and time seemed to stand still. I didn't know anything more after finishing this conversation than I did before I started it, and I desperately wanted her to stay. Instead, she turned slowly away, back toward the Drone. At the last possible moment she flashed her hand around the side of her body: *green trees.*

I stood there and watched her walk away, completely confused.

This place had defeated us, and in that moment I didn't care if the Associates were watching me or not. There was nobody left to guide me through whatever it was I was supposed to do with this information I didn't understand. I was lost.

———————

Later we were all sitting in Williams's class, and I was desperately trying to piece together the story of why America had abandoned its allies at the height of the War for Central Europe. Williams had thrown a couple of incongruous quotes on the display, asked us to create a pro and con list of the foreign policy moves America made in its retreat into global isolation. Kiki was explaining all the players to me, not for the first time, while Madison and Randall were tapping at screens and working on the list. "Teachers love Venn diagrams," he had said, "we got this." On my part, I just felt stupid. Not only was I falling behind in class, but also I had gotten absolutely nowhere with this mystery about Jazz and Mason and the book and the African flag. *Green trees* meant nothing to me; the conversation that I had been desperately counting on had turned out to be a complete waste of time.

"Ben," Liam said in a low voice, his gaze directed at the chart Maddy was sketching out. "Tell me one more time exactly what Jazz said to you."

I cut my eyes across the room to look at her. She was sitting with the Peeks, her back to Williams, laughing quietly. She hadn't looked in my direction once since we parted ways at the coffee station. There was enough going on in the room that I couldn't hear or see anything she was saying—and I had tried real hard to listen in on their conversation, one way or another. I turned away from her and shrugged; at least the noise gave me cover to talk with Liam.

"Green trees, Liam. Green trees," I said. "That, and like ten more times with all the hands up don't shoot."

Kiki heard us talking and decided to add to our sonic camouflage.

Right in the middle of a sentence on the Carpathian Front she smoothly transitioned away from information I actually needed to learn and into something more resembling gibberish, all the while trying to entertain Madison and Randall.

"And the U.S. had close to a hundred thousand troops stationed along the western edge of the Carpathians up until the signing of the Great Russian Treaty. At that point, it became clear that Drones were monitoring the rampant distribution of blue hot chips throughout the entire region—all of the smuggled contraband brought under the gym and up into the dorms—and so Admin decreed that nothing was to be done but to hold their middle fingers up to the Globes. And so they did, all hundred thousand troops in unison, on what posterity would come to know only as Middle Finger Day. To this day we still celebrate the occasion on the 11th day of every month with this short remembrance." She placed both her hands on the table, palm up, flashed the middle fingers and joined them together to make a rudimentary eleven. Randall and Madison were dying. The Venn Diagram remained just a couple of mostly empty circles.

Underneath her steady stream of noise Liam and I were able to speak with a little more freedom. "That's it?" he asked, turning to face me. "Are you absolutely sure she said green trees? Maybe you misunderstood her, right?"

I rolled my eyes. "No, man. I mean, she only said it like ten times. She definitely said green trees."

He stared off into space for a moment and snapped his fingers. "I know! Maybe she wants to meet you outside somewhere! There are some trees by the football field, right? Is she wanting to meet you out there? Where the two of you could talk with no one around?"

I sighed. "Yeah, I thought about that, too. I mean, there's a couple scrubby trees out there. But nowhere that the Associates won't follow. Or now, I guess, the Drones." I thought about that hovering hulk of metal trailing away after Jazz as she left the coffee station, pictured it waiting for her outside the door right now. It was freaking me out to imagine more of them floating around, staying in our business even more than the Globes and Associates were able to do.

Kiki hit pause on her monologue and looked around. "Y'all ever stop to think that Jazz is just playing games with you? I mean, she caught you spying on her that day of the Code Red or whatever, and now maybe she's just having a laugh at your expense." She shrugged and looked at me funny, got kind of quiet. "I mean, I'm just saying Ben. It might be true."

"I wondered about that, too!" Liam said, a little too loud about it. Randall glared at him and shook his head. Liam looked sheepish. "But, I mean, that still doesn't make any sense out of Mason and that book, right?"

"I'm starting to wonder," I said, exhausted by all this. We had been going around and around every little detail for something like two weeks now, and we were getting nowhere. "Maybe Mason just randomly picked me that day to go to In-School and maybe Jazz is just clowning on me. Maybe the book really was just an accident. Maybe she's sitting over there, actually just really pissed that I haven't returned it, or whatever."

I said it out loud, but it felt like a lie; I didn't believe it at all. I could still picture being alone in that dungeon with Jazz, the frantic way she moved her hands in silhouette on that wall, the urgency I could feel in her signals. *Ben, we don't have much time,* she had signed—the same thing she had said in the coffee line just a few minutes ago. It didn't make any sense at all, but it just felt way too real. Who would go to all this trouble just to mess with me? I was convinced that it had to mean something.

Williams rolled his chair out from behind his desk, stared at us for a moment, then flicked the lights on and off three times from his screen. Without control over the Globe, however, this painted us all with a weird kind of filter effect, as the soft glow it gave off never wavered. The room as a whole got super dark in this windowless space, but if you happened to be looking right at the Globe when the lights dropped it almost felt as if it were getting somehow brighter—like the Globe was blinking ominously at you, not that the room was getting darker. I wondered if he knew this, if he was trying to remind us of our place in this school, or if he was just doing that annoying thing teachers did when they didn't feel like standing up to get our attention.

"One thing about history," he said, still from his seat, "is that allegiances are constantly shifting." He dropped the screen into his lap and stared at the Globe as he went on. "One year our nation might be on the side of a country like Russia, fighting against a common enemy. Then for decades we become opposed, the collective interest of our Nations in an irrational conflict. And yet, on the other hand, as the War for Central Europe so keenly shows, this period of opposition can give way again to something that looks like friendship. But it is not, in fact, friendship. What feels like 'right' and 'wrong' are illusions. 'Good guys' and 'bad guys' are characters in stories read by children, myths told to make sense of a chaotic world. It is all fiction, little more than fantasy. History teaches us that in the real world there is nothing like a fairy godmother. There is only power. As the saying goes, history is written by the victors. All that matters is that, in the end, you find yourself sitting on the side with the winners. These are the 'good guys.' Being with the losers gets you nowhere."

He turned to look at the Peeks, almost a dare to Jazz. For just a moment I thought she was going to say something—she squirmed a little in her chair and even opened her mouth—but I guess she decided it wasn't worth it. She kept quiet.

Williams smiled, a slow creeping grin that made him look halfway like the Joker—if the Joker was a pale, middle-aged man content to terrorize a room full of captive teenagers. He turned to the Globe, then back to the room. "Madison, is your group ready to talk to me about America's choice to leave Europe and retreat from the War? Can you help explain the wisdom of our decision to choose Russia?"

Maddy shrugged, grabbed the mostly-blank list from Randall, stood up. *I got this,* she mouthed to the rest of us. I breathed a sigh of relief. I still had no idea what was going on with Russia. She stared at her list as she walked to the front, going over what little information she and Randall had managed to cobble together.

That's when the Code Red went off.

I could hear Kiki groan over the sound of the siren and the voice, then the clatter of bodies scrambling to the floor and under desks. Our seats were all a little out of alignment due to the group work we were doing, and I found myself right up next to Liam, his gangly elbow pushed up almost into my face. I saw Maddy look around wildly for a moment, panicked, before she took a free desk closer to the front rather than make her way back to the rest of us.

The voice blared on and on: "CODE RED. CODE RED. PLEASE FOLLOW PROTOCOLS AND ASSUME THE POSITION FOR YOUR OWN SAFETY. CODE RED."

Reflexively, I looked over to Jazz. At first I wasn't able to see her, hidden as she was by fidgeting bodies, and I just about gave up looking. Then, at the last second, I found her, saw her hair sticking out over Liam's shoulder. She was closer than I had anticipated—I had been looking all the way across the room at the Peeks, but she had taken a desk closer to me in the middle distance. I felt a surge of anticipation in the pit of my stomach. Had she moved closer to talk to me somehow? Then Liam shifted his weight just a little, my desk scudded a foot to the left, and I saw her face clearly for the first time.

She was staring right at me.

I caught my breath and reflexively looked around to see who else was watching. It appeared that no one in the room could see her as she started to sign to me.

Green trees, Ben. Green trees. Hands up don't shoot. Green trees.

Jazz! I signaled back. *I don't know what you're talking about! Please!*

She stopped moving her hands and looked at me a long moment. I held up my hands, not signing, just imploring her to help me. I willed her to understand; if ever I could believe in something like magic, it had to be now. I needed help. Finally, after what felt like forever, she rolled her eyes and shouted out at the top of her lungs.

"Mr. Williams!"

Kids twisted around under their desks to look at her. Students did not call out for the teacher during a Code Red; this did not happen. Williams didn't respond.

"Mr. Williams! Mr. Williams!" she called out again, getting louder, insistent. "Can you hear me?!"

And still the voice, over and over: "CODE RED. CODE RED. PLEASE FOLLOW PROTOCOLS AND ASSUME THE POSITION FOR YOUR OWN SAFETY. CODE RED."

Williams screamed over the Globe, "What, Jazz? What on earth do you want?"

"I was thinking about that whole thing you were saying, Mr. Williams, that thing about history being written by the victors," Jazz cried. She was talking to him, but she was still looking right at me. "It reminded me of something I read recently. It was about somebody who said they had no mercy for a society that would crush people. A society that would crush people but still punish them for not being able to stand up under the weight."

"Jazz!" he called back. "What in the hell are you talking about? Shut up!"

"CODE RED. CODE RED. PLEASE FOLLOW PROTOCOLS AND ASSUME THE POSITION FOR YOUR OWN SAFETY. CODE RED."

She pointed at me one more time, shrugged her shoulders and signed, *green trees, Ben, please understand.* Then she hollered at Williams again, "Okay, Mr. Williams, it was just something I read somewhere! I thought you would want to know!"

Then, finally, I caught a thread of thought, snatched it out of the air like a leaf floating slowly to the ground. Those words, they weren't just from "somewhere." They were from *The Autobiography of Malcolm X.* I had dog-eared the page because it reminded me of this building—a place that could crush children and blame them for it at the same time. I finally understood. The book was the key to all of this, but not for any reason other than that bookmark she had left me to find. The bookmark was the green trees.

It wasn't an African flag I had been given. We had foolishly been following an unwitting red herring. A stripe of brown at the bottom, a stripe of yellow in the middle, a stripe of green at the top. It looked enough like the African flag that we had gotten distracted, but it wasn't a flag. It was a forest. The thing is, though, we didn't have a sign for forest with our hands—only a sign for trees. We didn't need to talk about the outside much here, not forests or beaches or mountains. We hadn't invented words for most of the things out there in the rest of the world.

It was a forest on that card, not a flag. Jazz must not know all her colors yet, though, because for the first time ever I caught her making a mistake.

"CODE RED. CODE RED. PLEASE FOLLOW PROTOCOLS AND ASSUME THE POSITION FOR YOUR OWN SAFETY. CODE RED."

It wasn't *green trees* she had been trying to say to me all this time. It was *yellow woods.*

I closed my eyes and saw her, clear as day, holding that flashlight and signing to me in the shadows, reciting that Robert Frost poem. In a rush, I realized that she had only warmed up to me when I mentioned the poet, and that I had only mentioned him in the first place because Mason passed me the message. Mason! He was behind all of this somewhere, after all! But what did it mean, even still?

Two roads diverged in a yellow wood, I thought. But what roads? Where? If I knew where the other road was, maybe I could take it. But I wasn't even sure what road I was on, much less the other road I could be taking.

The door clanged. The light turned violet and the voice finally stopped as a gang of Associates came crashing into the room. Two of them went for Jazz, two for Orion, dragging them both out from under their desks. One went to guard Williams, two more at the door and others posted up outside. I had never seen this many Associates in one classroom before.

And then, suddenly, I knew exactly what I was supposed to do.

I don't know why it took me so long, but I finally understood. Two roads diverged in a yellow wood, and I? I had to take the one less traveled by, had to trust that it would make all the difference. Hands up, don't shoot. *Hands up, don't shoot. Hands up, don't shoot.* It was time for me to take that road.

I crawled out from under the desk and stood to my feet, ignoring Liam's bewildered stare. Even with the voice finally over, the room was noisy, so loud that it took a couple of moments for anyone else to notice me. Eventually Williams paused in the middle of a sentence he was directing at the nearest Associate, pointed at me and narrowed his eyes. The Associates hauling Jazz and Orion out of the room stopped, looking around at each other. I've never understood the chain of command without Admin in the room, but finally one of the Associates guarding the door lurched my way, hands on his taser. Another called out to me, "Code Violet protocol, son. Get back under your desk."

I kept my eyes on Jazz. When she heard the Associate speak she looked up, first at him and then at me. Our eyes locked and she smiled. I heard Randall risk a whisper to me, "Ben! What the fuck are you doing?" I grinned back at Jazz, finally feeling like we had some control over this place.

The Associate with the taser stepped between us and pointed it at my chest. "Sit down, son, or I'll have to give you an Infraction."

One of them, I think he was holding Orion, said, "What the hell are you doing, Derek? You can't shoot that kid. He's a Guest."

The Associate with the taser, Derek, turned around and waved the other one away. In that brief moment, I caught just one more glimpse of Jazz. She signed the words to me, again, *green trees, Ben, green trees.* Then she held up two fingers in a sideways peace sign. As crazy as this situation was, I almost laughed. Green trees, yellow wood—if only I'd put this together sooner.

Two roads diverged in a yellow wood. I had to take the one less traveled by, now that I finally saw it laid out before me. I took a deep breath, terrified of what was about to happen, looked down at Liam. He was wide-eyed, and though he was scrunched into a ball under the desk I managed to see his hand moving slightly against the floor.

Hands up, don't shoot, he signaled. I nodded.

I turned back to the Associate, saw Jazz get pulled sideways, away from me. She was whispering something, but if it was for my benefit I couldn't catch it. Slowly I raised my hands in the air, palms forward, looked into the opaque goggles of the Associate and said, "You can't take them away. They didn't do anything wrong, and you know it."

Williams laughed, a petty little sound. "History is written by the victors, Ben. Put your hands down and get back under that desk."

I looked at him. He was small, sweaty, unstable. His history was bullshit, and we all knew it. I rotated my hands inwards until my palms were facing me, then lowered eight of my fingers and gave them what they deserved—one hand for Williams, one for Derek. It was finally Middle Finger Day.

After the word "Infraction," the last thing I heard before I got tased was Madison gasping. Then my world went dark.

THE PROGRESS OF LIGHTS

If you stick a knife in my back nine inches and pull it out six inches, there's no progress. If you pull it all the way out, that's not progress. The progress is healing the wound that the blow made.

- MALCOLM X

CHAPTER 17
WAKE UP

"Ben, it's time for breakfast. You're going to be late to school if you don't hustle!"

I rolled over and blinked my eyes against the light. Mom had thrown open the curtains, turned off my fan. Suddenly, it was too hot and too bright in my bedroom. I groaned and shook the covers off, pulled a shirt over my head. Rolling over, I managed to get my feet on the floor. But I was just so tired.

"Mom?" I asked. She had already left, though, gone through the open door, off to the kitchen to get me breakfast.

My legs felt like lead, dragging, as I followed her down the hall. Why was I so tired? Had I stayed up too late the night before? It was hard to remember; my head felt thick, foggy. Last night was one big blank—had I been doing homework? Or was I up too late on the Stream?

Breakfast was strange, food Mom usually didn't make—bagels

and eggs that weren't quite yellow enough. The smell of coffee was overpowering, like she had burned it or something. It felt extra bright in here, too, somehow making my head hurt even worse.

"We have a big day ahead of us, Benny," Mom said, her back to me as she cleaned up a huge pile of pots and pans at the sink. "Your dad will be down soon to talk us through all the details. I hope you're excited!"

"Mom?" I said. She didn't turn around, but I went on anyway. "Were we out somewhere last night? I'm so tired, but I can't really remember why."

She didn't answer, just kept right on doing the dishes. The clatter and clang receded into the background against the pounding of my head. It was a monster of a headache, felt like it connected straight down through my throat and into my heart. My chest hurt, too; every beat felt like I was getting hit by an invisible hand. I picked at my breakfast, but it didn't look any good to me. I was just so tired.

Dad came into the room, all bustle and noise, holding a screen under his arm as he tried to put a tie around his neck. "Hey, buddy," he said, "you ready for your big day?"

For the life of me I had no idea what they were talking about—what big day? Dad came over and sat down across from me, but he was super distracted, looking around the room, chatting at Mom as she kept on crashing those dishes. I waited for him to tell me what was going on, blinking against the pain between my temples.

"Listen, buddy," he said eventually, still not looking straight at me. "I know you're not happy about this move." He paused, looked at his screen for a long time before going on. "But it's for the best, I promise. You'll make new friends there, get a great education, make it into a top college. In the end you're going to love it, I know. Your mom and I both know it." He looked over at Mom, passing the buck on whatever he was talking about.

"We just want what's best for you, Benny," Mom said, finally turning around and looking at Dad, all smiles. He nodded at her, curtly, and then he stood up and they both walked out of the room together.

The pain in my chest finally synchronized with my head—my heartbeat felt like it was pulsing something evil into my body. Mom called out from the other room, "Wake up, Ben. Wake up!"

"Mom?" I called. "I'm up, remember? I'm right here in the kitchen eating breakfast."

A knock at the door interrupted me, fast and insistent. At first, I ignored it—Dad would have work meetings here at all hours of the day, and no way my friends were here this early—but nobody went to answer, and the knock just kept coming, louder and louder. Where were my parents? Getting ready to go? But where were we going?

I stood up, my head swimming, and went for the door. The floor felt uneven under my feet and I wondered if I might be able to just go back to bed. The closer I got the louder the knocking became; by the time I grabbed the handle it felt like it was filling my brain, offbeat bumps fighting against the thrum of my heartbeat.

I opened the door and, mercifully, all the pounding stopped. I had expected to see one of Dad's employees on the porch, talking on one screen while tapping at another, doing three things at once as always. Instead, it was a girl.

"Ben," she said. "We don't have much time. Come on."

She was a couple of inches shorter than me, slight build, graceful looking. Her hair was pulled together in tight braids, and she was wearing some ridiculous orange jumpsuit. She looked familiar to me, somehow, and I blinked against the sunlight as I tried in vain to place her. It was weird—I didn't have all that many Black friends, but I could have sworn I knew her.

"You know my name?" I said, trying to smile at her despite the confusion. This girl just seemed so put together, so cool. Even if I was sure she was in the wrong place, it was nice to talk to her.

"Ben! We don't have time for this shit. Wake up!"

All of a sudden my head hurt like all hell again. I caught my breath and stumbled forward. She put her hands against my chest, not shoving me, but only to keep me from falling down. Her touch throbbed straight through to my pulse, kicked up the pain in my heart, too. I was sure that any moment now I would burst into tears in front of this strange, wonderful girl.

"What is going on?" I asked as the light began to flicker. The sun? No, it was night now, and the streetlights were blinking on and off. "What do you want from me?" I looked up at her and she rolled her eyes.

"BEN!" the wonderful girl screamed at me. "WAKE THE FUCK UP!"

I stared at her, suddenly afraid. Then, out of nowhere, a question came to mind. "What is jazz?" I asked her in a whisper. But before she could answer, in a rush, the whole scene burst apart before my eyes, shattering like the glass of a broken mirror.

I dropped to my knees, screaming.

———————————

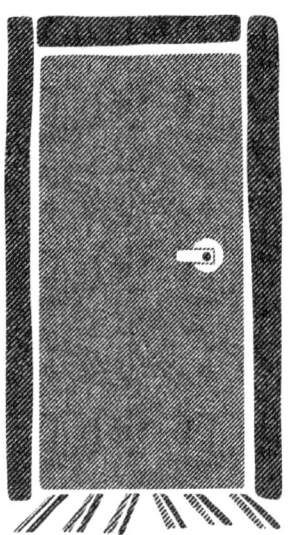

CHAPTER 18
THE INFIRMARY

I woke up on my back, lying on some kind of stretcher, staring straight into a bright light on the ceiling and sweating through my shirt. My chest hurt like hell, waves of pain radiating out from a spot just north of my heart. I groaned and tried to sit up, but my head started spinning so bad I immediately thought better of it and laid back down. On my left was a wall; after a minute I reached out my hand and pushed against it, used the resistance to roll over and face the room.

It was only then that I saw the Associate, standing quietly near the door, watching me.

He wasn't all that close, but I flinched purely by reflex, sending more pain coursing through my body. Suddenly the Associate wasn't the most important thing in the room, and I curled up, grabbing my knees into my chest. I had finally slowed my breathing down, closing my eyes and concentrating on my body, when I managed to remember—Williams's room, the Code Red, green trees and hands up don't shoot. I received a wicked Infraction, and I must be wherever it is they take the people who get tased in the middle of class here at 231.

"Ben, come on," the Associate said, "you going to talk to me, or what? They went to a lot of trouble to set up this little meet and greet. It would be a shame to waste the whole thing with you just lying around moaning, you know?"

My eyes shot open. I looked over at the Associate—he was the only other person in this tiny little room—and only then did I notice his face peeking out from under his helmet. Or, rather, I should say *her face*. Because, of course, somehow in the midst of all this craziness, it was Jazz standing there wearing that uniform.

She must have seen recognition in my eyes, because she smiled. "There it is. Hey, Ben. We need to talk."

She came close to me, pulled up a chair and sat down. She was wearing the uniform to the limit, all the tactical gear and the helmet and everything. The gasmask swung around wildly until she took the helmet off, and I noticed that she had pulled her hair together into a couple of afro puffs that at this point were decidedly squashed. I gaped at her and she gave a little flourish with her hand

"I know, I know, you're thinking, *she's a little short for a stormtrooper.* It was the best we could do on short notice." She put the helmet down on the ground, used it as a prop for her feet, leaned forward toward me.

My brain still felt dizzy, both with pain as well as the utter strangeness of this situation. It felt like I had gone from one crazy dream into another. "But how…" I started. I couldn't even finish; there were too many questions to pluck just one out of the swarm.

"We don't have a ton of time," she said, "so you're not going to get all your answers right now. You're just going to have to trust me." She glanced over her shoulder at the door, and only then did I notice a faint, sickly green light wavering from underneath it. She turned back to me and asked, "First, are you in, or are you out?"

I swallowed hard against a suddenly dry throat. "In or out of what?"

She shook her head. "Nuh-uh. You know enough to answer the question. I'll walk away right now if you say so, no hard feelings even with all this waste of time. Just tell me: are you in or are you out?"

I didn't hesitate again. Looking into her eyes, searching for something like courage, I said, "In. I am most definitely in."

"Good," she smiled. "I totally lied, I would have been really pissed off if you had been out." She checked her comm—standard Associate issue—and nodded. "I thought you were never going to understand *yellow wood* and Malcolm X. Shit, Ben, why do you think I recited you that poem? You almost dropped that ball right from the jump."

I was just a breath away from defending myself, telling her all about the misunderstanding, when all of a sudden I realized what we were doing—we were sitting inside of 231 and having a completely normal conversation, speaking unguarded words out loud. I panicked, choked on a protestation as my eyes skittered around the room, searching for the Globe. What the hell was Jazz thinking? I looked back at her in fear only to see that grin on her face get somehow larger. She laughed.

"Relax, Ben, relax," she said, still smiling. Just as she had done in In-School, she was leaning back in the chair, looking like she didn't have a care in the world. "We're in the infirmary. One of the few places at 231 that just so happens to be completely absent of Globes. Medical privacy and all, you understand. The lawyers ironed it out years ago."

No Globes? I searched the ceiling to see that it was true, and felt a certain kind of way when I realized she was right. For the first time in my entire stint here at 231, I was having a conversation in a room with another human being without being monitored. Curiouser and curiouser.

"So, like I told you," Jazz said, "we don't have a lot of time and can't get into everything right now. I'll just give you the highlights." She paused, waiting for me, and I nodded. "First off, sorry about the tasing. There are other places we can meet, later, but this was the easiest one we could bring you into. The plan got all screwed up after that fight with Colin, when they locked me up in solitary."

"The uniform?" I asked, pointing at her get-up.

"Part of the contraband Admin has been missing this past month."

"And you're, what, supposed to be on guard duty right now or something?"

"Yes, and that's our time crunch. We're on a tight clock or they'll notice I'm not at the door, send someone to look for me."

"The green light…" I said, remembering that blank hallway in the Z.A.'s office the other night. "You've got one of those snapbacks?"

She looked at me sideways. "Snapback, huh? I didn't even know y'all knew about these things over on your side of the chain link." She stopped herself, shook her head. "They clicked one onto you and Randall the other night, didn't they? They don't normally use them for Guests, but I should have realized it when he got all beat to hell and wouldn't tell Orion why."

"Nobody we talked to—nobody on our side—had ever seen that light before. It can't be all that common, right? Only a couple of folks had ever even heard a rumor about it."

"Well, we've got several in our possession right now," she smiled. "But anyways, yeah, we've got a few minutes free in here while the Globe out there covers for us. They actually call them 'rollers,' but I kind of like snapback." She nodded and gestured out toward the door and the hallway beyond. "It was the first thing we stole. Nothing else we have planned was going to fly without a way to cover our tracks."

"How do they work?" I asked. Again, so many questions, but this one had been burning in my mind since I watched them jump Randall under the gym.

She pulled the strange little triangle out of her pocket. "One twist of the top and it grabs any Globe in camera range and wipes it to zero. Meaning, it skims the Algorithm to take an overview of a typical view from that Globe at that timestamp, drawn from footage stretching back over the past year. Then it chooses the most common view and overrides the current picture. So, right now, it thinks there are a pair of guards posted up outside the door to the infirmary. Because more than half the time there are, in fact, a pair of guards posted up outside the door to the infirmary."

"And so the night they jumped Randall they could make the hallway look empty, because it was so close to lights dim and the most common view would have been an empty hall?"

She put the snapback into her pocket again. "Yep. It gives you five, ten or fifteen minutes, depending on how many times you click it, and it's completely untraceable. Whoever designed them ensured that they'd be dark even from the Algorithm itself. That way they have plausible deniability when they need to beat some Peek senseless for whatever bullshit reason they invent."

"Do all the Associates have one?"

She snorted. "Nah. Only a few. Most of them don't even know they exist. Same with Admin—they have to be up past a certain level to have even heard of it."

I remembered the Z.A. that night. "Yeah, the Z.A. on our Block told me it was just a glitch in the Algorithm, that it was 'pruning' itself or something."

"Shit, Ben!" Jazz exclaimed, crashing her feet off her helmet to the ground. "You told Admin about Randall? Why the hell would he let you do that?"

"He told me not to," I replied, averting my eyes. "I didn't listen to him." I'd thought a lot about how poorly I'd handled this, been over it with Randall several times. Reliving it with Jazz was not helping me feel any better.

Jazz was looking off into the distance, obviously thinking about something. "I don't know if that changes anything. We probably still would have brought you in. But I wish you hadn't done it. That was fucking stupid." Somehow being admonished by Jazz was the worst thing that had happened to me today, and that included being tased.

I tried to change the subject, embarrassed. "So what's the deal with Mason? Is he in charge of this whole thing or what?"

She shook her head. "All you need to know right now is that Mason is in. Just like you."

A thought occurred to me. "Would you have brought me in if I hadn't seen you and him talking that day during the Code Red?"

Jazz barked her little laugh. Up close like this it was somehow infectious, and it made me smile. I didn't even know what was funny, but I couldn't help myself. "Ben," she said, "did you ever think that I was the one who was watching you that day? That you saw exactly what I wanted you to see?"

I thought back to that moment, cramped under the desk, staring at her and Mason communicating, hidden in plain sight. I shook my head and laughed, a real belly laugh that made my chest hurt. "Jazz, nothing would surprise me at this point." I waved my hands around the room and added, "This whole thing is so crazy. Sitting here with you, wearing this?" I pointed at her uniform and trailed off. A goofy grin stayed on my face even after my laugh died away.

"So," I said, shaking my face back to normal, "what is the point of all this? What is it that's actually happening?"

She shook her head again. "Not right now. Even if we had the time, they're not going to let you out of here without a good talking to, and the less you know the better."

I caught my breath, sending another spike of pain through to my eyes. I hadn't thought of what they might do to me, of the questions they would ask.

Jazz put her hand on my arm. "Listen, Ben," she said, "they can't inspect you without probable cause, and they don't have it. But they can ask you a bunch of questions and annoy the hell out of you." She paused a moment and all I could feel was the pressure of her hand. "We wouldn't have brought you in this far if we didn't think you could handle it. Just tell them that you were trying to prove to some Black kid that the Associates would treat you the same way they get treated. That the kid said this place is racist and you said it isn't. Admin will eat that shit up, you acting like this place is some model of fair treatment."

This place was nothing like fair. I may not have known that before, but I finally understood. I took a deep breath and started to reply, but then the door opened. Startled, I turned to look, only to see an Associate in the doorway. Not just any Associate, though—it was Derek, the one who had tased me only a few hours earlier.

For just a moment I panicked, froze in place, certain this entire plan had gone up in smoke before I even knew exactly what it was. Then, suddenly, I jumped up, went for Derek with my fists out, hammering at him in payback for me, for Randall, for Jazz. Every indignity I had witnessed here at 231 came out in a flurry of violence that I took out on this one Associate.

At least, that's what I had hoped would happen when I leapt to my feet. Instead, I took just one step forward and crumpled to the ground, my head swimming. All my noble intentions lay down there with me, on the floor, only so much noise. I did my best to curl into a ball, trying to prepare for the blows that I was sure were coming.

Instead, I heard laughter.

I looked up, cautiously, to see Jazz leaning against the wall for support, seemingly laughing so hard that she would fall over without it. Derek clicked the door shut behind him and took off his helmet; he, too, was grinning as he strode over to me and held out a hand.

"Hello, Ben," he said. "My name is Agent Derek McKenzie. Let me help you back to bed."

I groaned and rolled my eyes. "More secrets?" I said to Jazz.

She pulled herself together, wiped tears away from her eyes. Whether they were real or not I couldn't tell. "Ben, what were you going to do? Were you trying to go after this grown-ass man? With those wobbly knees?"

For just a second I was super embarrassed, but then I realized how ridiculous I must have looked, lurching up from my infirmary cot in order to take on an Associate. Who did I think I was kidding? I smiled and shrugged. "I told you I was all in," I said.

"That's great, but we're out of time," Derek said. "In three minutes the roller will reset and I want to be back in place pretty much now." He turned to me. "I'm guessing you still have questions, but they're going to have to wait."

Jazz stood up, grabbed her helmet, turned to go.

"Jazz?" I said. Derek had already stepped outside, but she turned back. "You've more or less given me who and how. But I need to know—why? Why me?"

She paused a moment before answering, adjusted her helmet. "It's easy, Ben," she said, holding still and looking me in the eye. "We needed a Guest, and that Guest needed to be white. Randall trusts you, Orion trusts Randall, and I trust Orion." She waved around at the infirmary. "Here we are."

Again, for just a second I felt embarrassed. They picked me out just because I was a white Guest? I'd been sitting in here thinking that there was something special about me, that I had drawn Jazz's eye for some reason or another. But really it was just about Randall being willing to vouch for me?

It was almost like Jazz could read my mind. "Hey, Ben," she said, softly. "There's nobody in the world more important to me than Orion. Nobody. Anybody he says is cool with him is cool with me." She paused for just a second and smiled. "I'm glad it's you, though. I always hoped you might be all right."

She was grasping at the gasmask, swinging it back into place, when I said, "Hey, did you know that all that time you were really saying *green trees*? We don't have a word for *woods* and you messed up the color. I had no idea what you were trying to tell me." My feelings were still a little hurt; it felt halfway like I was telling her just to prove something.

She stopped and looked at me, her eyes glimmering, and I could tell that she was about to laugh. "Oh man," she said, "that makes me feel so much better. All this time I just thought you were kind of stupid."

She snapped the gasmask into place, squared up and saluted. "I'll be in touch, Benjamin Walker," she said, her robotic voice alien to me now. "And next time we're together let's invent a signal for *woods*."

She left the room and shut the door. It clicked and whirred, and I was alone, stuck in a space that was little more than a stretcher bolted to the wall. For the first time since I arrived at 231, though, I felt free from the looming presence of the Globes. It was intoxicating.

Less than ten minutes later, in walked the Head.

———————————

CHAPTER 19

ON THE INSIDE

In the end, Jazz was totally right about the interview. I was back in the common room just in time to catch the News.

The Head came in alone to talk to me. He left the door open, and I could see a couple of Associates milling around out in the hallway, but they weren't close enough to even be in microphone range. He walked in, one hand in his pocket, the other carrying a clipboard. He came close to my stretcher and sat down in the chair that only recently had been Jazz's seat. The contrast was funny enough that I had to work not to laugh at him.

"Benjamin Walker," he said, almost like it was a question. I nodded even though he wasn't looking at me. "Would you care to explain the...events...that took place in Mr. Williams's classroom this morning?" He pulled a pen out of his front shirt pocket and clicked it loudly, made a short note on his clipboard and paused, waiting. He still hadn't looked at me.

I took a deep breath and launched into the story I'd cooked up after Jazz left.

Yes sir, you see, it's like this. The other night at Recks a couple of kids from another Block started complaining about how unfairly certain kids were treated here. From the way they were talking I just knew they were talking about race, white kids versus Black kids, and I called them out on it. We got into a long discussion about how things went down here, nothing acrimonious, no big deal or anything, but afterwards I decided to show them the truth. They said that no white student would ever get treated the way Jazz did, and I knew that I had to prove them wrong. So, I decided that I would give a demonstration to show how disobedience was disobedience, whatever the student might look like.

It was bullshit from get to go, and it stuck in my throat to say it out loud. I had been with Randall that night underneath the gym; I knew how things really went around here. But Jazz was totally right. The Head ate it up.

"And when was this…conversation?" he asked, finally raising his eyes to me. He had taken assiduous notes throughout my story, his pen scratching almost nonstop.

"A couple of weeks back, maybe?" I said, deliberately vague. "I can't quite remember. It was sometime after the Testing for sure." I had a night at Recks in mind, one where we had argued basketball with kids from another Block for quite some time. I was hoping they wouldn't go searching for video, of course, but better safe than sorry.

"Yes, of course. And why did you wait so long to…perform your experiment?"

Shit. For some reason I hadn't anticipated him asking this question. "Oh, yeah, well…I mean, I guess I just chickened out at first. You know, I was afraid? Of doing the wrong thing even if it was the right thing?" I hoped that my evident reluctance to answer would come off as shy and not evasive.

The Head smiled—with his mouth but without his eyes. The effect was less than reassuring. "That makes perfect sense, Mr. Walker," he said. Then he wrote on his pad for a couple more minutes in complete silence. I was starting to get anxious before he finally looked back up at me. "I have spoken to your father, Mr. Walker." He paused a moment, probably to see what this news would do to me. I managed to stay stone faced. "I wonder if you could predict his reaction to your... creative act of obedience?"

I had no idea what my dad would say, but I knew how he would feel: frustrated that he had to deal with me; angry that I couldn't just stay off his radar like my older siblings. It was easy enough to answer here with complete honesty: "I don't know, sir. I know he wouldn't be happy."

"He was not happy. You are correct about that." The Head stood up and snapped his fingers, the two Associates jumping to attention from the hallway. "You will stay here for the evening, Mr. Walker. For observation, you understand. Please be assured that, as much as Admin appreciates your efforts to demonstrate racial equality within the walls of our beloved institution, we have the situation well in hand. Meaning, do not take lightly any Infractions subsequent to this one. A single blemish on your record, like today? That is easy enough for us to expunge."

He had been moving out the door, doing a little dance of exchanging places with the Associates in this tiny room, but here he paused and turned around, looked directly at me. "An additional Infraction, Mr. Walker, will be far more difficult for your father to handle. I'm sure you are aware of how delicate that situation could become for your family." He kept his gaze upon me until I nodded, confirming that I understood. My dad had pulled some strings for me, but he wasn't going to be able to do it again.

The Head turned on his heels and left.

———————————

An evening alone in that tiny room was no punishment. For a couple of hours I got to sit and think, replay the scene with Jazz in my mind on a loop. It felt like no time before they brought me dinner—I had missed lunch and was absolutely starving—and pretty quick after that they came to take me back to the dorm. I was shocked to realize that it had been hours since Jazz left. I had done nothing but think about our conversation, and yet the time had flown by so fast.

The common room went dead silent when the Associates walked me in. One second everyone was doing homework, playing around, talking and laughing. The next second was like a switch got flipped.

The Associates had entered before me, posted up on either side of the door, so after I came in there was a bit of a show with them leaving. They made a point to stare around the room as I stood there awkwardly, unsure of whether I was free to sit or not. Finally, one of them turned to leave while the other stepped up into my space. I took a couple of steps back until I hit the wall, but he kept coming. His helmet was inches from my face when he finally spoke.

"Remember what the Head said, Ben." He spoke this at full volume, theater for the dead silence in the room, but then his metallic voice modulated to a whisper; it was like listening to music through broken headphones. "When he gives advice, it is best to treat it as wisdom. There is no choice being offered to you here, Ben. No chance to frolic in the yellow wood or the green trees."

I tensed up for just a second, then realized who it was. Derek. Of course. It was all I could do not to laugh at how ridiculous this moment felt—here I was, taking advice from an undercover Associate who had, hours before, tased me for an Infraction. No reason to give the Algorithm anything to look at, though, so I just nodded and replied, "Yes, sir. I'll be careful to remember everything about my interview in the infirmary."

I hoped that made him smile behind his mask.

The moment Derek shut the door behind him, the common room erupted into a restrained explosion of questions. Where have you been? What did the Head say to you? Did you get inspected? How do you feel? Is there a scar on your chest? Are you in trouble? They were all moving chairs and cushions around, getting ready for the News to begin, and, of course, they were trying to play it cool for the Algorithm. But it was just question after question, overlapping and unending. I would barely get into one answer before another question began; then someone would return to the first because they felt I hadn't answered it properly. Most of the conversation I could more or less address truthfully, but one question kept coming up, over and over, forcing me to maintain the lie I had told the Head.

Why did you do it, Ben? Why?

I got a reprieve when the News came on. Sitting there staring at Dan and Donna gave me some space to work on my story, trying to make it believable enough for most of the Block to give it a pass. I knew my best friends weren't going to believe me, they would know it had something to do with Jazz and Mason, but hopefully they could keep their mouths shut until we had a chance to talk without the others around. I had no idea what I was going to tell them—some version of the truth, for sure. But I wasn't sure who I could bring in on the whole thing.

Another excellent day here for our City! Productivity is up, the stock market is booming, and the economy is humming along. Let's go to a story about a neighborhood watch group which is keeping their streets safe with armed patrols that double as book clubs...

It occurred to me that I had no idea how Jazz would contact me next. I took Derek's words to mean that I would not be taking an intentional Infraction anytime soon, that another infirmary meeting was off the table for the time being. I knew that with the snapback Jazz would be able to arrange another conversation, but I wish she had told me something before she left. Instead, it sort of felt like yesterday morning again—just watching and waiting.

At least now I knew that I was in. That was something I could hold onto.

Grim news coming out of our Federal Education Sites. Students continuing to run afoul of the rules. Terrorists in our midst. The Drone program threatened by a lack of law and order. Let's take a look at one school, 231, right here in the City, and see if there is any hope for its students to come out from under the thumb of chaos.

It was a trash take. My name wasn't specifically mentioned, though Dan did say that Jazz had potentially corrupted several Guests and that investigations were ongoing. They showed pictures of Jazz and Orion, the word "terrorist" labeled right up under their faces in giant block font. An interview with the G.A. who had walked me down to In-School was full of double-talk about the tremendous gains demonstrated on the recent Testing, coupled with complaints about the quality of the Peeks that the City kept sending to 231. Dan seemed ecstatic.

"Well, that's our City News for tonight," Donna said.

"Keep in mind, City, that it is our solemn duty to eliminate the darkness," Dan added.

"—but never forget to praise the progress of lights," Donna finished, with a smile.

On the way to bed Randall flashed me a signal. *That story you told was bullshit, right?* I nodded and signed back, *later.* Kiki was watching us, tapped her temple lightly and pointed at me. I cut my eyes over to Madison and Carlos and back to Kiki, then signaled, *no more, tell them, okay?* She nodded back.

I tried to read before lights dim but I couldn't focus at all. I kept picturing myself in the infirmary, sitting with Jazz, talking. Somehow, despite the utter strangeness of the circumstances, it was the only unmonitored conversation I'd had with a girl in something like two years. It may have only been about some undercover plan that I knew basically nothing about, but at the same time it was just so normal. I was in. I was in with Jazz and it felt good.

I rolled over and saw Liam staring at me from the top of his bunk. *No sleep?* he signaled. His signs were sloppy but I could at least understand them. I couldn't help but feel proud of his progress.

I can't fall asleep on a normal night. No way it would happen tonight. You?

He paused a minute. I couldn't quite see his face, shrouded in the shadows, and for just a moment I wondered if he had dozed off. Then his hands started moving again. *You saw Jazz. You talked Jazz.*

I froze. I wasn't planning on telling Liam—not out of disrespect, but only because I figured the fewer people who knew the truth, the better. I debated answers and finally went with, *what do you mean?* I figured maybe I could stall for time.

Jazz. You saw Jazz at sick room. Shit. Well, there's one more person who knows, nothing to do about that now.

Yeah, I saw Jazz at the infirmary. She wanted to talk and she thought that was the safest way.

A whisper cut across the silence between us. "Two roads diverged in a yellow wood."

Yes, I signaled back. *I'll tell you more later.*

A long minute went by with no motion, no noise. Then his hands suddenly rose to life for just one more phrase: *hands up don't shoot.*

Hands up don't shoot. I thought for a moment and then added, *except sometimes, when they shoot anyway.*

It was three days later before I could talk to Kiki, Maddy, and Carlos.

They had all huddled around me at breakfast the morning after the Infraction, but there was no chance I was going to risk this story with all of Admin's eyes on me—and it was obvious that I had been placed on some sort of watchlist. No one was posted up in microphone range, but it felt like every two minutes or so either an Associate or a Drone came down the aisle by my seat. Clearly, Admin was hoping to catch me saying something untoward. Damned if I was going to oblige by being their bait, though. They weren't going to find me talking about yesterday.

Similarly, I kept my eyes to myself. It took all my effort, but I managed to go the entire meal without looking over at Jazz and Orion more than once or twice. It was impossible to think that Jazz would do something foolhardy like try to talk to me today; it would have been stupid to even so much as consider the coffee station. Keeping my eyes off of her was the least I could do.

"Common room," I had said, the moment I sat down, before anybody could even ask a question. Then I changed the subject to our Nation projects and our *Frankenstein* papers. But that night we got to the common room at a time when it was usually dead, and David was sitting in the corner studying.

"Well, well," he smiled at us in an airless kind of way. "Look who's here. Hoping for a little private convo, Ben? Want to tell all your friends about what it feels like to get an Infraction?"

I was disappointed but wasn't going to give him the satisfaction. "Nice to see you, too, David. Just trying to find a quiet place to study."

It wasn't at all what I was hoping for, but that night was the first time I'd done any real homework in weeks.

I had already told Randall an abbreviated version of the story in the Meeting, of course, using our hand signs. He was the only one who understood enough to follow, though Kiki kept her eyes on my hands the entire time, trying to suss it all out.

I didn't know you and Orion were cool like that, I signaled at the end. *Jazz said she brought me in just because he vouched for you.*

Randall shrugged. *It's just,* he started but then he paused. *Don't take this the wrong way. Ben. It's just a Black thing. You wouldn't understand.*

He could have punched me in the stomach and it would have felt better. What the hell?

Ben, he signed, you're my boy. *Don't you ever doubt it. But, it's like… you wouldn't understand what it's like. Especially here.*

I summoned some maturity and signaled back, *No, I hear you. No worries.* It was a lie though. For the first time I was glad that it was nearly impossible to read tone from our hand signals.

Randall went on. *Did I ever tell you what Orion is in here for? Here in jail altogether I mean? How he got to the Peek side?*

My curiosity was up. I didn't know what anyone was in for here. Those were secrets tightly kept; I had no idea how Randall knew. *No, what?*

Then what felt like an intrusion from the stage: "Now stand for the Pledge of Allegiance."

We stood up automatically. Randall rolled his eyes and signed, *tell you later, for sure.*

Ok, yeah, I signed back. Then it hit me that we made it through the entire Meeting and my name hadn't been mentioned. I had been bracing for it—after they brought Jazz and Orion back to the display, I assumed that at least some sideways mention of my Infraction would make it to agenda. But there was no word at all. I wondered if the rest of the school even knew about it.

Maybe there was something to what Randall was saying; maybe there were things about being Black in this place that I just didn't understand.

———————————

"So this girl went and stole a fucking Associate uniform?!" Kiki exclaimed, her eyes shining as she slapped the table to underscore her words. She was rocking back and forth with laughter the whole story, interrupting for clarifications at every turn.

I laughed along with her. It felt like magic, what Jazz had done. "Yeah. I don't know how. But she did it."

After dinner that third night we finally got into the common room alone. Liam and Randall were playing basketball—they both wanted to be here for this conversation, but I knew it would look way too suspicious if they skipped the game at this point in the year. What passed for our end of year tournament was coming up, and the Algorithm definitely would have had questions. I asked Randall to fill Liam in as best he could tomorrow in the cafeteria; the Drones were still stalking me, but they could easily sit apart from the rest of us with their raisins and pretend to be talking strategy.

"But did she really say she was short for a stormtrooper?" Carlos asked. "You're not doing that thing where you tell the story the way you wish it would've happened, are you? You can't lie about a clutch line like that!"

Madison rolled her eyes and shoved Carlos backwards in his chair. "Carlos, focus on the important stuff. Nobody cares about who made up some stupid Star Wars joke." I looked over her head, nodded at Carlos and gave him a big thumbs up, but then Maddy turned around and shoved me, too. "Ben! But what comes next? What did she bring you 'in' to do? What is going on?"

I sighed. I had been going over and over this question for the last three days, to no avail. I had no imagination for what Jazz might be doing. "I don't know," I admitted. "We ran out of time and the snapback was wearing off or whatever."

Kiki cut in. "I don't understand how she managed to get herself put on guard duty that day, though. That seems dumb risky to me. Did she say anything about that?"

I hadn't told anyone about Derek, not even Randall. It wasn't like I had any particular reason or anything. At first, in hand signs, it didn't seem all that essential, but then the more I thought about it the more it seemed that maybe him being anonymous might be a good thing for the whole plan. Whatever the plan happened to be. I had an answer rehearsed already for this eventuality, though—I knew that folks were going to catch that detail.

"She told me there were people on the inside, undercover Associates or something like that. That's all she would say, and I had so many questions I didn't try to follow up." It was a believable answer because it was all true—it just left out a couple of key details. Fortunately for me, the three of them didn't seem to think twice about it.

"And you think it was your dad that got you out of there so quick?" Carlos asked, and I winced. I was embarrassed by my father's ability to pull strings from the outside, the way he could reach even inside this place. It felt like a superpower I didn't ask for and wasn't in control of, coming from a place of uncertain affection. To top it off, I had no idea what he was going to ask in return some day for all of this help.

"Yeah," I nodded. I took a breath, trying to think of what else to say, but Maddy was quick to change the subject for me.

"Undercover agents?" she asked. "You have got to be kidding. It's like you switched from Star Wars to some totally different movie!"

"No way! What about Lando in Jabba's palace?" Carlos said, but one look from Maddy shut him up quick.

"Think about it, though," Kiki said. "How else are they going to steal any of this shit in the first place without some kind of help, right?"

"Right," I said. "Jazz told me the first thing they took was a snap-back. There's no way they could have done that without a lot of luck or a lot of help."

"Probably both," Carlos said. He was fidgeting with a pen and paper, drawing patterns. He said it helped him think. "So I guess now we just sit around and wait? Cross our fingers and hope that something really amazing comes of all this?"

Kiki grinned. "It'll be amazing. Anyone who could steal a uniform off one of those clowns and make a stormtrooper joke about it? She won't let us down."

"Star Wars!" Maddy groaned. She scribbled something on a piece of paper, crumpled it up and threw it at my face. I smoothed out the page to see what she had written: *All of you should read more books.*

I mouthed back, big and exaggerated, *Like Lord of the Rings?*

Maddy lay her head down on the desk and began mock snoring. The door opened and the others started filing in for the News. Our conversation was over.

CHAPTER 20

VISITATION

"Incorrect again, Mr. Walker. I am saddened to see that your little brush with authority has failed to motivate you and your anemic study habits. You seem as lost as ever."

We were in Williams's class a couple of days later. I had been working triple time to catch up on all my work in Nation, but I stayed confused by the crazy way the big powers had divided up land after the War for Central Europe. It was something like dozens of countries that merged and dozens more that split, and everyone else seemed to be signing new economic agreements or double-crossing each other or both. The Great Russian Treaty had way too many sections; I just wasn't able to keep all of them straight. Williams had cold called me to list off four major geopolitical ramifications of the treaty, but I had gotten bogged down halfway through the third, trailing off in a hopeless muddle.

He had stood up and snatched my screen away, began to walk

around the room as he furiously tapped and swiped. I watched the display up front swirl together into a bewildering collage of images. Maps were jammed right up next to photos of world leaders; quotes were dropped over ancient newspaper headlines. It was impressive, dizzying, and completely unhelpful. "What you fail to grasp, Mr. Walker," Williams said, clearly relishing the moment, "is that the current prosperity enjoyed by our Nation is a direct result of the way that we exited this war. Without this treaty, so presciently signed by President Brashears, we would still be struggling to keep the lights on, so to speak."

I know I wasn't alone in taking a quick glance around the room. This ugly little place was supposed to be our prosperity? It was all I could do not to laugh. Biting my tongue, I managed to keep my eyes away from even a glance at the Globe. No reason to give the Algorithm any more reason to keep tabs on me.

For a moment it seemed like Williams was going to go unchallenged. But then, for what felt like the first time in forever, Jazz spoke up.

"Prosperity, Mr. Williams?" she said quietly, and everyone put their head on a swivel to look at her. She was in her usual seat, legs hiked up into the desk cross-legged. Her screen was nowhere to be seen; she seemed to be taking notes by hand with a pen and paper. Immediately after she spoke she placed her hands flat on the desk.

I turned back to Williams only to see his face break out into a sick little grin. He had been waiting for this, a chance to go toe-to-toe with Jazz again, make himself feel better about the way she had schooled him in the democracy presentations. Her time at In-School had only delayed what, for him, must have felt inevitable. For just a second before he turned he reminded me vaguely of a wolf sizing up a meal.

"And what else would you call all of this, Ms. Lewis?" He waved his hand around the room, at the cinder block walls, toward the display on the front, pausing for an extra flourish on the Globe overhead. "All of this marvelous technology, gathered together, here in one place?

And all for such a small gathering of teenagers? All in the service of educating young minds? Is this not prosperity? Is this not the greatest moment in the history of our Nation for students such as yourself? Prior to the advent of Federal Sites, Ms. Lewis, what educational hope do you think was available to somebody like you? This room represents nothing but opportunity for you. This room is your best possible path to prosperity."

He was really rolling, strutting around the room, something like screeching by the end. I watched him gesticulating with my screen in his hands, winced whenever he swung around. If he broke it, I would definitely end up paying to replace it. Mercifully, though, he paused and glared at Jazz. "Let's be honest," he added. "This represents your only path to prosperity."

For her part, she had done nothing but train her eyes on him as he roamed the room during his diatribe. I know she was watching him because I had been watching her. Her hands stayed flat on the desk; she was breathing slowly, her face a perfectly neutral mask. When he finished, she smiled, a sweet little-girl grin that was completely incongruous with her orange jumpsuit.

"You're probably right, Mr. Williams," she said evenly. "This probably is my only way out, at this point. And before they built these prisons? I would have been in some regular school, somewhere. Before they needed all these bodies to fill up these jailbird beds, I would have just been the girl at the top of her class in some shitty neighborhood school. But, since they picked me up and put me here?" She looked pointedly over at the Guest side of the room. "Well, now I get to compete against these fine folks. And still be top of the class, ahead of all their sorry asses."

Her hands flashed briefly into motion after she finished. *No disrespect, boys. But y'all got to know how sorry you are.* I heard Randall stifle a laugh next to me. I couldn't keep myself from grinning.

"Ungrateful child," Williams spat. "You go and make a mess of your life on the outside, and here we are offering you a second chance.

As if you deserve such a thing." He flicked at my screen and the mass of images disappeared, replaced by one of those inspirational posters, like the ones that used to cover the walls in elementary school. Half of it was a black and white photo of a skinny guy, scary looking with short, balding hair. The other half was of a light bulb flickering to life in some ancient lab. A name was superimposed across the bottom of the picture—Charles Baudelaire—and a quote across the light bulb:

Do not forget when you hear the progress of lights praised.

I rolled my eyes at the poster—it reminded me of the one of the kitten on the branch with the admonition to *hang in there!* I recognized the quote from the News, of course; Donna said it to us every night as the final word of her sign off. I wasn't sure why Williams was showing it to us—it was corny but whatever—and then Jazz barked out her laugh, seemingly unable to control herself in the quiet classroom. She sputtered a little, maybe about to say something, but finally put her face down on her hands. Her shoulders were shaking still with laughter.

Williams ignored her, turned his back to the Peeks and addressed those of us on the Guest side. "Do not forget the progress of lights, young people. Our Nation is getting better. It is slow. There are many obstacles. But, we are improving. You will leave this place and go on to do great things for society, improvements upon improvements. Until, finally, one day one of you just might figure out what we are going to do with this lot." He shot a thumb over his shoulder. "Do not let them lie to you. Never forget the progress of lights."

He pulled up short and stopped talking, seemingly spent of whatever manic energy had driven this speech. In the meantime, Jazz had managed to stop laughing—though her face was still buried in her hands—and the room was a creepy kind of quiet. Williams took a step in my direction, handed me my screen, went back to his desk. He gave another hard look at Jazz, ensured that he had silenced her adequately, and then sat down. He leaned back and picked up his own screen. Regaining control of the display, he flicked the Baudelaire guy away and replaced him with a battle map of the War for Central Europe—a return to his regularly scheduled lesson plan.

I looked down at my screen. The scary-looking face stared back at me, and all I could hear was Donna's voice in my head: *never forget to praise the progress of lights.* I shuddered and swiped the image away.

"Test next week, students," Williams said, holed up again behind the safety of his desk. "Fifty percent of your grade. I would encourage you to take advantage of this opportunity to live up to the prosperity that has been offered." He looked up and around the room, lazily, then returned to his screen before adding, "Most of the time, in real life, you will find that there are no second chances."

———————————

I was shocked, but not surprised, to see that my dad didn't bother to come to school for Visitation. He had only been to 231 once in the three years I had been a student here, and that had been on my Intake Day. Some time ago I had stopped expecting him to show up altogether.

Still, it was annoying that he wasn't here. I wanted him to see this place for what it was, not for what he and the people in the Mayor's office hoped it would be. When I'm home for our short little breaks, he always talks just like Williams, on and on about the equal opportunities everyone was being offered. The story I told the Head about my "protest"—the one I was going to have to repeat for my dad at some point—was easy to invent. I just imagined what he would say if someone cried foul; he would be quick to deny anything like injustice in the City. I had to believe, though, that if he could just see it with own eyes, if he could really look around, then he might change his tune. But he never showed.

They always held Visitation on a Sunday—it's the only day they don't schedule classes. Admin takes over the gym for the day, fills it with a jumble of tables and chairs broken up into irregular sections depending on how many parents had signed up. This Sunday was just for the Guests; the Peeks were only allowed Visitation twice a year, always on a Sunday when the Guests were home on break. From what I'd heard, it bore little resemblance to ours. On our Visitation days, the Peeks got stuck sitting in the auditorium the entire day, eating bag lunches and doing extra homework. No way Admin was willing to risk letting a Peek walk around and possibly scare parents of the Guests.

I got in line for security twenty minutes before my two o'clock appointment. The queue moved briskly; they were mostly just getting Credentials scanned, with only an occasional retinal read. When I got into the gym they funneled us into a temporary pen, set up with blocky felt walls. For a few minutes I milled around with the others who had drawn my time slot, nobody saying much in this tight space guarded by multiple Associates. Madison was the only other person from my Block; we stood close but didn't say much. At five minutes to two the Globes announced the turnover—*Parents of Federal Education Site 231, it is time for your Visitation to end; we look forward to seeing you here in the future.* A tremendous clatter rang over the walls and into our holding area, chairs and tables scraping over a mishmash of teary goodbyes. We could hear the Guests from the previous session push past us on the other side of the felt wall, headed back into the bowels of the school. I knew from talking to my mom over the years that the parents were having a similar experience on the other side of the gym. The only difference being that they moved across the football field, straight to the parking lot and their cars.

At exactly two o'clock one of the Z.A.s came through the make-shift doorway. "Let's go," he said, gesturing back into the gym. The fifty of us filed out of the pen, making double sure to remain as orderly as possible.

I knew what to expect, of course, but every time it took my breath away. Fifty metal tables set up around the room, cordoned off by fifty zones of tape. Three chairs at every table—only two visitors were allowed at a time, leading to the occasional family squabble—with a sad looking bouquet of fake flowers set upon every top. Each bouquet had one of those plastic holders showing a number. I checked mine again and looked around the room for the sign showing 38.

For a minute or so the gym was a scrum of bodies running around, everyone trying to find their table. Our visitors had all been let out of their area in a similar undifferentiated blob, and until enough of us spread out and reached our designated numbers the room echoed with a chorus of "excuse mes" and "my bads." I managed to catch sight of my mom across the room before I spotted the number—they were in order, sometimes, until suddenly for some reason they weren't—and she pointed toward a table on the edge of the room. On the way to meet her I saw Madison again, sitting at the table with what I knew were her mother and stepfather. She was already crying. For a lot of kids, just sitting down with people from the outside, talking face-to-face—it was enough to trigger a full scale meltdown. I knew from experience that Maddy would be a wreck later tonight; I also knew she wouldn't miss seeing her parents for anything in the world.

My mom was already at the table by the time I made it over. She was sitting alone; I could just about feel my dad's absence from a distance. She had bought me a drink and a snack from the canteen cart while she was waiting—one thing Admin didn't miss was a chance to sell to parents during Visitation. She stood up for a hug, pulled me in for just a little too long. When I felt the tears massing up in the front of my eyes, I pushed her away. I wasn't about to let myself cry, not in here at least. Not today.

"Hey baby," she said, wiping away the tears from her own eyes. She smiled weakly, trying to put on a brave face for me.

"Hey, Mom," I replied. I opened the drink, gulped down a little in an effort to reset the heat I could feel still rising in my face. "Thanks for coming," I added, and without even meaning to I glanced over at the empty chair that should have been my dad's. I quickly looked back at her, but too late. Instantly I knew she had seen.

"He wanted to come, baby," she said, shifting in her seat, looking nervously over my shoulder, almost as if he might show up suddenly in order to justify himself. "There's just so much going on at work right now. The primary is right around the corner, you know? He's working seven days a week sometimes."

"Didn't they just win the last election?" I answered, reflexively. "I thought things were going to be different after that?" I had told myself I wasn't going to get into it with my mom about my dad, but for whatever reason I couldn't help myself. There were just so many words, unbidden, fighting to get out of my mouth. My mom, reliably, changed the subject. Just like always.

"We got a message that said you got second place in the recent Testing? Ben, that's amazing! I'm so proud of you." She quickly corrected herself. "We're so proud of you."

She smiled again, pleading with her eyes, and I softened. Whatever else was going on, she was my mom, and it wasn't her fault that my dad was choosing to be busy on a Sunday during a non-election year. I smiled back at her, took another sip of my drink, opened up my snack and talked.

Just like always, the hour flew by. Several times we were interrupted by the humming whoosh of a Drone passing by; there were at least five of them roaming the aisles, mobile support for the Associates posted up around the room. My mom wasn't used to Drones—she had seen them on the Stream, of course, but they weren't common on the outside just yet—and every time one passed she would stop to watch it, wide-eyed and waiting to resume our conversation after it passed. More than once we were brought low by the sound of somebody in the gym breaking down into sobs and moans. Like a kind of dark magic, this display of emotion would cast a little spell of silence around itself until the student, or, just as often, the parent, got themselves under control. Staying quiet was a loss of our valuable time together, but talking over someone in such a state seemed disrespectful to all of us.

She waited for longer than I expected to bring up my Infraction, and I fed her my story. By now it was a well-polished tale, and I was able to hit all the right notes to guarantee she bought it wholesale. The

Head had already reported it back to my parents, of course—part of whatever deal he had struck with my dad to get me out of custody so quickly. But I knew my mom was going to want to hear it from my own mouth.

On my part, I waited until it was just about time to go before bringing my dad up again.

"Mom," I said, "can you please figure out a way to get Dad into the building next time? I want to talk about this place for real. There's stuff I just don't feel safe putting into a letter and trying to mail home."

My mom looked alarmed, though I didn't know which part made her more uncomfortable—the fact that I was purposefully asking her to confront my father or the realization that 231 might be anything less than perfect.

"Well, baby, you know he wants to be here!" she said, her eyes pleading with me to believe her. "I'll try to talk to him. It's just so busy right now with the primary coming up next year." Another Drone swished by just as the Globes overhead announced the fact that we had only five minutes remaining in Visitation. My mom got quiet, turned her head to watch the Drone hover away, then came back to me. "And your dad says this next election is going to be exciting! That they're really making progress on all the...problems...you mention here about your friends."

For the first time since I could remember I just snapped on my mom. It was partly the way she said *your friends*, as if I only wanted to talk about all the bullshit here out of some personal gain for me. But it was also that word—*progress*. It felt like I was back in class listening to Williams, watching him try to bully Jazz into admiring all this *prosperity*. Like I was sitting in the common room, forced to watch Donna tell me all about how we should be praising the City for all it's done for us.

"Progress?" I replied, getting loud. I couldn't help it. "Mom, what progress? I've been stuck here for three years and the only thing that's ever changed is that now we have cameras and microphones attached to floating robots, instead of just unstable guards." I waved my hand at the departed Drone.

"Well, Ben, I don't know" my mom said, stalling. She looked around nervously, but with the looming end of Visitation the room was rising in volume all on its own. Nobody was watching us. I could tell she was nervous, but I didn't cut in and she just prattled on. "Your dad says that this next election is going to be our real chance to show the other side what we believe in. That every day we're making progress working with—"

"Stop saying that word!" I was almost shouting now, probably past the point where we were going to go unnoticed. I was just so mad, and we only had a couple of minutes anyway. What were they going to do? "Mom! Stop saying that word to me. You have no idea what it's like in this place. You sound so ignorant, going on about 'progress' to me, like that makes any sense at all sitting around this fucking table!" I slapped at the top with the word; my empty bottle toppled and fell, rolling around aimlessly on the floor.

"Ben!" she said, making her whisper as loud as possible. "Please stop with all this!" Her head was whirling around, trying to get a bead on all the nearby Associates and Drones, looking for all the world like just any other student here sizing up the surveillance.

"No, mom, you stop it," I said. I managed to get quieter—remembering that this was 231, after all—but I couldn't stop the anger from saturating my voice. "There's no progress to be had in a place like this. It's not going to get better. The best thing Dad could do for any of the students here is to get us out of here. All of us, out of here. Somewhere new, somewhere built for us. None of this bullshit of doing school in a place built for this." Knowing they probably wouldn't pull footage of me in the crowded gym, I pointed at the Globe.

My mom was close to losing her shit. She wasn't crying or anything; she was way too buttoned-up across the board for something like that. But behind her eyes I could see the panic. "Ben, baby," she said, "just give your dad a chance. He's a good man, the Mayor is a good woman. They can make changes! They can help!"

I was about to go off on my own mother when a Drone hovered up. We had probably one, maybe two minutes left in Visitation, and we were making a scene. The Drone came right up next to our table, swiveling its primary eye back and forth from me to my mom. She caught her breath; she'd never been this close to one before. Watching her sit there and watch the drone, all of my energy completely dissipated, like a balloon deflating in a sudden burst. I settled back into my chair, ashamed of myself for giving my mom such a hard time, swallowing hard to get my vitals down in case it was reading me. After a long moment—soundtracked by the noise of multiple crying families—it floated away.

I looked at my mom, slackened my shoulders, exhausted. "Listen, Mom, I read something recently. It's all I can think about when you talk about the next election. Progress is good, I know. I'm not stupid. But if you've got a knife stuck in your back and someone offers to help? And then they only pull it out halfway? That's not progress. I mean, even pulling it all the way out isn't progress. It's only progress if they pull out the knife and then help you get stitched up. That's all I can I think of when you say *progress*." I looked around at the Drones, the Associates, the Globes. I listened to the crying families, thought about the Peeks all sitting in silence in the auditorium. I remembered Jazz stuck in that cell, Randall getting all hell beat out of him while they made me watch. I turned back to my mom.

"This place, Mom? They're worse than all of that. They won't even admit that there's a knife at all. They're looking at a wicked, bloody knife, stuck into an open wound, and they're pretending it's just the way it has always been. That's how fucked up this place is."

The Globes blared: *Parents of Federal Education Site 231, it is time for your Visitation to end; we look forward to seeing you here in the future.*

All of the students in the room stood up immediately. We were programmed to respond to those Globes when they spoke. The parents followed suit, a little more raggedly, my mom drifting slowly to her feet and pushing back her chair. She was finally crying, tears streaming from the corners of her eyes, streaking her mascara all down her face. She pulled me in for one more hug, buried her head in my shoulder.

Suddenly I remembered that when I started here at 231, she was still a good bit taller than me. I used to be able to give her a hug and lay my head into the crook of her collarbone. Sometimes I would come home from school—real school, the kind where you got to sleep at your own house every night—and at the end of a terrible day I could just let her hold me, wrap her arms around my shoulders and stroke my hair as I cried into her neck. Now, though, I towered over my mother. I must have been four or five inches taller than her.

We had entirely missed the moment together where we were the same height. That was something else this place had taken from me that I would never get back.

"Oh, Benny," she said, sniffling into my shirt. "What on earth is going on with you?"

Her question was the last straw. I burst into tears, and the Associates had to pull me away from her in order to clear the room for the next round of visitors.

CHAPTER 21

INCREASED ATTENTION

I met up with Madison out by canteen, and, for a couple of minutes before walking back to the dorms, we sat together in silence. She bought a bag of chips and we split it, more to have something to fill the quiet than because either of us was actually hungry.

"It's just so far for them to come," she said, eventually. "For only that one hour I mean." Her face was wrecked with tracked tearstains; she was still wiping at her nose and eyes, trying to pull herself back together. On the other hand, I had dried up immediately after I lost sight of my mom. *Later tonight,* I thought. *That's when it'll hit hard again, when I'm alone.*

"Do your parents take the channels? Or the streets?" I asked, trying to run with the conversational kickoff. Traveling through the channels from neighborhood to neighborhood was always the safer option, but it could take forever, especially if there wasn't a direct route. The streets were quick—because they were mostly abandoned—but that made them dangerous. If you were willing to spend enough money, of course, you could hire a guarded car to get where you wanted to go.

"The channels," she said. Then she laughed suddenly, turning her whole face aglow again. "I know we live on the Northern Arc, Ben, but we're not rich, you know. They couldn't afford to hire the right team to drive them here. And my mom would freak out if they tried to drive the streets alone."

I smiled. "Yeah, us neither. I mean, not we're rich, either. My dad can take a street when it's something for his job or whatever. But... yeah."

Getting back to my dad killed the conversation again, and we sat there for a couple of minutes even after the chips were gone, just watching folks come and go. Between the Peeks locked up in the auditorium and most of the Guests doing Visitation, the whole place was kind of dead. Eventually we pulled ourselves together and took off back for the dorms; everyone had planned to meet up there before dinner so we could walk together.

In some sort of unspoken agreement, we decided not to take the tunnel under the gym. With the Visitation area closed off to traffic, of course, it would be a hike to stay on ground level and go around; it might cost us an extra five minutes. But ever since they jumped Randall that night I hated walking under there, avoided it whenever possible. Maddy and I had never really talked about it, but I wasn't surprised at all when we both started taking the long way home.

We walked along in silence until we were almost back to the dorms. Drones drifted in and out of our orbit, Associates and Admin bustled around corners, the Globes hummed softly with their artificial light. Just a normal Sunday stroll at 231. Finally, only a minute or so before we made it to the common room, Maddy spoke.

"Ben, I wonder if you could check my make-up for me?"

I almost stopped walking. What? Check her make-up? I know she cared about how she showed out to Randall, but we both knew that Randall was aware of her deal with Visitation. He was ready for her to be a wreck coming back; he would probably worry more if she came back and acted like everything was okay. What kind of guy did she think he was, worrying about make-up on a day like today? I turned to her, nerves still raw from talking to my mom, probably about to say something stupid and cruel, and then I saw her fingers. Flashing in front of her stomach, over and over, she was signaling pretty much the only thing she knew how to say with her hands: *green trees green trees green trees.* I hit pause on my mouth.

Green trees had become an inadvertent code word with my best friends here on K Block. At first it was just kind of a joke—said as shade when someone wasn't following the thread of a conversation. It evolved, though, into something more, a kind of symbol of solidarity. Maddy and Carlos had learned how to sign it, and soon enough we were flashing it to each other in passing throughout the day. It acted like a lifeline in this place: we exist; there is something more. It was a symbol of hope.

Right now, though, it functioned as a signal that I needed to be cool.

"Sure," I said. "Definitely need to check those tear tracks." We rounded the last corner before our common room, passed the final Globe before the door. A couple more steps and then she stopped as I turned smoothly around to face her. I made a show of looking at her face, pointing at a couple of spots and calling them out loud for the sake of the Algorithm. But what I was really doing was watching her lips. It wasn't the slickest move, but with her back to the Globe we had maybe thirty seconds of freedom before it became too risky.

Fortunately, I was able to read Maddy's lips pretty well by this point, so she could talk fast. *Ben, you have to be careful. They pulled some of us out yesterday, grabbed us when you weren't around and asked us questions. Questions about you. They wanted to know about Orion and Jazz and you, they wanted to know about the stolen equipment. They wanted to know what you had to do with stealing it. Ben, they offered us scholarship money if we knew anything. They tried to bribe us with a way out. You have to be careful. I don't even know for sure who all they talked to—*

The door opened suddenly behind us and Carlos nearly walked right into me. "Ben! Madison!" he called out. "Where have you guys been?"

Maddy flashed the sign one more time—*green trees*—and then turned to Carlos. "We're back! Just had some chips to finish off before dinner, you know?"

The rest of our friends spilled out of the room—Kiki and Liam and Randall bumping up into Carlos, everyone talking and laughing. Randall sobered up quick when he saw Maddy's face, and he fell in line next to her as we headed toward dinner. Their hands brushed a little as they walked; this was as much physical contact as the Algorithm would ever allow them. Kiki was telling Liam and Carlos a story, a loud one that seemed to be killing it with both of them. Everyone was in the zone.

Except for me. I was sick at the thought of Associates pulling my friends aside and trying to get them to snitch on me, offering them money out of here just for secondhand information about Jazz. Apparently, this was standard practice on the other side of the chain link—Randall had heard that Admin offered all kind of bribes the day they marched the Peeks out of the Meeting. As far as anyone knew, though, it had never happened on our side.

Even more terrifying was the wonder of who else they had talked to. Outside of the six of us, I didn't think anybody else on the Block had enough information to be dangerous. But now I couldn't shake the doubt that maybe, in fact, we hadn't been as careful as we thought. What if all this *green trees* stuff had gotten out to someone who didn't have my back?

What if Admin found the right person to bribe, and I ended up ruining whatever Jazz had worked so hard to plan?

A couple of days later, Kiki and I were in the library, studying.

By that point I had managed to get a good idea of what had gone down with Admin's attempted bribe. From my core group of friends, only Liam and Maddy had received an offer. Carlos did some asking around, and he was pretty sure that on the rest of the Block only David, Ellie, and Jon had been approached. In other words, all the white and Asian kids, but none of the Black or Hispanic kids. Randall had shrugged when Carlos gave us the news.

"That's just the way they think," he said. "They know this is all about Jazz, and they know that we know it. So, they're going to try to flip you guys. Because they think we're more likely to be loyal to her." He held up his hands, wiggled his fingers to show me his skin.

Aside from Randall, I trusted Maddy more than pretty much anyone at 231. I was pretty sure that Liam was okay; he had stuck to us like glue ever since that first day, and there'd been no indication that he was anything but on our side. Jon and Ellie had each written me short notes, telling me what had happened and reassuring me that even if they had known something they would have kept it to themselves. I didn't really trust David, but I had no reason to believe that he knew anything at all.

So, at least for the moment, I felt safe.

Kiki coughed and I looked over to see her hands moving over the library table. We were working on our *Frankenstein* papers—big, end-of-year essays due sooner than we hoped—but taking occasional breaks from the writing to do problem sets for math. Kiki was a better writer than me, but she hated math. I didn't mind the problems, though, so we helped each other out, always better together than alone. I had been deep into a paragraph about Victor Frankenstein and his failure to control the technology he had invented, but I stopped on a dime to watch Kiki's hands.

Ben, you so important person here. I so happy to be friend.

Her hand signs were getting much better, but still choppy. I had no idea what she was talking about until she tipped her chin over my shoulder. Turning around, I groaned and hit pause on my work.

Two Associates and a Drone had come into the library, spreading out among the stacks. Ostensibly, they were probably on some sort of patrol, but things like this had been happening to me pretty much nonstop since Visitation. If I was on the sidelines watching basketball during Recks, an Associate would be posted up nearby. If I decided to take a walk over to canteen, a Drone would follow along behind me. Even though I knew Jazz wouldn't try to contact me at the coffee station again, I'd been over there several times—Kiki had pointed out that the Algorithm might notice if I suddenly stopped getting my caffeine, and maybe it would go back and run old Globe footage. Every time I moved in the cafeteria, however, somebody was there with a microphone. Apparently, the same was going to be true here in the library.

I looked across the table at Kiki and she grinned at me and flashed some more sarcastic signals: *me big important friend.* Then she mouthed the words, *probably they just want to read your Frankenstein paper.*

"I hear it's super amazing," she finished out loud with a whisper, and it was all I could do not to laugh.

She went back to her work, but I couldn't keep my eyes off our visitors. The Associates ambled up and down the cramped aisles of books, making what amounted to a lot of noise. The library wasn't all that big, and during free time it was usually pretty dead. There was no way to have a private conversation here, so we only showed up when we needed to get work done. The presence of two armed guards was almost comically intrusive. The Drone, on the other hand, didn't play around at all. It hovered straight over to Kiki and posted up behind her, stayed still save for its revolving primary eye. It was close enough that if I coughed the Admin on the other side of the microphone would be likely to catch a cold.

I wrote a couple more terrible paragraphs, but it was quickly apparent that my time of productivity had come to a crashing halt. Closing my book just a little too loudly, I looked up at Kiki and she nodded at me, started packing up. Not coincidentally, the Associates finished their tour of the stacks at the same time, and they rapidly made their way over to meet up by the Drone. We were halfway to the door before I looked back, expecting them to be following us. However, one of them was tapping away at some control panel on the top of the Drone. It looked like they were stuck with another malfunction.

I smirked, turned back to Kiki, moved my hands to flash her the signals for *dead laughing*. Then I ran smack into Orion.

At least, I realized it was Orion a few seconds after the impact. At first, all that registered with me was a bump and a stumble; I had been twisting sideways to see the busted Drone and wasn't prepared to stop short. My books went flying, my screen smacked on the ground. When I recovered enough to check my surroundings, there was an orange-jumpsuited Peek sprawled out on the floor next to me, thrashing around to get back to his feet. It was only then that I realized I had knocked Orion down.

Yet another Associate was hovering nearby—presumably Orion's guard, as Peeks were only allowed in the library by appointment and under escort. There was no chain link here, but still nothing like the ability for us to be together. The guy didn't seem to be in any hurry to help Orion to his feet, though, so I tried to move in and give him a hand up. The handcuffs were making it difficult for him to rise on his own, but, even still, he brushed me back.

"What the fuck, Ben?!" he snapped, throwing his shoulder away from my hand and glaring up at me. "What can't you look where you're going?"

"My bad, Orion," I said, taken aback. He was really pissed. "I was just watching…" At the last second I stopped myself. No reason to tell the Algorithm I was paying any attention to my unofficial guard and the busted Drone.

Orion lurched to his feet, a difficult proposition with his hands cuffed in front of him. He bucked up into me, getting louder. "*My bad? My bad?* Yeah, Ben, it's definitely your fucking bad!"

I froze completely. Orion was stepping up on me, and I had no idea what to do. I turned to Kiki, but she looked as stricken as I felt. "Orion," I said, trying to smooth things over. "Listen, Orion, I didn't—"

"Fucking Guest!" Orion shouted. "Stop saying my name like you're some kind of hostage negotiator!" Then, in a flash, three things happened that demonstrated my complete lack of control in this entire situation.

First, Orion shoved me—hard, right up against one of the stacks. Several books rattled out of place and fell to the floor; one hit me in the head. At first he grabbed my collar with both hands, using it to keep me pressed against the stack. The chain between his handcuffs was swinging back and forth between our bodies; it hit me in the chest several times. Then he was working his elbows into my ribs, knocking the breath out of me, all the time hollering at me about how I needed to pay attention to what I was doing. The ferocity of the attack was made all the more intense by how unexpected it was.

The second thing that happened was that Orion's guard slammed into the both of us, spilling more books onto the ground. He hit Orion square, like a football tackle, and Orion glanced off of me and into the stack. Then they both tumbled to the floor. Orion put up a bit of a fight, kicking and screaming still, but the Associates who had been watching me were there quick, truncheons out, smashing his legs and back as he thrashed around. He went still at that point, just muttering over and over, "Okay, I'm good, okay, I'm good, okay, I'm good."

The third thing that happened was that when I stood up and straightened my clothes, trying to hold back tears, I found an envelope in the inside pocket of my jacket.

Relief flooded over me, and it was only then that I broke down and started crying. I'm sure Kiki and the rest of the Associates thought that I was hurt or embarrassed or something like that, but I was just so happy that Orion and I were cool. I had thought for sure that he and Jazz were through with me, that I was being pushed out of whatever was going on. Instead, it was just the opposite. They were sending me a message.

The Associates hauled Orion to his feet and dragged him out the door. He watched me the whole time, playing his part to perfection; if you didn't know any better, you'd have thought he had murder in his eyes. Kiki ran over to me, a panicked look on her face, and I thought we should keep the theater going for the Algorithm. I let her worry herself for just a minute.

"Ben, what the fuck?!" she asked, putting her arm around me and leading me out the door. There were only a couple of dozen students left in the library at this point, and they were all staring at the two of us, watching our departure. "I haven't seen Orion that hot since the thing with Colin. What did you do?"

I did my best to look shook up. The further we got from the situation—once my breathing and heartbeat slowed up to normal—the more I realized that I wasn't hurt at all. Orion had shaken me and knocked me around, but none of it had actually stuck. Meaning, I was having a hard time not laughing.

"I don't know, Kiki," I said, trying to keep a quaver in my voice. "I just bumped into him accidentally and he snapped." I turned around to give the library one last look, hoping the Algorithm clocked the worry in my eyes. Then I turned back to Kiki and trudged along beside her, gave a ragged sigh for good measure.

We slow-walked in silence, me leaning against her just a little bit for effect, all the way back to the dorms. Right after she shut the door behind us, though, before she had a chance to say a thing to anybody else in the common room, I squeezed her arm and smiled for our friends. "Green trees, Kiki," I whispered, "green trees. Just be cool." Then I made for the group and started complaining loudly about how little I'd accomplished on my paper.

Kiki was only a beat behind me on the couch. She may not have understood it all, but she didn't say a word about Orion. We'd tell the others later.

CHAPTER 22
THE LETTER

I didn't get to open Orion's envelope until the end of the night. Instead of taking a shower, I stuck my head under the faucet, got my hair good and wet, then jumped right back out. It was an old move here at 231, but it could always buy you five minutes of privacy to sit and read in a room without Globes. I knew folks that did it sometimes just to sit, to get the chance to be alone and still while the shower water ran on down the drain.

For the first time I examined the envelope; it was completely unmarked. I wasn't surprised at this—the hope being that if the delivery had gone wrong, then it would just get tossed out with the trash—but even still I tore it open with a little anxiety. It was crazy to think that it could have been an accident, not after what Orion went through to get it to me, but I was going to be nervous until I knew for sure.

It was a single sheet of paper, unlined, filled front and back with tiny, cramped writing. My eyes went immediately to the end of the letter. Again, I wasn't surprised to see Jazz's name. Nonetheless, relief flooded over me as I quickly began to read.

Hey Ben,

Sorry about the theatrics involved in getting you this. A couple months back I could have just passed it through Mason, like the book, but I think we're past that point now. They're watching us more than they ever have. We've always had Associates in our rooms, at all hours of the day or night, but just recently they've brought in a double shift and a Drone. We never had much freedom, but now they're taking even that away.

The Drones. Ben, this is all about the Drones. I can say more later, but what you need to know right now is that the Drones are more than some new tech that just happens to be rolling out in Federal Sites. There's a reason no one on the outside has seen one in action yet. They're experimental research, Ben, with the emphasis on experimental. And they're dangerous, in ways that aren't obvious. They're designed to run off the grid, completely untethered from the Stream, and that takes a tremendous amount of power. More power than they can store from solar cells and lithium batteries. More power than they can pull at night when they're offline.

Ben, the Drones are nuclear powered. Each and every one of them is a potential bomb just floating around the halls of 231. The City is testing its first wave of nuclear robot tech here at our school. It's not enough that they watch us every minute of our lives. It's not enough that they knock us around for no good reason. They have to add to that. Somewhere in the greedy mashup of Admin and City, someone gave the okay to letting our lives double as an atomic test site. Bombs are watching us.

And it's not going well, Ben. You know it. You're the only Guest who knows it, who's seen the bunker beneath the building, who's seen the Drones laid out in surgery on the table. They are literally playing with nuclear fire underneath our school. Playing with our lives in order to make a fortune selling them after they work out all the bugs. But we're not going to let that happen, Ben.

We stole a Drone.

Someday I'll explain it to you, how we got it. Someday I'll tell you about the agents embedded in this building, the people dedicated to exposing this injustice. This plan is years in the making, you and I late additions. For today, though, just know that we stole the Drone, and someone else deactivated it, and someone else figured out how to hack into it.

We're going to finish this, Ben. We're going to expose this school for what it is—a thin mask stretched over a group of white men trying to make money off of Black bodies. And we need your help.

One week from tonight, after Recks, after you get back to your dorm, you need to come back out. Meet me at 9:15 in the tunnel under the gym. I know that's where Randall was jumped. I know you don't go there anymore. But they won't expect us to be there.

Hopefully Orion provided you some breathing room today. Hopefully they'll decide you don't have anything to do with the missing Drone or the snapbacks or the uniforms. Hopefully you'll be okay for a minute, until the first teams play ball here in a couple of weeks. We'll know soon enough.

Stay away from the gym. Orion and I will be there every night practicing. Go get coffee every day like you've been doing, but don't expect to talk to anyone there. Just try to act normal, like before you got mixed up in all this. You won't hear anything from us again until the tunnel.

You know what to do with this letter.

Green trees, Ben. Green trees.
- Jazz

I read it three times, then turned the shower off. When the water had slowed to a trickle I held Jazz's letter up under the nozzle, moving the paper around and taking on drops until the ink bled and the fragile sheet started to pull apart. Then I sat down and shredded it into long strips, balled them up and ate them one by one. They went down easy.

I took a towel and mopped it around on the floor to make it damp, changed clothes and stepped outside. Dropping the towel into the bin,

I caught Kiki watching me. I nodded at her and mouthed a single word.

Drones.

———————

It took five days to piece together a conversation that covered the events of Jazz's letter, letting my friends in on its contents and the way it was delivered. We had only snatches of time to talk freely in the cafeteria, working around the constant interference of patrolling Drones. At night, Randall and Liam were on the court full time, getting ready for the game. The situation created a lot of backtracking and double looping, catching up with Randall during the Meeting, sending Kiki or Carlos to talk to Liam during breaks on the court.

"Damn, that's slick," Kiki said when I first told her about Orion and the letter. "And I would have gone into the common room all hot if you hadn't given me the green trees."

"I wish they'd let off watching you, though," Randall said, looking around nervously. "Even after Orion, they don't trust you." Just then an Associate came close to our table, slow-walking his way past us, microphone blatantly pointed in our direction.

Liam picked up the thread, filled the space for the Associate's ears. "Can someone help me with my math homework? I was too tired after basketball practice to even glance at it." When the Drone followed right on the heels of the Associate, we gave up and moved on to basketball and math.

Orion was gone for two days after the incident in the library. When he returned, Randall confirmed that he had been put in In-School.

"He said it wasn't so bad, just boring as hell," Randall added. "He was so bored he wrote like five hundred words on his *Frankenstein* paper."

"That place down there is straight out of *Frankenstein*," I said. "Someone should write a paper about that."

Carlos affected Mason's voice, leaned back and peered at us

through invisible lenses. "Compare and contrast the ongoing Drone program with the experiments of Victor Frankenstein. Provide at least three examples, cited in the text." David looked up at us when everybody started laughing, and we cut that conversation short, too.

"So you really think they were doing nuclear work on that table?" Maddy asked the next day during lunch. "In the basement, right under our feet? I mean, that's insane, right?"

Kiki smacked her teeth. "Listen, if Jazz said it, they're doing it. She's got no reason to play with all this."

"I guess," Maddy said. "It just feels, like, how could they do that to a bunch of kids? Testing nukes all over the school? For what? Money?"

"You ever heard of Tuskegee?" Carlos asked.

Kiki and Randall nodded. The rest of us shook our heads.

"I'd tell you to look it up, but they wiped it from the Stream," Carlos said. "Point is, the government's been testing on Black and brown people for centuries. It just feels new to you because, finally, some white people are caught up in the whole mess."

Randall's alarm went off, and we had to start getting ready for the News.

"How are you going to get out of here to meet Jazz?" Carlos asked that night. For the first time since the letter, it was just us in the common room. Three of us, at least—Randall and Liam were in the gym; Maddy was there, too, so that we didn't look too suspicious all clumped up together. Per Jazz's instructions, I hadn't been to the gym in days, but we didn't want to change everyone's schedule all at once.

I sighed. "I don't really know. I guess I could go get my Credentials authorized for something, right?"

"You could do that homework thing again," Maddy said. "Ask the Z.A. to authorize your Credentials so you can go back to the gym and look for something?"

"That won't work," Carlos said. "What if the Z.A. just starts running Globe footage like last time, looking for whatever Ben says is missing? That could be a disaster for Jazz."

"I'm not worried about Jazz," I said. "She definitely knows what she's doing. But, yeah, I don't know what to do on my part. I don't know why Jazz didn't give me any idea about how to get out of here." The common room door burst open and half the dorm walked in at once, talking and sharing snacks. We were done.

The day of my meeting with Jazz was extra busy in Mason's class. We were in the final round of editing our *Frankenstein* papers, sitting in tight circles with our group and passing conclusions around for feedback. Today we'd been all mixed around—too much time with our best friends, Mason said—and I was sitting with Kiki and David from the dorm, in addition to Anthony and Brie from the Peek side. I wondered if Mason was being extra careful to put a lid on the conversation I so desperately wanted with my friends. At least I would get some work done today.

"It's solid, Ben," Brie was saying about my pages. I felt like I had made a pretty good case for what Randall had said during that first class conversation: Victor Frankenstein was kind of a terrible person, a deadbeat creator. He was nobody to feel sorry for. "I like how you really try to consider the story from the monster's point of view."

Kiki nodded. "Ben can write, for sure." She slapped me on the back so hard my desk moved. "When he gets the right person to help, I mean."

David huffed a little. "It's fine, yeah," he said, "but it lacks a certain…authority?"

I glared at him, annoyed. I usually didn't put any stock in what David had to say, but I wanted this paper to be perfect. I felt like I needed to prove to Mason that I deserved to be on the team. "What are you talking about?" I asked, trying to keep my voice level.

He waved his hands at the papers spread out before him. "I mean, it's just so much about responsibility and technology and not enough about what was going on in Europe at the time. That's the ultimate connection that you're missing, to Williams's class and the inevitable war with Russia. And what on earth is this book you quote a couple of times? *The Autobiography of Malcom X*? What is that?"

Kiki, Brie, and Anthony all fidgeted in their seats. It was clear that Jazz's book hadn't only made its rounds around my group of friends—it was also known on the other side of the chain link. I tried to hide a smile.

"Just some book Mason gave me," I replied, not untruthfully. David rolled his eyes.

"Well," he said, "it doesn't make any sense what some American man in prison has to do with Victor Frankenstein." He looked at me and I shrugged. If David didn't see it, that didn't matter to me. "Just my opinion, of course," he added in a voice laced with shade.

I was just about to respond—unwisely, for sure—when Mason walked up behind us. "Ah!" he said, "it seems I have stumbled upon the foundation of education—the spirited discussion." He looked at each of us in turn through the lenses of his glasses. Because he was standing up and we were all seated, he really had to lean back to see us. If it had been anyone else besides Mason, he would have gotten laughed at, looking down at us from such a weird angle. As it was, our whole group lit up under his attention.

"Yes, sir," Anthony said. "We were just talking about Malcolm X. David was wondering what he had to do with *Frankenstein*."

"Ah," Mason said, cutting his eyes, ever so quickly, to Jazz. I followed his gaze, saw her sitting in a group with Maddy and Jon and a couple of Peeks I didn't really know. She was talking rapidly, moving her hands around to make her points. As usual, Maddy was taking assiduous notes. Her paper would probably be better than all of ours.

"Ben," Mason interrupted my thoughts. "I need you to run to the Admin wing. I believe I left a book there when I was eating lunch."

I blinked, tore my eyes away from Maddy and Jazz, stood up. "Sure, Mason, no problem," I said. "What's the book?"

"It's called *The Secret Agent*, by Joseph Conrad. You might remember that he also wrote *Heart of Darkness*."

My whole body tingled at Mason's words. There was no way this was a coincidence—The Secret Agent? Finally, here was a connection back to Mason. I looked up at him, but he was very deliberately not making eye contact, instead merely holding out his hand for my Credentials. I held my wrist out and he made a couple of swipes at his screen.

"I think I left it by the coffee machine," he said, walking away. He turned back and added, "You know how distracting a good cup of coffee can be, right, Ben?" He smiled and strode over to open the door.

I stood up in a daze. Listening to David pontificate about his own paper, glad I didn't have to stay and critique it, I followed Mason. He didn't look at me again as I left, and I turned toward the Admin wing, my thoughts all whirled up. Had Jazz changed our meeting? Was she somehow going to get out of class and meet me right now? It seemed impossible, but so much of the last couple months would have seemed similarly impossible if I'd thought about it ahead of time. And yet, these things happened.

I rounded a corner and almost walked right into a Drone. I skidded left, squeaking up the silent hallway with the sound of my sneakers, and it stopped dead still, rotated its primary eye to face me. I couldn't help but feel a shiver up my spine. It was crazy to think that I was so close to a tiny, experimental nuclear reactor. I instinctively backed up a step.

"Credentials, please, student of 231," it clanged, the robotic sound of its voice harmonizing with the small whirrs given off by whatever allowed it to hover. I'd never been alone with just one of them before; the noise was instantly unsettling. Wriggling my Credentials to loosen them from my wrist, I held my arm out.

The Drone scanned them and immediately its primary eye went red. "Warning, Benjamin," it said, "you are out of area. Please explain your actions, or be prepared to face consequences."

I froze. How could I be out of area? The eye rotated away from me and back while I tripped over a response.

"Um, Mr. Mason sent me to the Admin wing for a book of his? He authorized my Credentials just a few minutes ago. I just left his class?"

I held them out again and the Drone did another scan. Its primary eye stayed red.

"Warning, Benjamin. You are out of area and your explanation has proved insufficient to justify your presence. Please return to your authorized location immediately, or be prepared to face consequences."

I didn't need to be told twice. Spinning around, I hustled back to Mason's room. I could hear the Drone hovering along behind, though once I made it to the main classroom wing it lingered at the intersection, content to merely watch me. I was breathing heavy by the time I knocked on the door, but not from exertion. I felt like somehow tonight's plan had already been messed up, and it wasn't even my fault.

Mason answered the door and gave me a curious look. "Ben?" he said, "did you run the whole way there and back?"

It took us just a minute to clear up the confusion. After hearing my explanation, Mason checked his screen and laughed. "Sorry, Ben! I accidentally post-dated your authorization. That Drone was right—you didn't have any business in the hall at this time of the day." He turned to me, his back to the Globe, and winked. "No business at all. At this time, at least."

It felt like electricity surging through my body. Mason asked Diana to go get his book—"Ben has missed enough class today, I think"—and I sat back down just in time to talk about Brie's paper.

I managed to focus on the work, repay the favor Brie had already done me by helping with my writing. But my thoughts kept skittering away from *Frankenstein* and toward tonight. I had no way to know for sure, and it was going to be an act of faith to prove it, but every time I felt the weight of my Credentials on my wrist I felt certain I had a ticket out of the common room. Mason had authorized me to meet

Jazz in the tunnel, put up the subterfuge of the book for the sake of the Algorithm.

The rest was going to be up to me.

CHAPTER 23
ACTIVE PARTICIPATION

I spent the rest of the evening playing a brutal game of waiting. Now that the burden of getting out of the common room seemed to be lifted, I was free to imagine what Jazz might say to me under the gym, what the next phase of the plan could be. I have no idea what we did in science class later that afternoon; I couldn't tell you what we ate for dinner. Kiki and I wandered around during Recks and talked about Mason and the Credentials the entire time, me telling her the story in fits and starts—using hand signs and words—whenever we found enough cover to communicate. Canteen was boring; the News nothing but babble. All I could think about was meeting up in that tunnel.

"*Well, that's our City News for tonight,*" Donna said.

"*Keep in mind, City, that it is our solemn duty to eliminate the darkness,*" Dan added.

"*—but never forget to praise the progress of lights,*" Donna finished, with a smile.

Randall turned to me as we were straightening up the common room. *How you going to get out, my man?*

I shrugged my shoulders and signaled back. *I think Mason got me the green trees. I hope.*

He nodded and turned to Maddy, mouthed the words *Mason green trees.* We were all headed toward the dorm when I saw Maddy tell Liam. Kiki had already told Carlos. Now everybody knew what was about to happen. Or, at least, what I hoped was about to happen. I twisted my Credentials on my wrist, hoped that I was right about Mason, took a deep breath and turned around.

"Guys, I can't find my book," I said. "I must have left it in the classrooms." The entire Block stopped to watch me as I flipped back to the common room.

"You can't go out there!" David scoffed. "You'll get all of us in trouble for being out of area." A couple of folks murmured in assent. Carlos and Kiki were nodding along, grumbling theatrically, and I had to suppress a laugh.

"I'll go to the Z.A., don't worry about it," I said, not looking back as I rounded the corner toward the main door. Pausing for just a moment, my fingers on the handle, I heard Mason's voice in my head: *no business at all at this time.* I let them rattle around up there for just a moment, drumming up some courage.

Then I opened the door and stepped outside.

There were no Drones or Associates in sight. Relieved, I turned in the direction of the tunnel and flashed my Credentials over my head, began walking toward the Globe. For just a second it felt like my entire life was hanging in the balance. I'm not sure exactly how much trouble I would get in if Mason's hint ended up being a dead end, but for sure it would raise flags with Admin and the Algorithm—me being out of area twice in one day was not going to harmonize well with the Head telling me to keep my record clean. I crossed my fingers, wished upon a star, and walked forward.

For what felt like forever, nothing happened. I kept walking; no news is good news, I figured. But then, just as I got underneath the Globe, pretty much to the spot where continuing to stare at it was going to get weird, I saw that small flash of dark purple that meant my Credentials had, in fact, been authorized.

Mason had done it again.

I fought every urge to hurry, forced myself to walk along at a normal pace and keep my head on a swivel, looking for my "missing book." It was dead quiet out here, super unnerving. I kept my ears peeled, but whether Jazz was pulling strings from somewhere, or whether I just got lucky, the result was the same. I didn't have to run my Credentials to anyone, man or machine. Just so long as the Z.A. kept watching his game show, and not the Globe feeds, I was in the clear.

I could see the green light glowing from around the corner before I even made it to the tunnel. Jazz had beat me here. I sped up just a bit, bounded down the three steps to the turn, and rounded to enter the hallway. The moment I entered the green light, however, I froze.

Two Associates were standing in front of me.

My ears went red and I felt my pulse jump. For a second I couldn't force a breath at all, and when it started coming it was in short, ragged bursts. That green light was hot against my face, and I felt seconds away from throwing up. I didn't know whether to turn and run or just to calmly show my Credentials. Either way, I was completely fucked.

Then one of the Associates laughed, a barking little sound chopping through the gasmask and filling the hallway. My body calmed down instantly, like muscle memory for something safe. It was Jazz.

She took her helmet off, grinning at me. "Sorry about that, Ben," she said. "You're a minute earlier than I expected. You must have walked fast." The other Associate opened up his gasmask and goggles, but I didn't recognize him. Relieved beyond words, I wondered how many agents there were working on the inside here at 231.

"I did my best to walk normal," I said, trying to sound collected about the whole thing. "But, you know. It's a lot going on right now."

She laughed again, pointed at me. "Washington, this is Ben. Ben, this is Washington." We nodded at each other.

"Nice to meet you, kid," he said. He was a good bit older than Derek, like my dad's age at least, a tall Black guy with a scraggly beard. He pulled a small box out of his pocket and handed it to me. "Let's take care of business, quick."

I took the box and glanced at Jazz. When she nodded, I opened it up to see a snapback, sunk into a little bit of foam to keep it from rattling around. Next to it, also set into the foam, was a set of Credentials. I looked up, curious.

"Jazz says you already know about the rollers," Washington said, pausing for me to nod, "but you need to know that this one has been modified. Instead of giving a specific amount of time, it will go green for only the duration that you're in range."

"It lets you stay on the move," Jazz said, looking down at something on her screen.

"Right," Washington said. "It'll cause a Globe to go green when you're in sight, and then it'll revert to normal when you're gone. Turn it on when you want to go dark, and turn it off when you're ready to come up for air." He paused again, waiting.

"Got it," I said, swallowing hard. What were they going to ask me to do that I need to be *on the move*? "Who modified it?"

Washington grinned. "I did. I also modified the Credentials. You don't have to wear them, just hold them in your hand. For exactly fifteen minutes, though, during the basketball game you will be able to use them to do three things that your Credentials can't. First, they will get you through Mr. Mason's classroom to the Peek hall, and then into the elevator down to the lower level."

"Then," Jazz looked up from her screen, "they will drop a bug onto a Drone down there."

"A bug?" I asked, confused.

She smiled. "A bug that will blow that thing to hell."

I stared at her. Certainly, she was joking. However, both she and Washington kept their eyes level, their faces impassive. Nobody here was messing around.

They wanted me to set off a nuclear reaction in the basement.

"Listen, Ben," Washington said, "it's perfectly safe for the students. That site down there was built to weather the storm of a full-scale nuclear assault above ground—a bomb will just collapse the area back into earth and rock. You'll go down, target the first Drone you get close to. There won't be any people present outside of school hours—it's considered a security risk to allow even guards down there at night. The roller will keep you off the cameras. All you do is scan the Credentials and drop the bug."

"After that, you run like crazy," Jazz said, "back to the gym and the game. You'll use the snapback the entire way—the halls will be empty until you get to canteen. We'll have a couple of Associates posted at the perimeter. Pass the bogus Credentials and the snapback to one of them and they'll provide you cover to make it into the gym, mix you in with the crowd of students. When the Drone blows, they won't be able to connect any of us to the explosion."

I was still staring at her when her screen started beeping. She looked down at it, made a couple of swipes, turned to Washington. "They're coming down from the Guest dorms on this side. Let's head to the middle so we can keep talking."

Washington jerked his head at me, and they started into the tunnel. I hustled to follow. It was only then that I noticed that Jazz wasn't carrying her school-issued screen—the device that had told us to move was of a kind I had never seen before. She kept it cradled in her hand, half an eye on it the entire time we walked.

She turned over her shoulder to look at me. "They only run one manned patrol per Area, and this tunnel connects two separate Areas. There's no reason for any of them to walk down here at all. Drones pass sometimes, but the guy on the other end of this"—here she held up her device—"can keep us posted about where the patrols are, and when we can dip out."

As we walked the Globes turned green just ahead of us, a strange kind of magic. It was all I could do to believe the situation at hand; it was like some surreal joke—a Peek, a Guest, and an undercover Associate walk down a tunnel together, plotting a revolution.

"What happens after the Drone blows?" I asked. They had both stopped moving; we had come far enough, apparently. Jazz grinned as Washington sighed through his lips, an imitation of an explosion. His fingers burst outward from an invisible center.

"All their research burns to hell," he said, "and their illegal operation comes to an end. A big, messy, public end."

Suddenly Jazz's device began beeping wildly. She tapped at it and held it in front of her face. "Go for Lewis," she said. Her voice was calm, but I thought I could see a certain something in her eyes.

"You've got to get out of there," a voice came through. It might have been Derek; I couldn't tell for sure. "The patrol in Area 3 seems to be heading for the tunnel. You've got just a couple of minutes to get out on your side ahead of the Area 7 team."

"Shit!" Jazz exclaimed, and she immediately began stripping off her uniform.

"What are you doing?" Washington said, checking at his gear and tightening some straps. "You stay here undercover. I'll get Ben back to the dorms safely."

"No way in hell," Jazz said. She had just about the entire uniform on the ground by this point, underneath she was wearing her basketball clothes. A small bag materialized from the Associate gear, and she stuffed everything inside but the helmet. Handing it all to Washington, she repeated, "No way in hell, Wash. If they catch me, I'll just end up back in solitary. If they catch you?" She smacked her teeth and shook her head.

He nodded and took the bag from her, grabbed the helmet, tucked it under his arm. "If I hustle I can dump these in a hideout before they see me." He paused for a flash, looked at Jazz, and said, simply, "Thanks." Back to me and a glance at the box I was clutching in my hand. "Good luck, Ben. A lot of us are counting on you." Then he took off running down the tunnel, away from us, toward canteen and the looming patrol.

Jazz grabbed my arm and tugged. "We need to get out," she said, and we began sprinting down the hall in the opposite direction.

The heavy tread of Washington's feet immediately disappeared, covered up by Jazz's lighter step and my squeaking sneakers. She pulled ahead of me, handily, despite the fact that I was running faster than I would have thought possible. As the Globes clicked green in front of us, I risked a glance behind. Far off down the tunnel, almost out of sight, I could see a glimpse of green—Washington must be almost out. In between our two snapbacks was an encroaching zone of white, looming like an angry sunrise.

Jazz hit the brakes at the end of the hall, stopped on a dime and checked her screen. I huffed into place next to her, was about to say something when she put her finger to her lips.

No noise, Ben, she signaled. *They're too close. We're going to have to run the wrong way and hide.*

We're going to hide? My fingers said the words, but my face had all the emotion. Where in 231 could we possible hide from a patrol?

Jazz winked and crossed her fingers. *Let's do this,* she signed, and grabbed my hand. We sped around the corner and up the three little steps. At the top was the branching hallway, left or right. One way back to my dorm and, apparently, a patrol. It might have been a trick of my imagination, but I almost thought I could hear them coming. Jazz peeked around the corner and squeezed my hand lightly.

Then we went the other way, down a hall, around a couple of turns, and into a part of the building I had never set foot in before.

———

We walked quickly but quietly down the hall. It twisted and turned, doors leading off on either side, Globes blinking off in front of us.

Where are we? I asked Jazz.

She signaled back, *this was In-School Suspension, before the bunker.*

What's our plan? I was starting to panic. Being invisible to the Globes was one thing, but I had no idea what they would do to us if they caught us out here. I was fairly sure that in the history of 231, nothing like a Guest and a Peek out together after curfew had ever occurred.

We should be able to loop back to the classrooms and hide out there— "Shit!" she interrupted herself out loud. I had heard it, too: a noise from up ahead around the corner.

She pulled me backwards and, still holding hands, we ran stealthily back the way we came. When we lost the noises behind us I started to breathe a little easier, but only until I could hear the patrol in the other direction. I was freaking out, wondering if her plan was just to run right into them and make up some story, when she stopped so suddenly that I lost my balance. In the green glow of the befuddled Globe she dropped to her hands and knees, began to examine the baseboard.

"What are you doing?" I whispered. "Are we out of options?"

She waved me away. Now that we weren't moving at all, I could hear voices coming from both sides. I had finally decided to give up hope, prepared a lie about Jazz and I on a secret romantic tryst, when she suddenly let out, "Ah, here." She flashed her Credentials and waved them over the wall, and a thin crack appeared. Widening ever so slightly at the push of her hand, it showed itself to be some kind of doorway. She looked up at me and smiled, then pulled her snapback out of her pocket.

"Come in here, Ben," she said, backing into the dark little opening. Seeing no other alternative, I dropped down and crawled in there with her. Using a handle on the inside, she pulled the door almost shut, then pointed out into the hallway.

"Three…two…one…" she said, and she twisted the snapback off. The Globes went from green to white, and at almost the same moment she pulled the door shut on us altogether. The darkness covered us immediately. We were alone in the stillness.

It was a cramped little space. I couldn't have stood up above a crouch, and even sitting with my back against one wall my feet bumped up against the other, forcing me to raise my knees. Except for our breathing, the silence was absolute. A moment earlier we had been listening to two patrols of Associates and the ever-present background hum of the Globes. In here, however, there was nothing. It smelled of us—government-issue soap and sweat.

Jazz's face flared to life in the light of her special screen. She was watching something that gave off a series of flashes, then she turned the glow to face her hand against her leg.

You good?

We were sitting against opposite walls, our legs pressed up against each other in the tight room. In the glow of the screen, I could see now that it was little more than a closet, some kind of storage room. It was so small that we couldn't have fit another person in here without laying them on our laps. I placed my hand on my knee next to hers and signaled back.

I'm fine. You?

I stay good, Ben. I stay good.

What is this place?

Jazz shrugged. *We don't really know. Some kind of a safe room, but we don't know why. They're all over 231.*

Do you think this will work?

Yeah, we should be okay in here—

No, the thing with the Drone. Do you think that blowing it up will put a stop to all this?

She put her hand in front of her mouth for a moment, suppressing a laugh. *No, Ben, I don't think this will put a stop to all this. But I think that blowing up their bullshit research is a good start to something.*

Do you think—I started to signal and stopped suddenly. We'd started to hear some noises from outside, growing louder, but now for the first time I was able to place the sounds in my memory. They were the same beeps and squawks I had heard that night they jumped Randall.

A flash came to my mind, bathed in sick green light. Randall and I on the ground, the Associates walking away waving those weird devices over the walls, the clatter trailing off as they left us behind. I didn't know what they had been doing then, but I knew now.

They were searching for these safe rooms.

My whole body went tight and for a long moment I felt like I couldn't breathe. In this cramped space Jazz could feel the change in energy; she looked at me, alarm on her face.

What's wrong, Ben?

I couldn't even think of the best way to explain what I knew using hand signs. I grabbed her screen and pointed it at my face, blinding myself in the process, and mouthed the words to her: *You hear the noise from those devices? I've seen them before, the night they got Randall. They were searching the walls for something. They're searching the walls for us, right now. We're not safe in here.*

I pointed the screen back at the ceiling, diffusing the light. I couldn't see a thing at first, but as my eyes adjusted I saw Jazz sitting across from me, her knees pulled up to her chest. Her eyes were shut and her mouth was moving a mile a minute, so fast and loose that I couldn't follow.

Suddenly, I realized she wasn't talking to me. She was praying.

The beeps closed in on both sides, started to cross over and harmonize with each other. The hope I'd felt when we first climbed into this safe room was gone; all I could feel was dread. Jazz stopped talking to whoever she was talking to, opened her eyes and looked at me, mouthed three words to me—*I'm so sorry*—and leaned her forehead against my knee. Her skin was slick with sweat; I tried to stop myself from shaking. However bad it would have been to get caught together in the hallway, it was going to be far worse being in here.

A voice broke through. It sounded like it was right outside.

"Walton!" he called, "they're calling us all back to Admin wing."

"The hell?" another voice called out, slightly more distant. "They just sent us out here with all this gear to search and now he wants us back?"

Some scuffling and bumping from outside but, mercifully, no more beeps or squawks. Jazz was still leaning against me, but I could feel her lips moving again. I closed my eyes and tried to pray, too. It had been a minute since I'd done anything like that, but now felt like a pretty good time to get back to it.

Mason in my head again: *there are no atheists in foxholes.*

"Whatever," the second voice said, closer, and a bang against our door so loud I was shocked it didn't burst open. "He's the boss. Whatever he wants, he gets."

"They're saying that some kind of information just came in," the first voice said. "Time for a new brief, I guess."

Another bang, and then the voices trailed quickly away. Soon all I could hear was our breathing again. Jazz pulled her head off my knee and looked down at her screen. We sat there in silence for I don't know how long—our legs were still crammed together side by side, and something about the contact synchronized our breaths. I watched Jazz watch the screen.

After what could have been forever she let out a long sigh. She pulled her snapback out of her pocket, held it up into the light, looked over at me.

"They're gone," she said, her voice loud in the dark. "Let's get out of here."

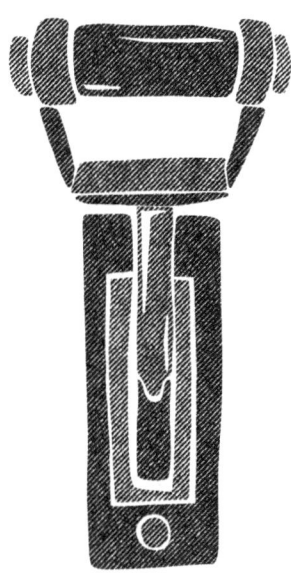

CHAPTER 24
THE BIG GAME

Our walk back to the dorm was entirely unremarkable, save for the moment we almost ran right over a Drone.

We walked quickly, and in silence. By all rights I should have been nervous, but it was almost as if I was too exhausted to spare any energy toward such a feeling. At this point, either Jazz was going to get me home or she wasn't. Easier to trust her and follow along than to worry about things I couldn't control.

My heart was about fit to explode, though, when we rounded the corner and had to duck out of the way of the Drone. Jazz saw it first, of course, and she spun out of its path, putting her back flat against the wall in one smooth motion. She looked every bit as graceful out here as she did on the court. On my part, I froze in place, terrified. Only after Jazz reached out and grabbed my hand, pulling me against the wall with her, was I saved from getting plowed over by the machine. For a couple of seconds the hallway was all squeaking shoes and heavy breathing. The Drone, though, hovered straight by, unperturbed.

Jazz squeezed my hand, let go and pointed at the green glow emanating from the Globe. *They can't see us when it's green,* she signaled, *it's like we're...*

She paused, searching her mind for a signal, gave up and grinned. *Invisible,* she mouthed to me.

We kept walking, made it almost all the way back to my dorm when suddenly Jazz stopped. She pointed at the Globe.

"Watch how we do this. It's important how you turn the snapback on and off. If you do it the wrong way, you'll just appear out of nowhere. The Algorithm can't help but notice shit like that."

I nodded, and she pushed me tight up against the corner. We were at a T, and she stepped across the hall to the other corner, directly opposite me.

"Always click it when you're turning," she said. "See how the Globes in all 3 directions are green right now? If we time it just right, we'll round the corner at the same moment the lights change. The Algorithm won't think twice." She pointed back the way we had come. "I'll go and wait at that last turn—we can't appear together or anything. I'll turn onto my hall at the same time that you turn onto yours. Easy."

"What about your disguise?" I replied. "Won't you get into trouble for being out here?"

She winked. "Don't worry about me, Ben. I know what I'm doing out here after curfew."

"Jazz?" I interrupted. Something was on my mind that I couldn't shake. "Remember when you were talking to Washington, and he volunteered to be the one to take me?" She nodded. "You said something about what they would do to him if they caught him?"

I waited, but she didn't step into the gap. I went on.

"What would they do to him, Jazz?" I almost didn't want to hear, but I was certain that I needed to know.

She looked away for a moment, then into my eyes. She sighed.

"They would kill him, Ben. For sure. They would kill him, and it wouldn't be the first time. There's more going on here than I can tell you tonight. There's more going on here than I even know."

I caught my breath, then pointed at the snapback. "Let's do this," I said.

"Hey, Ben?"

"Yeah?"

"Green trees, man. Green trees." She gave me one last, long look, and then she was gone, at the other corner, counting back from three. We turned away from each other at the exact same time, and, suddenly, I was on an empty, well-lit, perfectly normal hallway, all by myself.

I walked into the dorm just minutes before lights dim.

"Couldn't find my book," I announced to the room. "But I had a good walk, at least."

Without making eye contact with anyone, I stepped into the bathroom to wash off the dried sweat before bed.

———————

One thing about 231 is that, as frustrating as it can be when you are itching to talk to your friends, there is no better situation when you are trying to keep a secret. And I was sitting on the mother of all secrets. With only a week to keep it safe, I was in no rush to tell anybody about my night out with Jazz.

I filled Randall in at the Meeting, of course, but also told him that we needed to keep it to ourselves for the time being, that I would let other folks know but only slowly. I caught Kiki up that night while we were walking around, and Maddy the next night when she came back from basketball a little early under the pretext of wanting to study. All three of my friends were floored by the plan, asked a whole list of questions. Every one that I answered, I got just a little more anxious.

True to her word, there was zero contact between me and Jazz. I went to get coffee but didn't even so much as look toward the Peeks.

Even in class Mason was keeping us in rows, away from our groups. It was like the calm before the storm. Everything was so steady that if I didn't remember the safe room so well, I might have thought the story about the Drones was only a dream. But I could close my eyes and imagine the fear in that tiny space, hear the whisper of Jazz praying for our safety. As the days went by the memory only became more intense.

In the end I didn't tell Liam or Carlos. At first, I fully intended to get to them. But by the third day—watching all the Associates and Drones, knowing for certain how hard they were watching me—I realized it wasn't the worst thing to keep the plan quiet. I decided to have Randall and Maddy help me out, told them to give Liam and Carlos a shortened version of the night, one that left off the specifics. We let them know that something was going down soon, but that I was still on a need-to-know basis with Jazz and her team. I felt a little bad about the lie, but I was terrified of messing something up.

The day before the game, when they started pulling students out of class for "questions," I knew that I had made the right decision.

They grabbed a few folks at a time all day long and through the next morning. The last batch, taken from math class just a couple of hours ahead of the game, included Maddy, David, Liam, and Kai. We didn't see any of them again until lunch. I spent all of Williams's class worrying, trying to distract myself by going over final details of the War for Central Europe, preparing for our test. They had gotten every Guest but me and Randall by this point, making some kind of low-key statement by leaving him behind. Kiki had gone the day before with Carlos, but I hadn't been able to get a moment alone with either of them to touch base about the questioning. All I'd received from Kiki was a thumbs up and a smile.

It was reassuring, sort of.

When the word had come down for Maddy and them to report to Admin wing, I risked a glance at Jazz. She wasn't looking at me, but her hands tried to calm me down. *Green trees, Ben. You got this. Green trees.*

A few hours later Maddy walked into the cafeteria, alone, straight to the table to drop her books off. When she slipped and a book fell out of her hands, I quickly reached down and picked it up, sliding out the note she had written before handing it back to her. It was a move we had done hundreds of times in one form or fashion. Reading her short words, I was not encouraged.

They're coming hard, Ben. They offered more money than last time. For anything at all we could tell them about Jazz or Orion or you. Split us up, left us in rooms alone. Real detective movie stuff. You've got to be so careful tonight. They know something is going on. They just don't know what.

I crumpled up the note, thought about stuffing it into my milk carton, decided to just eat it instead. Looking around, I saw that Maddy and Kai were the only ones back; Admin still had the others. For a flash I felt grateful that I hadn't told Liam anything about tonight, but that turned to shame real fast—he hadn't been anything but a solid friend to us since he showed up. It had only been a couple of months, but time here passed different than it did on the outside. It felt like I'd known him forever.

I don't remember anything from class the rest of the day. Liam showed back up at the very end of dinner, but we didn't have any time to talk—he wolfed down some fast carbs and went straight to the court, even before Recks officially began. They almost never allowed students, Peeks or Guests, to leave the cafeteria early. The final basketball game between the first teams, though, was a guaranteed exception.

Anticipation was higher than usual this year—between Jazz being in In-School and Randall's "accidental" injuries, a proper roster of the first teams hadn't played in months. Now that Randall had finally returned to practice, I didn't need to ask why Jazz and her team had chosen tonight for me to sabotage the Drone. So many students showed up for last year's game that they had already announced the closure of every part of 231 except for the gym. Every student, and, more importantly, every Associate in the entire building would be there. Except for me, the halls would be empty.

After dinner they gave us fifteen minutes to go back to the dorm, drop off our stuff, and get to the gym. I had worked out a plan with Kiki a couple days back—we'd take the long way, tell people we just wanted to stretch our legs after all our studying for Williams's test. If we dragged our feet, we could be the last people at the turn toward the classroom wing. At that point she would move on ahead, and that would give me easy cover to head the wrong direction, away from the gym.

Except that it didn't really work out that way. The first phase went fine; most of the crowd took the short way through the tunnel. At this point everyone was used to us avoiding it—even if they didn't know the reason—and nobody asked questions when we said we would walk around. The few stragglers in the hallway got caught up in one of Kiki's stories, and she pulled out in front of me as I slow-walked my way to the back of the line. But then, right before the turn for the classrooms, a group of kids came marching up from behind us, late arrivals from some other Block. I froze, unable to think of any reasonable explanation for me to just stand there for the next minute while I waited for all of them to get ahead of me. I had just decided to turn around, pull the old I-forgot-something card again, when Maddy called out to me from the group listening to Kiki's story.

"Ben!" she said, and I spun around, startled at the anguish in her voice.

She was at the corner, leaning against the wall, crying. I moved quickly toward her, obviously worried, but all I could think was, *not now Maddy, not now.* I came as close as I dared but she didn't even look up at me, just sobbed and shook; even as upset as she was, she made sure not to touch me in front of the Globes. She was saying something about Randall and Williams and basketball and the Testing, but I couldn't follow any of it. The group from the other Block passed us by, heading for the gym. A couple of them caught my eye and looked curious, but I shrugged my shoulders. There was no need to fake confusion—I had no idea what was going on with Maddy.

Suddenly she pulled away and looked up at me. Her makeup was smudged; there was snot running out of her nose and down her face. Then she grinned. With her back to one Globe and our height differential shielding her from the other, she was invisible.

Good luck, Ben, she mouthed. Green trees. *But please be safe.*

She turned around, wiping her eyes again and whimpering softly.

I stood there for as long as I thought I could get away with, looking like I was feeling a certain kind of way about Maddy. I hoped the Algorithm wasn't smart enough to know that I could never do that to Randall. Her footsteps faded away, and, except for the Globes watching my every move, I was alone.

I put my hand in my pocket, got a grip on the snapback. I pulled it out, hidden in the palm of my hand, and took one last look around, still trying to appear sad. There was nobody in sight. Recks started in two minutes, the game shortly thereafter. It was now or never. I took a deep breath, turned the snapback, saw my world turn to that greasy green light.

At the same moment I turned around the corner and, effectively, disappeared.

I dropped the snapback into my pocket and took off down the hall, watched the Globes turn green just ahead of me running into their range. A Drone was hovering off in the distance—as planned, all the Associates seemed to be in the gym already—but I didn't even break stride as I made my way past. It was wild to be so close and not have that primary eye rotate to stare at me; for just a second I wanted to give it a shove and see what would happen. Instead, I kept running.

The other set of Credentials were in my hand before I even made it to Mason's door. This was the next test of Washington's special equipment, and I couldn't help but wonder what would happen if the door didn't open. Fortunately, just like the snapback, the Credentials worked like a charm, the door giving off that familiar buzz as it swung into the room. I jumped inside and quickly pulled it shut behind me.

The room, like the hallway, was bathed in the now-familiar green light. I made a mental note to loop back here if something went wrong. It was safe in this room—there would be no reason for Associates to be patrolling in the classrooms. Walking across to the Peek side, I was surprised to see that the display was on. A single quote illuminated the empty desks, made me stop and smile. It was a line I had quoted in my essay, one of my main points of argument as to why the scientist was actually the bad guy.

Listen to me, Frankenstein. You accuse me of murder; and yet you would, with a satisfied conscience, destroy your own creature. Oh, praise the eternal justice of man!

The line had jumped out to me on a second reading of the book. It felt like 231, blaming and punishing even as it dealt in destruction. Mason was wishing me luck, even if he couldn't be here with me. I hoped he would like my paper—no way that monster was as bad as his creator. Energized, I kept moving.

The door to the Peek hallway opened at the special Credentials, no retinal scan required. The Globes were green by the time I could even see out there—a glance in each direction confirmed that I was alone, and I took off to the right toward the elevator. The hallway had seemed so tight with the G.A. and the Associate that day; at the moment, I felt exposed in the emptiness. Squeaking to a halt at the end of the hall, I ran the special Credentials for the third time. The elevator rattled open, and I stepped inside. Spinning around, I waited for the door to shut behind me, then cranked the arm down.

The elevator didn't move.

I stood there for a second, waiting. Sweat was trickling down my back, dripping in my eyes, tickling my legs. It was hot in here, like that day with Jazz in In-School, almost as if they turned the air off during the night. I looked around the elevator in vain for another button—nothing but smooth metal walls and that single lever. Then I remembered the Globe.

I looked up into the green light and swallowed hard, said a little prayer to whoever had kept Jazz and me from those Associates the other night. Then I cleared my throat and spoke, hoping my voice had more confidence than I felt. "It's me," I said, hoping I remembered the words of the G.A. correctly.

The elevator started to drop. Washington had done it again.

The ride down to the bunker took much longer than I remembered, more than enough time to imagine a dozen scenarios where the room at the bottom would be filled with Associates. Convincing myself that the jig was up, I found myself creeping back against the rear wall of the elevator, pressed against the metal. I was shaking in time with the rhythm of the room.

The door opened. Save for half a dozen Drones, the bunker was empty.

The whole room had gone green before the door was even halfway open. The Drones were wandering around aimlessly, their eyes whirring back and forth, looking for intruders. Still a little cautious, I stepped inside extra slow, like I was trying to evade a pack of wild animals. Eyes whirred right past me. I was still invisible.

The other Credentials in hand, I stood for a moment and waited. For a long while the Drones seemed almost to be avoiding me, triggering my anxiety, but eventually one of them hovered near. I watched it closely, trying to clock its path, then matched its pace and approached. It was making a slow arc around the table—no turns, only a veer—and I came close, like a satellite trying to catch up to the orbit of a distant moon. For a couple of steps I just walked alongside it, holding the Credentials a foot or so away, ready to turn suddenly if it did. Then, confident in Washington this time, I waved the bracelet in front of its scanner. Instantly, it stopped moving, and its primary eye swiveled to me.

I barely had time to think before I heard a voice. "Ben!" it crackled, "this is Derek. Can you hear me?"

"Yes?" I answered, quietly. It didn't appear that the Drones could hear us either of us, but speaking still felt unsafe in this vast space.

"Ben, we've had a setback. There's a problem we didn't anticipate."

"What kind of problem?" I asked. My voice was shaking; I hoped Derek couldn't hear it.

"I can't get into it right now, there isn't time. We've had a security breach—they've taken Washington into custody, but we're not exactly sure why."

"Washington!" I cut in. "Is he okay?"

A brief pause on the other side. "We don't know for sure."

My Drone had stopped, frozen in place as Derek's voice incongruously emitted from its speakers. I had to keep my eyes on the others, though. I was fairly sure they wouldn't crash into the stuck Drone, but I didn't know what would happen if one bumped into me. My eyes skittered around as Derek kept talking.

"But, Ben, more importantly, Washington was unable to perform his final task for the operation today. He was scheduled to be the last one out of the bunker. His job was to clear the In-School Suspension room of students."

His words hung there for a moment as I waited for him to continue. Then, suddenly, it registered.

"There are students back there?" I said.

"Student. Just one. And you have to go get him."

"What? How am I supposed to do that?"

"Your Credentials should open the cell," Derek said, then stopped. "I hope. But you've got to run, now. The countdown on the explosion has already begun."

I took a step away from the Drone, queasy. It's not every day you find yourself standing next to a nuclear bomb.

"You already started it?" I dodged out of the way of a roving Drone, and then moved back toward Derek's voice.

"You started it, Ben," he said, so quietly I had to lean in to hear.

"The moment you ran the Credentials the timer started. It's at just over sixteen minutes right now."

"Shit!" I said. "Shit! Shit! Shit! And you can't pause it or stop it?" My heart was racing; I'd thought I was done with my part of this night.

Another pause. "No, I'm sorry. Washington might have been able to do it, but I just have no idea. At this point, it's just…" He trailed off.

"Boom," I said quietly.

"Boom," Derek repeated.

I pulled out my screen and set a timer for fifteen minutes, figured that rounding down was better for this situation than rounding up. I looked into the primary eye and nodded. "Just one student?" I asked, taking a deep breath, sliding the Credentials back into my pocket.

"Yes, Ben," he said. "The basketball game just started, so you should still be able to make the rendezvous point in time. I'm so sorry about this."

"I got it, Derek," I said, spinning away, taking off for the tunnel to In-School Suspension. In a moment of inspiration, I nabbed an Associate helmet off the table, tucked it under my arm like a football. Then I ran like hell.

It took me almost two minutes to run down the tunnel to the cells. I spent the whole first half staring at the dim light at the end, waiting for it to turn green. When it did, I risked a glance over my shoulder, saw that the central bunker had gone back to Globe light. Washington didn't deserve what was happening to him—that guy was a genius.

Slamming to a stop just shy of the doorway, I jammed the Associate helmet over my head. I was breathing hard, huffing in big, ragged breaths, and now I could taste my own stale air. I blinked hard against the dizzy feeling and stepped inside the small room that connected the cells. I couldn't see much through the goggles, so I had to get right up against the bars, shining my screen into each cage, looking for the student stuck down here. The first two were empty, but in the third I saw someone sitting up in their bed, scrunched against the wall, almost as if he was trying to disappear from me.

The student was David.

I stopped dead. Though he might not have known it, for just a moment David's life hung in the balance as I saw the events of the day in rewind. They pulled him out with Maddy, put the pressure on him, and somehow—but how?—he knew something, gave them something, led them to Washington. Right now Washington was being tortured, or worse, because David gave in to Admin's bribes. He thought he was getting out to his new school, but then they left him here, headed for the game, said they'd come back tomorrow to find out what else he knew. For just a moment, I was so sick of him I thought about turning around.

Nobody deserved to die today, though. I shook my head, told myself that I'd have to get him out, whatever he'd done.

But I sure didn't have to like it.

I kicked the bars with my shoe, tried to scare him by starting a little rattle, but they didn't budge. I thought about what I would do if the Credentials didn't work, but when I ran them in front of the scanner the door clicked softly open. I stepped into the cell, over to the corner, grabbed David roughly by the arm.

"Get up, kid," I said, trying to lower my voice and sound more like an adult. "You've been granted an early release."

David didn't budge. He ran his eyes from me to the Globe and back again; I could almost see him trying to square the green light with my obvious lack of a uniform. He pulled his arm away and squeezed even tighter into the corner.

"No way," he said. "I don't know who you are, but they told me I had to stay put. They told me they'd be back tomorrow. I'm going to stay here until tomorrow. Just like they told me." He was talking too slow, all air and space in his breath. He was probably in shock or something; his eyes were still jittering around, and there wasn't much to see here. I checked my screen. We had only eleven minutes to go until we were both going to be fried to death. For just a moment I caught myself wondering what that would feel like, whether or not I would even feel anything at all.

I sighed, shook my hands out a little bit, and slapped the shit out of David's face, backhand, hard.

He gasped, put his hand to his face. "What the hell!?" he said, in a more normal tone of voice. I grabbed his arm again.

"Son," I said, "we've got to move, now. This whole place is rigged to explode any moment. These fucking kids smuggled a bomb in here."

His eyes went wide, and for a second I thought I had pushed him back into shock. But then he stumbled to his feet, followed me to the door.

He paused in the central room under the Globe, stared up into its green light, but I grabbed him by the shoulder and gave him a shove to the exit. "We've got to run," I said, and I didn't stop pushing him until he took to his heels.

Well over two minutes back down the dark tunnel; David wasn't moving nearly as fast as I'd wished. Between the heat of this place, the exertion of the running, and that heavy helmet on my head, I was sweating hard. By the time we made it into the big room it was all I could do not to rip it off so I could breathe easy.

David tried to stop and gawk at the sight of the room—it made me think they'd brought him down here blindfolded, that this was the first time he was seeing this crazy place with its impossible height. I pulled him over to the elevator, dodging a couple of Drones, ran the Credentials and opened the door. Pulling him inside, I threw the switch upward as soon as it shut. Just under eight minutes to get to the gym and try to blend into the crowd. "It's me," I said.

The elevator didn't move.

"It's me," I said, a little more forcefully. David stared at the bare walls of the elevator, rested his eyes on my decidedly non-standard-Associate-issue shoes.

Feeling a certain kind of way about him at the moment, I flicked my leg behind his knees, knocked him to the floor with my arm. "On the ground, you lot!" I said. He was never going to believe I was an Associate, but I wasn't going to give up the subterfuge. I used my foot to turn his face away from me and lifted the mask up, spoke in my normal voice.

"It's me." The elevator lurched to life and started rising. Seven minutes. I dropped the helmet back over my face, took my foot off of David. After the brief moment of air, the gas mask tasted even more like metal.

I watched the time click down on my screen. How long was this elevator ride again? Was it a minute? More? I was so focused on the seconds ticking by that I didn't realize David was muttering to himself. He had curled up into a ball on the ground, still on his side where I had knocked him down, his words a fast little jumble. The shock he had felt back in the cell had given way to something more manic.

"They kept asking what I knew," he said to himself, "and I kept saying I didn't know anything. They kept asking me about Ben and the Peeks and I kept saying I didn't know Ben like that and I didn't know any of the Peeks at all but they ran my retinal scan and said it was weird and then they offered me a scholarship back to my old school and I want to go back there so bad but I didn't know anything to tell them and I didn't know what to say but they just kept asking and asking and asking…"

He trailed off into a mumble just seconds before the elevator jerked to a stop and the door slid open. Six minutes.

Was David telling the truth? Maybe he wasn't the snitch, after all. I didn't have time to worry about this right now, but the thought did make me feel a little bad about how rough I'd treated him. No time for that either, though.

I pulled him back down the hall, into and through Mason's classroom, just a little more gently than before. He was too overwhelmed to even react, so I gave him a nudge back toward the dorms.

"Go on," I said through the helmet. "Go back to your bed and wait there. Someone will come get you soon." I was lying; I had no idea what would happen to him from here. But at least he wouldn't be dead.

Fortunately, he started walking, allowing me to cut back the other way toward the gym. A couple of turns and past a Drone, Globes turning to green out ahead of me, and I checked my watch again. Five minutes. I just about had it made.

That's when I heard the patrol.

Shit. They shouldn't have been out here quite yet. They should have been at the game. I spun around and bolted back for the classroom hallway, no real thought other than maybe I could find somewhere to hide out until after the explosion. In no time I skidded back to a stop in front of Mason's door, pulled the Credentials out of my pocket, flashed them in front of the scanner. They wouldn't check for me in here; I'd be safe until after the explosion and then I'd figure something out.

The door didn't open. Washington's magic had run out.

I looked at my screen. Four minutes.

I could hear the patrol coming around the corner, and, in desperation, I decided to book it for the cafeteria. The Credentials had timed out; there was nothing I could do about that now. My best hope was to try to get lucky, make it to the turn before the Associates came onto the classroom hallway.

Halfway there, though, I slammed on the brakes. The Globe at the corner wasn't turning green. Was the snapback on a timer, too? Washington hadn't said anything about that, but I was just a handful of steps away from being fully visible to the Algorithm.

I could still hear the patrol; they would make the turn at any moment. I wasted precious seconds trying to decide which was worse: to be seen by the Algorithm going into the cafeteria without permission, or to be caught out of area by a pack of Associates. Given that I was holding a dysfunctional snapback and a bootleg set of Credentials, I decided to risk the cafeteria. I took a big breath for an all-out sprint, but the clanging buzz of a door opening stopped me in my tracks.

"Ben, get in here," a voice said.

It was Jazz.

———————————

CHAPTER 25

BEST LAID PLANS

I didn't waste a moment on being surprised. Instead, I dashed through the door she was holding open—some math classroom I'd never been in before—and checked my screen. Three minutes.

She shut the door behind her, holding her finger to her lips as the soft click sounded. We both knew the room was completely sound-proof, but it was easy enough to slip into silence after the panic I felt in the hall. She crossed to the other side of the class, leaned against the Peek door, motioned for me to follow. The Globe was green; apparently her snapback was still working.

She was wearing her full Associate gear, helmet in hand. Looking at her, I realized I had dropped my own helmet somewhere back on my run from the bunker. Did I leave it far from Mason's classroom like I had planned? No way to know at this point.

Suddenly her screen crackled to life, cutting through the quiet room. "You've got less than four minutes, Jazz. Do you have him?"

"Yes," she replied, looking at me and smiling. "We're safe in here. As safe as we could be, I guess."

I checked my screen as I moved to be near her. My timer was close to two minutes. I'd totally forgotten that I'd purposefully set it lower down in the bunker.

"There's a patrol outside," Derek said, "but I think in about ninety seconds you should have a window to make a run for the infirmary. Be ready."

"Got it," Jazz said, and looked up at me. "We meet again, Benjamin Walker. I can't help but wonder if you're stalking me or something. Everywhere I go!" She batted her eyes at me in a ridiculous kind of way.

I grinned in spite of myself. "What the hell are you doing out here, Jazz?" I asked. "Shouldn't you be playing in the game? Wasn't that the whole point of bringing me in?"

She shrugged. "Yeah, well, plans changed after they took Washington in."

"Is he…" I couldn't go on. Now that I had a moment to catch my breath, the look of fear on his face that night in the tunnel was haunting me.

"We don't know," she said. "Word is that some parent called Admin, complaining about their kid learning about 'somebody named Malcolm X,' wanted to know what kind of radical ideas they were teaching us here at 231."

My heart went into my throat. I could hardly breathe. Without a doubt, I knew that parent had been my mom.

Jazz went on. "They ran some search parameters through the Algorithm, searched Globe footage from the past couple of weeks. The only hit was a copy of *The Autobiography* that Washington accidentally left on his desk. That's why Mason gave you an unmarked book the other day—just in case some shit like this went down."

"Jazz," I started, but balked. How was I going to tell her that I got Washington caught?

She looked at me, but when I didn't speak she kept talking. "They took Washington in for questioning right before the bunker cleared out for the evening. Just dumb bad luck they left a kid down there that he was supposed to move up topside." She shook her head. "I don't know if he broke or not. I don't know what else they have on him. But when Derek passed me word, I faked an injury on like the third play of the game, and he took me to the infirmary. It didn't take me long to make it here."

I could hardly listen to her story. All I could picture was my mom, telling my dad about Visitation, him calling the school and complaining about the crazy ideas his innocent son had been exposed to. I knew mom was freaked out that day in Visitation; I knew I had been just too much for her. But it never occurred to me that it would get as far as all this. She and my dad had almost ruined everything, completely on accident. And it was all my fault.

Jazz's screen sounded. "Both of you, move. Now. You've got two minutes."

She ran her Credentials and the door buzzed open, spilling us out onto a green hallway. She grabbed my hand and took off to the right, past the elevator and around the corner, further down the Peek hall than I'd ever gone before. She kept one eye on her screen and the other on her route.

"This loops back to the infirmary," she managed to get out in between breaths. "We should be able to blend in there after the explosion." I could barely nod, we were moving so fast.

A couple of turns and I was completely lost. If Jazz had left me at that moment, I never would have found my way back to my side. Suddenly, though, after the fourth or fifth turn she pulled up hard.

Her face said it all, but I looked at her hands anyway. *Shit. They're coming from that direction.*

Without wasting another second she pulled me back the other way, flashing over her shoulder: *To the dorms. Uniform. Cover.* I couldn't figure out what her plan was, so I just kept running.

Another couple of turns and Derek's voice popped out of the

screen again. "Jazz! You've got less than a minute. Where are you?"

She didn't answer, just let go of my hand and started pushing her body even harder down the hall. Even in all that Associate getup, she was still so fast that I couldn't keep up. I was giving it all I had, but it was just no match for her. That is, until she stopped on a dime and cut back into me.

I managed to slide to a stop without knocking her down, just bumping up against her and knocking her off balance. She spun, kept her balance by bracing her arms against the wall.

"Another patrol," she said. "The fuck!" For a moment she stared at the ground and I thought we were done. Then she turned to me, grabbed my hand again. "Back to the classrooms. Maybe after the explosion they'll have to put people in the cafeteria or something, and we can blend into the crowd that way." She didn't sound at all optimistic about this Plan D.

We took off running again, but I was really dragging. At this point I had been sprinting in terror for well over fifteen minutes; my adrenaline was done and I was totally out of gas. She was pulling ahead of me, looking back, beckoning me with her hand, starting to slip away completely, when I heard Derek's voice from the screen again. I couldn't understand what he was saying, could only grasp the urgency in his voice as he called out to us. Jazz stopped running suddenly, tucked her legs against her chest, rolled to the ground and slammed against a wall. I tried to make it to her but pulled up short, breathing too hard to go on. Then it happened.

The world began to shake.

It started slowly, a vibration in the floor that spread upward, through my shoes and into my body. The walls cracked, and the ceiling started to crumble. Big parts of it sheared off altogether, crazy chunks falling around us in dusty crashes. Underneath this chaos was a noise that started as a dull sound, almost like swimmer's ear, increasing rapidly from a hum to a roar to what felt like a racecar revving its engine past me. I stumbled to my knees. For a moment I tried to get to Jazz, dodging sections of falling ceiling, but soon I gave up, curled into a ball and covered my ears with my hands. I started screaming; it felt like the only way to counteract what was happing in the building.

After what felt like forever, the noise started to recede and the floor began to feel solid again. I stood up, cautiously made my way over the Jazz. She rolled over and looked at me with wide eyes. For just a moment I forgot that we were being hunted by gangs of Associates, grown men who would probably beat all hell out of us when they found us here. In that instant of stillness, I was only able to feel relief that we were both okay.

Then the hall exploded.

In front of us, right where we would have been standing if I was just a little bit faster, a ball of flame shot out from the elevator. The explosion beneath the building had forced its way upstairs and into the hall. The doors blasted open, the flames licked down the walls toward us. The power went out altogether, even the Globes, the darkness now lit up only by the fire. I felt the heat push into me before I even realized what was happening, threw myself onto Jazz, tried to cover my hair. For a moment I was certain we were dying, burned up in the aftershocks of this thing we had done. The roar of the flames was almost as loud as the earthquake of the explosion.

Then, though, the heat and noise let up just a little, and I looked toward the elevator. The fire seemed to be contained at the corner, the hallway apparently lacking fuel for it to push forward. Score one for the cinder block, apparently. I rocked back on my hands and heels, instinctively trying to get my face away from the heat, and nudged Jazz with my foot.

"You okay?" I asked.

She uncurled her body, rolled her head sideways to see the fire, turned back to me. "As good as it gets," she said, rising up to stand. I scuttled backwards as she stretched her legs, then offered me a hand. She pulled me to my feet and we took a couple more steps away from the blaze. The smoke was pulling back in the other direction—toward the cafeteria—and for a moment we just stood there watching the surreal sight of 231 on fire. It was beautiful.

"What do we do now?" I asked, turning around to look back toward the Peek dorms and the impending patrols. "Just wait?"

Jazz tapped at her screen a few times, then put it into her pocket. "The whole grid is down." She looked up at the Globes; they were still dark. "This is crazy. The plan was always for you to be on the other side long before now."

"Yeah, well, I heard somewhere that plans can change," I said. She looked at me and smiled. In some unspoken agreement, we started walking toward the patrols. It was like we both knew it was just time to give up.

For a minute it got darker as we moved away from the flames. The heat lessened and I stopped sweating; the noise of the fire dampened away. Any moment I was expecting to see a flashlight shine from ahead, hear the sounds of Associates shouting, feel a truncheon against my gut. In what would have been an unthinkable move a month ago, I reached out and grabbed Jazzlyn Lewis's hand. She gave it a squeeze that said as clearly as any other method of communication: *It's been nice knowing you, Ben. See you never.*

Then I heard an unusual sound. It was a low hum, a strange monotonous buzz accented at times with higher pitches. At first I assumed it was part of the Globes malfunctioning, maybe the Code Red system trying in vain to come back online. The noise tugged at my mind, however, and though I couldn't place it, I knew it was familiar from somewhere. Suddenly, I saw a patch of gray against the blackness ahead, and I realized what we were hearing.

It was the sound of crickets, crying out into the night.

We stood there in the opening, staring out into the back of 231, breathing the fresh night air. Off in the distance I could see the lights of the City, the channel that led here from the center lit up like a string of jewels. Whatever was drawing the smoke toward the cafeteria was creating a breeze here, pulling fresh air into the building. I spread my arms wide; the wind felt like being on top of a skyscraper. Off in the distance, dull and thin against the song of the crickets, we could hear the noise of a Code Red. A part of the building must still have power, but it all felt like some kind of distant memory.

The hallway leading to the Peek dorms had collapsed here, creating this opening. For the moment, we were cut off from the patrols that had been hunting us. Sequestered into safety by fire and rubble, we were alone.

"What's out there?" I asked. Nothing was lit on this side of the school grounds. I assumed there were fences, but from what we could see it looked like the woods started just a few yards away. Stars winked on and off everywhere, but there was no moon. Even so, it was lighter out here than it was in there. An owl hooted nearby. It was all so terrifyingly normal.

"I don't know," she said, staring off into the night. "We're on the opposite side of the building from the Recks fields. And there are no windows on our side of the chain link. I've never seen any of this."

A beat went by, and in that moment I knew exactly what would happen.

We would run. Out into the woods. Make our way to the channel, follow it back to the City. Find somewhere to hide out, hook up with someone who could give us some work. Save enough money to buy passage on a truck headed north, or west. Leave the City behind, never look back. My family wouldn't even miss me. Not this version of me, at least. We could disappear for real.

"Let's go," I said, grabbing her hand and pulling her with me into the night. She took a couple of steps forward and my heart leapt. Then she stopped.

"I can't," she said. "I'm chipped."

I turned to her and she pulled her hand away from me, rolled her sleeve up past her Credentials, tapped at a spot to the side of her arteries.

"During intake they inject a tracker into all the Peeks," she said. "If I walk even a couple of steps away from 231, it'll activate. They say it makes you sick as hell. But, more importantly, they'll be able to find me out there as easy as they could track a Drone."

My stomach dropped. Of course they had her marked. Of course they did terrible things to the Peeks that they would never do to us. Of course we were stuck.

"You should go, though," she said, taking a half step back toward the building. "Get the hell out of here before they put out that fire and come find us."

Another beat went by, a long moment where I saw a totally different future.

I would still run. Through the woods, alone, and then follow the channel back into the City. But this time I would go to City Hall, find my dad, somehow convince him to take me back home. We would get my mom on the phone, make up some shit about how I was brainwashed—whatever it took to get her to come pick me up, help me move up north to be with my sister or one of my brothers. It could all happen. I was so close to getting out of here I could taste it.

Instead, I turned back to Jazz.

I shook my head and came close to her. "That doesn't seem fair," I said. "I can't let you get all the credit for this." I waved my hands over the building, taking in the wreckage around us.

For just a moment I thought she was going to argue with me. I worried that I would lose my nerve, was certain that she could convince me of anything. Then she smiled and sat down on a section of busted-up wall.

"Ben, you know that quote they say at the end of the News? The one about remembering the progress of lights?"

I nodded. "Williams said it the other day and you laughed at him. I could tell he didn't know why, though."

She laughed again, that little bark getting swallowed up instantly in the night. Somewhere not too far away some animal skipped through the trees, momentarily silencing the crickets, filling the space with the sound of crashing branches.

"I saw it once on this old movie," she said, turning to look into the woods. "Some story about a bunch of criminals, and one of them is telling his story to the cops and blaming all the others, so eventually they let him go. Then you find out that it was him, all along, that he was the main bad guy. And he says this line, something like the greatest trick of the devil is to convince you that he doesn't exist."

She paused and I waited. I didn't know where she was going with all this, but I was going to soak up every word in the time we had left. We might not ever see each other again, not after they caught us. Might as well take what I could get.

"But the line isn't originally from the movie" Jazz went on. "It's from that poet Williams put on the display, some French guy from around the time of Mary Shelley. He writes this crazy-ass story about a night he spent partying with the devil, and he's got a much better version of the line. *Do not ever forget, when you hear the progress of lights praised, that the loveliest trick of the Devil is to persuade you that he does not exist.*"

She took my hand, gave it a squeeze. It was the first time she had done so in a moment of stillness. "This place, Ben? This place is a trick of the devil. They tell us every night about the progress, but it's really nothing but pain. Somewhere somebody decided to close the News with the line, like some kind of sick joke. Just one more cruelty as they keep us in our place—praising progress when really the devil runs around like all hell."

She looked around into the dark, then I saw her close her eyes. "It's why we had to blow it up. We had to show their progress for what it really is. So now the devil can't hide here anymore, at least."

"Jazz—" I started, but faltered. How could I tell her that I got Washington caught? That I was the reason we were sitting here right now? In just a few minutes I was going to be taken in and roughed up, but I still had rights. I still had my dad. There was no way for me to know what would happen to her.

I paused so long that she opened her eyes and looked at me again. She was so close I could smell her again, that government soap. I found the words.

"It was my mom," I said, looking away. "I got so frustrated with my mom during Visitation that I said something about progress and the knife blade—that Malcolm X quote. I'm sure it was my parents that called the tip in. I know it. She went home and told my dad, and he looked it up and freaked the fuck out, called in with words for the Head." I gave out, suddenly exhausted, the events of the past hour catching up with me all in a rush. I turned back to her. "I'm so sorry, Jazz. This is all my fault."

She looked into the woods again. "It doesn't matter," she said. "They were going to catch me at some point. I wasn't going to stop until they did. Better with a friend than alone, you know?"

I let the silence sit between us, covered in the sound of crickets. The stars kept up their blinking and the crickets kept up their chirping and then, for whatever reason, even the Code Red in the distance stopped sounding. It was just us and the night, the most normal thing I had done in months—sitting there in the dark, holding hands with Jazzlyn Lewis.

And that's when I had the greatest idea of my life.

I jumped up, snatching my hand away from Jazz. Scampering around, I grabbed a couple of smaller pieces of rubble and piled them up behind us.

"Ben?" Jazz asked. "What the hell are you doing? You're really ruining the vibe out here."

"They don't have to catch both of us, Jazz. They only have to catch one of us." I stopped piling bricks for a moment and turned to face her. "They found that helmet I dropped by now. They know someone is out here. But if one of us stands outside all obvious, listening to the crickets or whatever, the Associates will swarm." I went back to my work. "The other can hide here in the broken wall, let them run past. If there's even a little bit of a fight, they can come out in the Associate uniform, blend right in. There will probably be dozens of Associates within a minute. It'll be easy to get back to the dorms and go clear with the Globes again. The Devil's not the only one who can hide in plain sight."

Halfway through my idea she had stood up and began peeling away the Associate uniform. Dropping gear to the ground, pulling off boots. I was so busy stacking bricks that it didn't immediately occur to me why.

"What are you doing?" I asked.

"Giving you the uniform, obviously," she said with a wink. "I'm not sure I like you enough for all that right now."

My neck went hot. "No, that's not what I mean." I dropped my bricks, grabbed her arm, stopped her from pulling off her other boot. "I'm staying, Jazz. Not you. You're going back to the dorms."

She looked at me as if she hadn't even considered it. To her credit, she probably hadn't. "No, Ben, that's stupid," she said. "I brought you into all of this, but you've got your whole life in front of you. You're the third smartest kid in our grade. You get caught here and you can say goodbye to whatever the scouts might have offered you next year."

"And you?" I asked, quiet enough that I was worried she hadn't heard me. The look on her face, however, told me everything I needed to know. "They'll do far worse if they catch you, Jazz. I can't just walk away and let that happen. I knew what I was doing when I said I was in."

For maybe the first time ever, Jazz Lewis wavered—waiting, thinking. Then she shrugged my hand off her body and began again to pull off her boot. But it was a half-hearted, tepid sort of action. Even if I wasn't quite sure, she seemed to know exactly what they would do to her if they caught her out here.

I picked up her other boot, gave her a little push back to our make-shift seats, and knelt down at her feet. She stopped fumbling at her boots. "Jazz," I said, "you saved me. Bringing me out of the lies on the other side of the chain link, inviting me out into the light? You saved me." I managed to get both boots squarely back on her feet and began to tie up the laces.

For just a second I could feel her leg flex against my hands, like she would kick me off and do what she wanted to do. Just like always— Jazzlyn Lewis, alone, against the world. Instead, she relaxed, hunched forward, put her head in her hands.

"Okay, Ben," she said, so soft I could barely hear her. "But I owe you one."

I smiled, helped her to her feet, handed her the gear she had dropped on the ground. Once she was dressed we added a little shape to the blind in the bricks. Finishing the work in silence, we went back to the opening, as far out as we dared while still ensuring we could hear inside the building. The draft caught us again here, my hair blowing slightly into my face as I tried to catch the last few moments of my regular life. Any minute now I was never going to be the same.

"It's been a hell of a ride, huh, Ben?" she asked. Her helmet was in her hands, ready to pop into place the second we heard them coming. Her hair was a mess—all squashed puffs coming undone, blowing in the wind. She turned to look at me and grinned in that way that she had, letting the world know she wasn't going to let any of this beat her down.

Between the breeze, the crickets, and the grin, I just kind of lost my mind for a moment. I leaned in to kiss her. It had been almost nine months since I'd last been near a girl like that—just a brief little thing while home last summer—and the moment kind of overwhelmed me.

I didn't get anywhere close to her lips.

She put her free hand on my chest and shoved me back. Not far, but decisively. "No, no, Benjamin Walker. That's not how any of this goes tonight. I've never been with one of you, and I'm not about to start right now."

Everything was so surreal that all I could do was laugh. I didn't feel any shame; I took a shot and missed. It was like trying to get with someone the last night of summer camp—we were probably never going to see each other again, so no big deal.

"One of me, what? Like, you've never been with a boy?"

She barked her little laugh again. "Vain one, aren't you, Ben? You think just because a girl turns you away she must not be into men, huh?" She popped the helmet on her head, kept the gas mask swung away, nodded back into the building. "Hear that? They're coming."

The mood iced over instantly. My stomach dropped as I swung around to stare into the darkness of 231. Jazz was right—off in the distance I could hear shouts and cries.

"Go," I said, turning back to her and waving toward the hideout we had crafted. "I got this." I wished I'd felt as confident as I tried to sound.

She didn't move. Instead, she took a step closer to me, got right under my chin and looked up at me from the depths of that helmet. I locked eyes with her and tried not to think of all the things I couldn't say. After a moment she put her fingers to her lips, kissed them, then moved them to my mouth. She pressed them up to my lips, left them there for a long, lingering moment. Somehow, it was better than kissing her for real. I closed my eyes and almost fell apart.

"I've been close to a couple of boys, Ben," she said, and my eyes flew open real quick. "I've just never been with a white kid before. I'm not sure what my Yaya would think if I ever brought you home. God knows, I've disappointed her enough." She smiled, took her hand away from my face, mouthed the words *thank you*. Then she turned and made her way into the hole.

I have no real memories of anything that happened after that. Rather, at some point during my interrogation they showed me footage of my capture, over and over, trying to imprint me with the danger I had brought upon myself, the shame they said I had introduced to my family. I know I turned back to face the outside again, because the footage starts with that first Associate squaring up on me from behind. He screams at me to turn around, put my hands in the air, get down on the ground.

I begin to comply—turning around slowly, keeping my eyes trained relentlessly into the camera, desperate not to reveal Jazz's hiding place through some inadvertent glance. For a moment there is an eerie calm as Associates circle slowly around me. It almost looks as if they are going to take me peacefully, cuff me quickly and pull me back inside.

Instead, one of them trips me from behind and slams me to the ground, causing my head to crash against a small pile of bricks. This is probably where I lose consciousness, but you can't tell for sure because suddenly I am being kicked, over and over, bandied about on the ground like a sack of soccer balls in some training exercise. My body bends and flops in ways I never could have imagined. Later I will learn that they fractured my jaw and broke three of my ribs. One of my teeth snapped in two and cut the hell out of my mouth. There is blood everywhere.

The other thing you can see on the video is an Associate who, for some reason, doesn't kick me. He dances around the edge of the circle until the rest of them finally stop, then he kneels down to touch my prone, broken body, taking my pulse and checking my breathing. "Vitals are steady," he says in a scratchy voice pitched just a little higher than you might expect. He's a little short for an Associate, but not so much so that you'd notice in the chaos.

Then he wipes my hair out of my face and stands up. A couple of bigger Associates push past him and begin the process of getting me inside, exacerbating my injuries when they take no care to be gentle.

The short Associate turns around and gets ahead of me into the building. He steps off the frame of the camera and disappears safely back into 231.

Every time they try to show me the beating, I watch this Associate instead, and I have to hide a smile. Then I say to myself, *we did it.*

We did it.

———————————————

EPILOGUE

Two weeks later I walked into the cafeteria on my own two feet. Sort of. I was using a set of crutches—my side was wrapped so tight I could hardly move—but I made it through the door on my own. Given what I'd been through, it felt like a victory.

I'd been kept in the infirmary for a couple of days, in and out of consciousness. Apparently they tried to question me, attempted to get me inspected, but before I was awake enough for the process my father showed up and raised holy hell. He had three lawyers with him, one of them more than a little famous in the City, and they threatened to wipe the rest of 231 off the map if I wasn't released to a private hospital immediately. They say the Head just laughed.

The negotiation took several days, back and forth from one team to another. I woke up, still at 231, mostly remembering what had happened but not entirely. Nobody would talk to me until everyone but me had signed the deal; every question I asked was ignored. I'd been moved to a small room, presumably in the old In-School Suspension wing—a bed, a desk, and nothing else. My screen had been taken away and I had nothing but pen and paper. With nothing else to do, I wrote.

Later I learned that the Drone program had been entirely destroyed, even the machines up on ground level had their processors fried when the bomb went off beneath. They spun it on the News like it was a business decision to discontinue the entire program, a "disappointing performance of the technology" unrelated to the "small fire" that had broken out near the Peek dorms. We had been halfway successful. They had used 231 to experiment on children, trying to make money from what went on in of the halls of our school, and we broke that pipeline clean in half. Unfortunately, it seemed as if they had gotten away with the main thing—nobody had to serve any time or even so much as admit to any wrongdoing. It was a bitter pill to swallow.

They never caught anybody else on our side. Washington was arrested and then fired "under suspicion," but he was never charged. My father worked out a deal where I accepted responsibility for being brainwashed by reading *The Autobiography of Malcolm X*—"a very dangerous book," he called it in the contract—and I accepted responsibility for being out of area, coincidentally, on the night of the fire. He kept me from getting inspected, but, combined with my actions in the classroom that day of the Infraction, he couldn't keep me from punishment altogether. They drummed up the Z.A., who testified that I'd been out of area without permission the night I came to his office; they pulled Drone footage of me being out of area when Mason feinted with the Conrad book. Three strikes at 231 and you were out, and I was up to four in a little over a month. I hear that the Head raised his hands in the air and smiled at my father.

"There's nothing we can do. It's regulation," he said. They had no proof of anything, but they got me nonetheless.

I hobbled into the cafeteria that day and the whole place instantly went dead quiet. Associates flanked both my sides while I made my way to the table, tripping over backpacks as I tried to negotiate my crutches. Every eye in the place was on me, all across the room. I turned to see Randall, Maddy, and Kiki, looked the other way to cast a glance at Jazz and Orion. Another glance back at Liam and Carlos. I hadn't even seen a mirror since my injuries occurred, but the shock on their faces made me realize how I must look.

I sat down, leaned my crutches against the empty seat next to me. The Associates lurked for a moment, but walked away as the room slowly buzzed back to life. Someone brought me a tray of food and I tried to eat. I got elbowed by my neighbor, not unkindly.

"Hey, Benjamin Walker," she said. "Long time no see."

I looked over at Jazz and smiled. "Long time no see, Jazzlyn Lewis."

Orion grinned from across the table, held out a hand for me to slap. "Welcome to the family, Ben."

I reached out to reciprocate, caught sight of the new orange jumpsuit chafing at my wrists. "How do you guys live with these things?" I asked. "It feels like they mixed cardboard in with regular clothes or something."

Jazz laughed and my heart leapt. "Ben, that outfit is the least of your problems. Just wait until you see the space in the dorms we made for your bed. You're going to wish your daddy had got you out of here for real."

They all broke out into laughter and, just like that, I felt like I belonged at my new table. In my new dorm. With my new people.

From my seat I had a straight shot across the cafeteria to see my old table. For a moment I watched Randall and Liam talking animatedly about something—basketball, probably—saw Carlos whisper something to Maddy, Kiki nodding her head to some unseen beat. It caught up with me then, suddenly, the events of the past month. Who knew when I'd ever get to sit with any of them ever again? Even surrounded by new friends, I felt lonely at the thought.

Just then Randall happened to look up at me. Without breaking eye contact he whispered something to Liam, who turned to interrupt

Kiki. She elbowed Carlos, who tapped Maddy. Randall smiled and looked around, then back to me. *No Drones,* he signaled, and nodded. *Well done.*

I hope it was worth it, I signed back to him.

Green trees, Ben, he said, and turned away. He nodded at Liam.

Liam looked up at me and smiled. *Green trees, Ben.* Then Kiki. Carlos. *Green trees. Green trees.*

Finally, Maddy. *Green trees, Ben. Miss you so much.*

My eyes widened at her skill with her hands, and she shrugged. *It's time. Got to be ready. Maybe one day soon.*

Got to be ready, I said back. *Green trees to all of you.*

She looked away when an Associate passed between us, returned to her conversation with Kiki.

I turned back to my new table, to Jazz. She had been watching me. "You good, Benjamin Walker?" she asked.

"Yes," I replied. "And no. It's complicated, you know?"

She laughed again. "Yeah, I know. Life has a funny way like that." She looked at me for a moment in a strange kind of way, then she whispered, "Green trees, Ben. Green trees."

———————